EMPIRE AT GLORAN

FIRST CENTURION KOSNETT
BOOK 5

BLAZE WARD

KNOTTED ROAD PRESS

Empire at Gloran
First Centurion Kosnett, Book 5
Blaze Ward
Copyright © 2022 Blaze Ward
All rights reserved
Published by Knotted Road Press
www.KnottedRoadPress.com

ISBN: 978-1-64470-318-2

Cover art:
Illustration 114296096 © Luca Oleastri | Dreamstime.com

Cover and interior design copyright © 2022 Knotted Road Press

Reviews
It's true. Reviews help. Even a short one, such as, "Loved it!" So please consider reviewing this book (and all of the ones you've read) on your favorite retailer site.

Never miss a release!
If you'd like to be notified of new releases, sign up for my newsletter.

http://www.blazeward.com/newsletter/

Buy More!
Did you know that you can buy directly from my website?

https://www.blazeward.com/shop/

This book is licensed for your personal enjoyment only. All rights reserved. This is a work of fiction. All characters and events portrayed in this book are fictional, and any resemblance to real people or incidents is purely coincidental. This book, or parts thereof, may not be reproduced in any form without permission.

ALSO BY BLAZE WARD

First Centurion Kosnett

Encounter at Vilahana

Consensus at Aditi

Hegemony at Dalou

Princes at Ewin

Empire at Gloran

Domain at Yaumgan

The Jessica Keller Chronicles

Auberon

Queen of the Pirates

Last of the Immortals

Goddess of War

Flight of the Blackbird

The Red Admiral

St. Legier

Winterhome

Petron

CS-405

Queen Anne's Revenge

Packmule

Persephone

Additional Alexandria Station Stories

The Story Road

Siren

Two Bottles of Wine With A War God

The Science Officer Series Season One

The Science Officer

The Mind Field

The Gilded Cage

The Pleasure Dome

The Doomsday Vault

The Last Flagship

The Hammerfield Gambit

The Hammerfield Payoff

The Bryce Connection

The Science Officer Series Season Two

Alien Seas

Buried Among the Stars

The Lazarus Alliance

Escape

Return

Rebellion

Revolution

Liberation

Retribution

Alliance

Shadow of the Dominion
Longshot Hypothesis
Hard Bargain
Outermost
Dominion-427
Phoenix
Princess Rualoh

The Handsome Rob Gigs
Can't Shoot Straight Gang
Can't Shoot Straight Gang Returns
Hunting Handsome Rob
Handsome Rob, Assassin

Earth Force Sky Patrol
Birth of the Star Dragon
Flight of the Star Dragon
Call of the Star Dragon
Shadow of the Star Dragon
Trial of the Star Dragon

Hunter Bureau
Mirrors
Latency
Pleasure Model
Inhuman

PROLOGUE: KOSNETT

DATE OF THE REPUBLIC MARCH 1, 412 RAN
URUMCHI, MEERUT ORBIT

Phil considered his image in the mirror.

Just over a year since they had arrived in the Balhee Cluster, with all the ground-quakes and repercussions from that still building in many places, while passed and receding in others.

At least he hoped so. Even a First Centurion could only be in one place. At least he had all his various ambassadors safely delivered to the *Aditi Consensus, Dalou Hegemony, Ewin Principalities*, plus those sent on to the *Gloran Empire* and the *Yaumgan Domain*.

People in the Cluster were talking. Slowly. Painfully. Awkwardly, even, when everyone had spent the last several centuries working towards the sorts of stupid autarky that had made the piracy problems around here all the worse.

And if they didn't start to come together soon, the pirates would return eventually. Phil knew that he had broken the *Zen-Mekyo Syndicates* as an organized body, and hounded many of the players out of business. At least for now.

Or trapped them here at *Meerut* and then offered them a chance to go straight. Many had taken him up on it. Others had come in later, once they understood that his offer of leniency had an expiration date on it and that he was serious.

There were still more out there.

Historically, this would be the point where any sound empire faced a bandit problem. Worse than pirates in a way, because they were a local issue, rather than a semi-formal, semi-legal business operation with rules and understanding.

What he had now would be rats that didn't want to go down easily.

The man in the mirror looked back and Phil could see the gray coming in on his temple. It would make him look august in PR pictures, but right now made him feel a little old and tired.

Nearly a year and a half at sea would do that, especially with all that he'd seen and done in that time.

Nobody would ever forget *Kosnett's Voyage of Discovery*. Now, he just had to make sure he didn't screw anything up as he came into the home stretch.

A knock at the hatch and Markus stuck his head in a moment later.

"Priority comm for you, boss," he said immediately. "*Hollywood*, and she won't talk to anyone else."

Phil nodded and stepped out of his bathroom into the main sleeping chamber. As First Centurion, he had a nice suite, but he kept it fairly spartan in here. Xue Yi could have accompanied him, but the kids, Yi Wen and Yong Sheng, were at that late teenage stage where being home on *Ladaux* and able to prepare for Academy or university would be a better choice, so she had stayed.

He took a look around the plain walls he hadn't upgraded from the basic watercolor art that someone had been paid to put in here. Probably should have bought himself something. Or had one of his artist friends send something along, but it hadn't been that high of a priority then.

Wasn't now, either.

He followed Markus out.

Hollywood had gone straight. And turned herself into a businesswoman of some power and reach around here.

Whatever she had to say though, if she would only talk to him, didn't sound promising.

MEERUT

ONE

DATE OF THE REPUBLIC MARCH 1, 412 RAN
URUMCHI, MEERUT ORBIT

Heather had learned it from Phil, back when she'd been his Tactical Officer on *CS-405*, and the lessons had stuck. She kept regular bridge watches, even though other Command Centurions were known to spend more time in their day office while they let their First Officer handle things most of the time.

She wanted to know everybody. So she sat watches. And rotated officers through the Emergency Bridge, Auxiliary Control, and even Phil's Flag Bridge on a regular basis. It helped when you knew everyone, at least as close as one got while sitting boring watches with them and talking.

Plus, she had two outsiders on the bridge today. Well, not outsiders. But two young women who weren't citizens of the *Republic of Aquitaine*. Nor were they likely to want to be, later.

Nam—Senior Officer Namrata Nagarkar—was an officer of the *Aditi Consensus* navy who had been seconded to *Urumchi* to learn their ways, and take some secrets home to her bosses, except that they weren't secrets. They were lessons on better ways to run a navy, at the end of the day.

And Nam had turned into an excellent Senior Centurion equivalent in the nearly one year she'd been with them. Had qualified to command a Pulse-Two battery and fought a battle there. Had sat bridge watches as the senior officer in charge of making decisions for the ship.

Solid, which was as high a compliment as Heather could offer. This crew had sailed into the unknown darkness to explore it. *Because it was there.* Everyone here had been selected from three hundred or more competing for each slot.

Nam belonged.

It was the other one that was causing interesting chatter among Heather's people.

First off, the girl was still just fourteen, when her peers would normally be twenty-one or older. She had been sworn in by Phil as a Cornet though, which was the rank you got just out of Academy, before you qualified as a Centurion. Everybody in the *RAN* was a Centurion, as the joke went, because so few billets opened to move up. Competition was fierce and you had to prove yourself, again and again.

But Kohahu Kugosu had asked to temporarily enlist as an officer trainee in the *RAN*, and Phil had allowed it. Heather hadn't been surprised that the youngster had been up to the task. She might look young, but she was the middle daughter of the Shogun of the *Dalou Hegemony*, and maneuvering herself to become the first ever female to hold that title at some later date.

Better, Phil's extended squadron included the *Dalou* Command Cruiser *Storm Petrel*, on which served the Crown Prince of *Dalou*, Shingo Yosan. Heather understood that those two had some level of agreement that would likely see the Shogunate and the Imperial House unified again for the first time in centuries. A revolution.

And Kohahu Kugosu, *Cornet, RAN*, was training as a naval officer. Sitting on Heather's immediate left today, handling communications, which was a good way to learn things. Plus, it let her talk to warships of the entire Cluster, in addition to everyone Phil had brought with him, including *CG-506*, back from escorting Lord Morninghawk to *Urwel* and helping found a new colony there that would revolutionize trade across at least three nations. Four with *Meerut* as a neutral player.

"Command Centurion, I have an observation," Cornet Kugosu offered now, apparently falling back on her old life in the Shogun's Household.

Science Officer Leyla Ekmekçi might have started that conversation with a dirty joke. But Leyla was like that.

Heather turned to the young woman. Gods, they were all young. Heather had fourteen years on Nam, and Kohahu was young enough to be her daughter by a ways.

Still, she smiled at the young woman as a prompt to speak. Needed to break her of the habit of not speaking up if something was important.

"The vessel that just arrived is the former *Hamath Syndicate* Picket *Tralfa*," Kohahu said. "According to the notes forwarded by Captain Ward, that vessel normally takes the *Meerut*-to-*Derragon* run. They were the ones assigned to let the *Gloran* Emperor know that Phil wished to call on their capital next. However, when they came out of Jump at the lagoon, they transmitted a priority message to their commander immediately. She called the First Centurion within three minutes."

Heather considered the team aft that had been awarded their own piratical nickname as *The Pixies* after cracking *Ewin*'s top naval codes in their spare time.

"Have we deciphered the original message?" Heather asked.

Kohahu was at a confused loss, but there were certain things that she might not have been told about. And Leyla was asleep currently.

Instead, Heather opened a comm line to Communications and Cryptography.

"Senior Chief Abadjiev," the man answered instantly.

Harman was one of the few people Heather had had to get into arguments to get included in her crew. He had too many little black marks in his personnel dossier, but if you read them closer, that was because people kept ordering him not to crack any code that he came across, friendly nation or not.

Oh yes, she knew Harman Abadjiev quite well.

"Comm traffic, *Tralfa* to Station," Heather said. "Supposedly encrypted. Any chance they forgot to code it properly?"

"Stand by, Command Centurion," he replied.

His image froze and she waited. He was probably hacking it apart on the fly. Harman could be like that. Kid in a candy store with a ten-Lev coin on his birthday. He wanted it ALL.

"Shit," he said, which meant that he had thought it, said it, then unfroze his comm line to repeat it. "Your screen number three."

Heather didn't even ask how he had taken command of her console from his station. She didn't need to. She'd hired the man over more qualified candidates with fewer black marks.

Who couldn't do what he'd just done.

"Shit," Heather agreed. "Owe you one, Harman."

He nodded and cut the line. Heather routed the fully decrypted message to the flag bridge, where Phil would be almost ready to talk to *Hollywood* Ward.

Right about now, Heather might have also ordered the ship to alert, but they were a long sail away from the emergency, and it had happened more than three weeks ago.

Still, shit.

TWO

DATE OF THE REPUBLIC MARCH 1, 412 RAN
URUMCHI, MEERUT ORBIT

Phil got settled at the command table with the big 3D holographic projector. Command Flag Centurion Harinder Abbatelli sat across from him like always, watching her own screens. The rest of the table was empty. The flag bridge itself was only about half-full, but that was because they were in a safe port, surrounded by a friendly fleet.

Phil could have everyone at their stations in three minutes if he had to.

"Heather has something for you to read before you talk to *Hollywood*," Harinder said succinctly as he got settled and Markus got his coffee into the clamp.

Phil grunted and opened the message on his screen. Read it. Read it again.

"Shit," he muttered under his breath. "They know we're reading their mail?"

"*Pixies*, Phil," Harinder grinned at him.

Pixies. Certainly. Capable of hacking apart encrypted codes because somebody had gotten bored enough to route things through the nav computer, still the most powerful machine on the entire ship when you had a lot of numbers to crunch.

He sighed, took a deep breath, and opened the line. Heather, *et al*, had wanted him to know the entire message that had been transmitted to *Hollywood*, presumably to see how much of it she would immediately pass along to him.

Good test, too, considering.

Hollywood Ward, captain of the Raider of the same name. A tall, stout woman in her mid-fifties, so about a decade older than Phil. Hard as nails, but honorable, once she'd gotten over her piracy days and started acting like a businesswoman.

Phil had high hopes that she could help him build the future of the whole Cluster. He wondered as her screen came on if she was about to burn it all.

"First Centurion," she said immediately. "We have a problem. There was an attack on *Carinae II* several weeks ago that appears to have been a pirate and slaver raid. Evidence accumulated by the *Gloran Empire* investigators suggests that the *Hamath Syndicate* did it. I think we're being framed. In fact, I'm pretty sure of it. In any case, I'd like to accompany you on your mission to personally eviscerate the asshole who ordered it when you catch him."

Well, that grounded things pretty well. Leaving out only a few details that weren't all that important, and touching on the all high notes she'd received from *Tralfa*.

"What makes you so certain?" Phil asked.

"*Hamath* hasn't operated on the *Gloran/Aditi* border in three years, Phil," she replied. "We ceded that territory to *Ingham*, which was why *Tango* and Basant Utkin happened to be at *Vilahana* when you first arrived. Long sail for one of our old hulls. Plus, all of them are accounted for."

Phil leaned back and read the message again.

Carinae II hit from orbit to destroy the warning beacons and the small orbital station. Raiders then landing on the ground in shuttles and opening fire. Phil noted that the casualties were older people and males, suggesting that many of the women of the colony had been…abducted. Nice word for it.

Because slavery was the sort of thing that got you chased to the gates of hell and beyond. Suggesting to the women under his command that some man had decided to accumulate a harem meant that hell wouldn't be safe enough for the stupid punk.

"Accounted for?" Phil asked.

They were on a secure line. At least as secure as a comm could be when people like *The Pixies* existed. He would need to have her come aboard *Urumchi* if he wanted an entirely private conversation, but Phil supposed that the whole system would hear about this soon enough.

Especially if he gave orders to move up the departure, currently set for three days from now.

"Accounted for, First Centurion." She turned serious. "*Hollywood*, *Halberd*, and *Insured Asset* were the only Raiders currently active when you arrived. I'm here and the other two were making their way here once messages caught up with them in hiding. *Triumphant* was our only Enforcer hull after *Glorious* was retired due to battle damage. Again, before your time."

"Are you suggesting that someone is specifically framing *Hamath* for the attack?" Phil asked, turning strategic with his thinking.

"We got a lot of enemies, First Centurion," she replied. "Plus, I'm going straight, so there are two other options. First, they want to make you doubt that you could trust me and the rest of the former pirates. Second, they don't want me building out your Pony Express network because trade and communication might suddenly break out."

She was smiling at the end. Phil was not. He relaxed his scowl before she thought it was aimed at her.

Who benefited from the increase in trade and decrease in piracy? Almost everyone. Ergo, if they didn't want that, then they were benefiting more from the old ways.

Phil had expected a couple of dead-enders to go down fighting. Heads on stakes as bandits, or something similar. People who couldn't walk away from the lifestyle.

At the same time, they had to know he'd come after them with a ten-kilo maul for this.

Were they counting on it?

No, they were counting on Phil going off half-cocked. Except that something like this required more planning if it wasn't just a smash and grab. *Hollywood* had gotten her Pickets flying faster than even Phil had expected, because she had a purpose and a mission; and funding had come in from a number of investors who wanted a piece of what they all saw as a huge and ever-growing pie.

He zeroed in on *Hollywood*'s projection.

"Would the Emperor go off half-cocked?" he asked. "Shoot first and not bother asking questions?"

"That describes the man, Phil," she replied. "*Gloran* folks get extremely touchy about their honor and this sort of thing is likely to rile a lot of people up."

He nodded. Turned to his right-hand expert, across the table.

"Harinder, I need a map projected, with *Meerut* and *Carinae II* at the edges," he ordered. "No, throw *Derragon* on there as well. Not sure where we'll go first."

Harinder did her magic and *Hollywood*'s image moved to one side. An internal map of the Balhee Cluster appeared next to her.

Meerut sat on a corner between the *Dalou Hegemony* and the *Ewin Principalities*, literally inside the wall of the Cluster itself. *Urwel* sat at the other end of the long frontier separating the two nations, then you crossed over into the *Aditi Consensus*, pivoting a little to your left as you did to get to *Derragon*, deep in the heart of the *Gloran Empire*.

Urumchi and his *RAN* vessels could make the run nearly thirty percent faster than any local hull. Folks around here were waking up to the fact that his JumpSails were as advanced as his weapons, compared to everyone else.

"*Hollywood*, who do you want to take with you?" Phil asked. "Assume *Urwel*, then *Carinae II*, then *Derragon*."

She caught her breath almost silently. Almost.

"*Varmint* is already attached to your squadron," she replied after a moment. "*Tralfa* just came back, and that's their normal run. Throw in my Raider and that's it. Not sure you should take anybody from one of the other Syndicates right now, as I can't really vouch for those people personally. And this feels personal."

"Sharply personal, *Hollywood*," Phil replied. "Somebody is playing with fire, in a room filled with oil. I need to stop them. And stomp out all the tendencies from someone else to try it again later. How soon can you depart?"

She blinked. Pirate, sure, but still getting used to how *Aquitaine* did things. Nobody in the Balhee Cluster moved quickly. It was a cultural thing dating back centuries and nothing he would fix in his lifetime.

It also gave him an advantage right now, because his people —and he could stretch to include the full squadron of attached cruisers after they had sailed with him this long—could move as soon as the orders came down.

"*Tralfa* needs to resupply," she said. "If I bump her to the front of the line, Captain Rosa can turn it around in a day or so. As I understand it, everyone else was almost ready to go anyway."

"Indeed," Phil replied. "In fact, I might not wait for *Tralfa* at all, because she is fast enough to catch up with us on our next stop."

"Where's that?" *Hollywood* asked.

"*Urwel*," Phil smiled. "We're going to call on Lord Morninghawk before we get involved with *Gloran*."

THREE

DATE OF THE REPUBLIC MARCH 1, 412 RAN
URUMCHI, MEERUT ORBIT

Phil didn't have time to call a full council of war, or whatever it might be called. No time to round up all his various command centurions and others. Not if he wanted to move.

And he needed to be gone quickly. Even the three week delay receiving *Tralfa*'s message was bad. The situation felt like it was spiraling out of control again.

Or still. Just as soon as he got one nation settled, the next had stepped right up to cause trouble or threaten to fall apart. *Carinae II* was on the *Gloran* side of an amorphous and squishy border, drawn to contain colonies established that didn't remotely follow any sort of straight lines.

Ewin and *Dalou* were calm for now. *Yaumgan* was off on the far side of *Aditi* from the new scene. That left the touchy warriors of *Gloran* and the corrupt businessfolk of *Aditi*.

Phil wasn't silly enough to fall for *Aditi*'s surface republicanism. Not after spending nearly a year getting reports from various ambassadors and reading the general news with a fairly cynical eye.

He was in the forward conference room, just because he

wanted a change of scenery from the flag bridge or the others. Everyone had to walk through Sergey's arboretum to get there, but Phil didn't have any traveling foreign ambassadors.

Well, not counting Nam and Kohahu, both wearing black and green. For whatever that said.

Instead, he had the big, transparent oculus forward, staring at stars and the wall of the Balhee Cluster. If he walked over and stuck his nose to the glass, Phil was pretty sure he could see the twin blue giants that marked that edge of the system and made the gravity wells so insanely complicated around here.

Didn't need to.

He studied Harinder and Heather. Iveta and Leyla. Nam and Kohahu.

Some fool had captured and presumably carried off any number of women from the colony after raiding the place. He had six women around the table with him, all seething to one degree or another.

"We trust *Hollywood*?" Iveta asked as they got settled.

"She was not aware that I had read the same report she had in front of her," Phil replied. "She left out a few things, but nothing important. Then transmitted the full brief when we were done talking. So yes, I trust her. Especially if someone is trying to make *Hamath Syndicate*, or at least *Hollywood* Ward, look bad."

Iveta nodded. That was all the woman needed. She had developed a certain calmness over the last year. One that made her even more deadly than she'd been when Heather had hired herself another Jessica Keller clone as Tactical Officer. Iveta might be Jessica's tactical peer now, as scary a concept as that might be.

Nam looked like she had swallowed a live goldfish. Phil focused his attention on the woman.

"It is not my place to speak out of line, First Centurion," she explained carefully. "Anything I might say here is personal, and not representative of Kaur or her Directors."

Kaur Singh. Commander of the *Aditi Consensus* Heavy Cruiser *Aranyani*, from which Nam had been forwarded, back at the beginning.

"Given," Phil agreed, nodding to prompt her to talk.

He would have liked to have Kaur here, but didn't have time. And didn't trust that messages couldn't ever be read. Just look at his *Pixies*, after all.

"I would not suggest that the *Aditi Consensus* engages in anything like piratical activities…" Nam said, trailing off.

"But?" Heather prompted now, leaning in and spearing the young woman with her fierce eyes.

"But I would be lying if I were to suggest that we never did that in the past," Nam continued. "Everyone did, funding the pirates and others to do things to their enemies. As you have noted, none of us have engaged in any sort of big, formal war in a long time. That just means that everything is generally under the table instead."

"Would *Aditi* pay someone money to frame *Hollywood*'s people?" Harinder asked.

"Without a doubt, Harinder, if they thought they could get away with it later." Nam replied. "What I can't speak to is who. It could be another Syndicate with an ax to grind, if we assume that *Hamath* wasn't involved?"

"We do," Phil said. "For now."

"Or it could be some faction at the *Consensus*," Nam nodded. "It could also be someone on the outs with the *Gloran* Emperor. They aren't quite as bad as *Dalou* or *Ewin* for renegade princes, but that doesn't make them saints, either."

"I agree with Nam," Kohahu spoke up, sounding more like a senior advisor and less like a youngster watching her fifteenth birthday approach. "The Shogun has entire budgets dedicated to such things. Or did in the past. It is my understanding that some of that money has been routed to colonization efforts. Such as Lord Morninghawk at *Urwel*. I don't know how much, though. Probably not all of it, with the remainder being a budget for espionage and juvenile delinquency."

Phil wanted to growl, but both women were messengers here. Experts on their respective cultures being tapped for that knowledge.

He didn't know Cruiser-Captain Adham Khan of *Juvayni* all that well. He did know that the man saw himself as a pure warrior in the old model, and dressed that way in public, a uniform that combined black leather, bronze-colored chain mail and a few plates, plus those tall, leather boots. Starkly primitive, at first glance, but it always had the feel of something rather more anachronistic than anything. Phil assumed that it was intended to contrast with the simple cloth uniforms everyone else wore, because on a starship, you controlled the temperature and humidity, so you could get away with whatever you wanted.

"So *Gloran* sees themselves as warriors," Phil said to the group, eliciting nods. "*Ewin* were all about Princes of the Blood. *Dalou* is a culture of stability and hierarchy. *Aditi* is an open republic that we all agree is probably the most corrupt of all of them, if only because they don't make any bones about the sorts of things they do. How do the warriors react here?"

"Aggressively," Iveta spoke up. "*Tralfa* ran as hard and fast as they could, trying to get the message to *Hollywood* because they were afraid that a war might break out behind them, and didn't have the authorization to just pop out at *Aditi*, even flying *RAN* transponders that would have at least made people stop and listen."

Phil turned to Nam and Kohahu again.

"Will they start a war without a target?" he asked. They both looked at him confused. "Will the *Gloran* Emperor assemble his fleets and send them out to crack heads together, even before he identifies a target? Reprisal raids against whomever?"

"Who would he hit?" Heather asked. "The pirates don't advertise their bases. And many were mobile, like our first mobile drydock in *Aggregator*. They could just sail off."

"My fear is that *Gloran* decides that *Aditi* was involved, and hits them," Phil said. "Or maybe the Fleet-Captain in command has an entire squadron handy and decides to see if he can capture some *Aditi*-aligned world while nobody is looking. How would *Aditi* react?"

"Badly," Nam nodded. "Escalating, as a matter of fact, because they would sail out to drive *Gloran* off. Or hit one of their worlds. As unstable as everyone is, that might trigger a real war."

"That is my fear," Phil said. "I've long been of the opinion that if we could navigate everyone past the uncertainty of the first few years, we might turn the Balhee Cluster into a paradise. What if someone doesn't want that?"

"Who wouldn't?" Nam asked.

"Anyone profiting from the chaos," Kohahu replied to her. "Bad blood. Old rivalries. Maybe they want to bring down the Emperor or the Speaker of the Assembly, or at least weaken them. Look at what that fool Russand did at *Ewin* for his own petty motives. And he was an amateur at that sort of thing."

"Anyone profiting from the chaos," Phil echoed the young woman now. "Lady Kugosu, I need you to transmit a message to the Shogun."

He waited as she blinked once and got serious. And a little scared. He hadn't addressed her as Cornet Kugosu. Or Kohahu. But Lady Kugosu, daughter of the Shogun, who she also was.

She nodded silently.

"I intend to take my entire force with me," Phil said. "That includes all the local auxiliaries, plus *Hollywood*. *Meerut* is not unarmed when I do, but at some level of risk, at least until they finish repairing those three cruisers we took from Russand."

"Yes, sir," she agreed.

"I need you to remind him that we have signed treaties of trade and friendship, Lady Kugosu," Phil ground on. "The Republic and the Hegemony. I expect them to be honored, just as I expect Prince Kalidoona of the Eastern Fleet at *Ewin* to mind his manners while I'm gone, but he's focused inward."

"What message would you like conveyed, First Centurion?"

"I have about had enough of fools playing with live blasters," Phil let his face turn utterly grim. "Now I have to fly off to keep *Gloran* and *Aditi* from marching into a potential war that could have been avoided. If anybody else chooses to test me at this moment, I will have no choice but to escalate my response to levels previously unheard of."

At least she was smart enough to pale at those words. This force probably couldn't fight a pitched battle with the complete Home Fleets of either *Aditi* or *Gloran*. Or *Dalou* with all of their battleships home.

He could, however, request that Petia Naoumov, First Lord of the Fleet, send him a squadron of Heavy Dreadnoughts with full escort wings.

With eight such monsters handy, nothing in the Cluster could resist him blowing them all up, up to and probably including the philosopher/kings of *Yaumgan*, who had been helpful and reticent up until now, possibly because they wanted everyone else to behave.

Or face the consequences.

Phil had no doubts, however, that even *Yaumgan* was looking for their own Yan Bedrov or Lady Moirrey to jump their tech up to a level where *Aquitaine* wasn't utterly dominant.

"I will make sure he understands, First Centurion," Lady Kugosu replied, bowing her head in submission to his wrath.

Because that's what this was.

Wrath.

He'd set out to be an explorer and diplomat. The successor to Tomas Kigali and all his navigation records, rather than Jessica Keller. It was still possible to make the fools of the Cluster see a brighter and better future.

Not, however, if they refused to grow up. In that case, he might crush them.

Or he might just embargo everything and sail home, original mission accomplished.

Phil wanted a win for the history books here, not a blood bath.

If they would let him.

FOUR

MOUNT PENMERTH, DALOU COLONY URWEL

Makara Omarov, Lord Morninghawk, read the report delivered by special courier and tried not to scream in surprise or rage. Both were on the tip of his tongue. He looked out over the valley below from his vantage on the rear patio of the home he had had built and bit his tongue, gesturing the messenger away.

Samnang, Lady Morninghawk now, smiled carefully at him from across the breakfast table, waiting patiently until they were alone again. At least until someone came with more food or coffee.

He handed her the note rather than speak. She read it. Looked up at him. Smiled.

"It's not that bad," she said. "I would think you would be looking forward to seeing all your friends again."

"Not that," he nodded. "If they had come earlier, they would have seen the plans. Later, and we might have completed enough to be impressive. Right now, this is more of a dream than a reality."

He turned back and looked. He had specifically chosen this low peak for the view as the sun traversed the northern sky.

River valley below with the first city laid out of what would eventually become his capital.

The city below was being built no faster than his hilltop fastness, but partly that was the lack of workers. Not enough people willing to move this far from everything they knew, even for a new start on a new world. There were half a dozen *Ewin* worlds closer, and nearly a score *Aditi* planets.

It gave him a corner from which he could trade. And stand alone facing all those potential enemies, but he was *Morninghawk*. He would not quail.

"The house is mostly done," she reminded him.

That had been the first thing they built. A house that would serve as his private residence for the several years it would take to design and build a proper castle. Merely decorative, given modern weaponry, but a statement of purpose that Morninghawk had planted his flag here and here he would remain.

Hopefully, it would even work.

"It will impress them all," Samnang said, smiling at him like she did. "You have created something where there was naught before. You will continue to do so. Eventually, even *Aditi* and *Ewin* will be forced to recognize that. Then they will come with trade."

Makara wasn't so sure, but he trusted this woman with his soul, as well as his life. If she said it would be so, it must be the case.

"And they are already in orbit above us," she reminded him from the note. "They will be here soon and there will be a reception and they can all lionize you yet again."

At least she was grinning. That helped him smile. Makara felt like he had smiled more in the last year than in all of the previous ones combined.

"But the Crown Prince and Lady Kugosu will be accompanying them!" He tried a different tack.

"And both are where they are because of you, Lord

Morninghawk," she countered just as easily. It was like she knew all his weak spots or something. And still loved him. Weird. "It will be good."

Makara looked at his plate and decided that he was done. Stress always put him off food. He dropped his napkin and rose. Samnang was close enough to done and rose with him.

"But I see that you will need to plan," she noted serenely.

He grinned back. She wasn't wrong. His own agitation was a persona thing. And she understood him.

First Centurion Kosnett had come to *Urwel*. And brought his entire fleet with him.

Something didn't feel right.

FIVE

DATE OF THE REPUBLIC MARCH 6, 412 URWEL COLONY

Heather had surveyed it all from orbit with *Urumchi's* scanners, so she was prepared for the atavistic feel of things that Omarov had started to put into place as they took a tour. At the same time, the palace grounds that had been cleared at the peak of the hill would have an unmatched view of the valley on two sides when it was done, and there was a starport going in across the valley and the river down there.

Trade would flow. Just not yet. *Ewin* needed to get their heads out of their asses. *Dalou* needed to re-calibrate nearly half a millennium of inwardness. *Aditi* would probably sniff first, but they would be cautious, expecting some sort of trickery on Morninghawk's part.

The *Dalou Hegemony Mystique*.

Except that there was no mystique here. You got Lord Morninghawk, the man who had ordered his own crew to ram an enemy vessel in battle, in order to protect Heather and *Urumchi* from somebody else trying to do the same thing.

As Iveta had said, the rest of the Cluster would have nightmares about that man coming for them.

Or now, Morninghawk was standing at that awkward corner

where *Dalou*-claimed stars came to a breakwater, a salient on a map thrust in between *Ewin* and *Aditi*. Again, interrupting the flow and forcing you to deal with him first.

The group of tourists had come to a rest on the spot where Heather knew that Omarov would build a wide patio for parties. It had exactly the right elevation and view.

Lord Morninghawk walked next to Phil, with Harinder and Samnang Sobol, Lady Morninghawk, close. Iveta was in charge upstairs, so Heather had brought Nam and Kohahu down, in addition to a few others. All the captains and command centurions had come.

All of them. Even Omarov had gawked at that. Captain Sugawara off *Forktail*. Captain Yukimura off *Storm Petrel*, with the Crown Prince in his naval uniform.

Yet another thing that might have gone a different direction at *Ellariel*, but for Lord Morninghawk taking charge and making sure that all of Dalou understood what Phil's arrival meant.

Makara Omarov really didn't understand how many people owed him. Or the depth of those debts.

Phil had been right when he said the man had single-handedly saved the Balhee Cluster from itself.

Now, they had to do it again. Pity that he was too busy here to join them on this joust.

Heather drifted close as the group turned back from the quick tour of flat earth where stone walls would rise soon. The walk to the current Morninghawk House wasn't far. Kohahu fell in beside her. Nam was a step behind. Interestingly, Crown Prince Shingo was tagging along as the larger group stretched out into several pieces, like a snake munching mice.

Samnang Sobol caught Heather's eye with a nod that promised a conversation later, but nothing that needed doing now, obviously.

At least Omarov had kept things light and easy. Heather could see a cocktail party being laid out in front of them, with some of the more prominent locals invited to attend, once the Lord had had his chance to talk to the conquering heroes.

Heather was glad they had come, but worried about what would happen next.

SIX

DATE OF THE REPUBLIC MARCH 6, 412 URWEL COLONY

Phil smiled as the crowd began to sift and surge like tides. Not for him formal receptions with speeches and posturing. He much preferred talking to people on an even footing, and Morninghawk had done just that.

They had landed, been greeted at the starport and then flown up to the peak. Gotten to say hello to old friends, then taken a quick tour of what was coming. Lord Morninghawk had apologized several times for not making more progress on the colony, until Phil explained his surprise at how much had been accomplished, starting from absolutely nothing.

Well, not nothing. *Urwel* had been an illegal colony on and off for a generation at least, with people being chased off regularly and others sneaking in. It was only when the Shogun had put his foot down that things became official. Those folks here could swear allegiance to a new Lord, or depart. Quickly.

Many had stayed. More had come, and were coming every day.

But today had turned into a surprise party, since Phil had outrun news of his coming. He could do that when there weren't messengers and couriers going every which way with news.

Speaking of…

He nodded *Hollywood* to step closer when she emerged from the crowd, still a little uncomfortable in these situations, since she had been on the other side of the law for so long. Lord Morninghawk was busy holding court with Heather and several others, but Samnang was close. She felt Phil's gaze and turned his way.

"Is all well, First Centurion?" Samnang asked as she also drew close.

"I know you have met Captain *Hollywood* Ward in passing," Phil replied. "I have asked her to start a new business, and even provided some funding to help. I thought that perhaps she could have a most beneficial conversation with you today, since your husband is currently occupied."

They all glanced over there as someone told a joke or brought up a funny memory. It was good to see the man laugh, as he had been so dour and stern before.

Driven by duty even more than Phil and many of his officers were, which was a truly impressive level to achieve. Still, he needed to take time to relax. Everyone did.

Phil stole those moments when he could, understanding that after this adventure, he was probably going to be tied to a desk, a lectern, or just retire entirely.

How does one top this? Well, there was a way, but he had already quietly been in communications with the First Lord about that, and it would hopefully be Heather's mission, one of these days. At least if everything worked out.

Phil smiled and turned to the two women close by.

"What this Cluster needs, at a cultural level, is communication," Phil continued. "To that end, *Hollywood* here is in the process of building up a network of retired, piratical Pickets, temporarily flying *RAN* transponders until all the details get worked out."

"To what end, First Centurion?" Samnang asked carefully.

"She has dedicated couriers running from *Meerut* to each of the other capital worlds on a regular cycle, carrying news and messages," Phil said. "I would like to expand that."

Hollywood made a sound that sounded like a strangled yelp of pain, but really, she should have seen this coming, if she was any good. Probably wanted to complain about the difficulty in hiring enough women captains and female-heavy crews, even with all the pirates to pick from.

Finding crews wasn't a problem, but command-level officers still were.

Not his problem.

"Expand?" *Hollywood* managed after a false start and suffering her voice breaking in the middle of the word.

"*Urwel*," Phil said simply. "*Belamel* on the *Aditi* side. *Toulouse* on the *Ewin* side. A triangle connecting three of the five nations of the Cluster across extremely short distances."

The two women looked at him expectantly. Phil smiled.

"I also need to share a secret with you two, and hope that you will refrain from sharing it on for a while," he said wickedly.

Oh my, that got their attention. As intended.

"My crews have been working on exploring the strange fold in physics and gravity that is *Meerut*," Phil said. "They have not succeeded yet, but that is entirely a factor of time, as I have run from one fire to the next. However, the mathematics involved suggest that there is at least one path out of the back of *Meerut* into open space outside the Cluster. Possibly three, but we're currently inventing the sensors to determine that now."

Eyes HUGE. *Hollywood* understood the implications immediately. Samnang took all of about a half-second.

"What about *Vilahana*?" Samnang asked.

"Oh, I'm still negotiating a treaty for warehousing and shipping through there," Phil nodded. "My scientists assure me that even with improved sensors over what *Urumchi* and *Viking* have currently, you'll utterly precise maps and timing to make those runs. However, it turns *Meerut* into a potential competitor to *Vilahana*, when it comes to trade from *Aquitaine*."

"And *Fribourg*," *Hollywood* noted. "They are closer on that front. Will you tell the Emperor?"

"We're pen pals," Phil grinned. "However, I suspect that this will, for a time, qualify as a military secret at a reasonably high level. At least until such time as the rest of the Cluster, and in this case, galaxy, catches up with us technologically. I will remind you that I brought smart people, added more people, and they are out on the bleeding edge here."

"More people?" Samnang asked.

"Senior Officer Namrata Nagarkar of the *Aditi* Navy has been serving on my flagship for nearly a year, and currently wears an *RAN* uniform," Phil replied, nodding to the woman. "The tall, slender woman standing next to Heather Lau."

Again, all eyes turned. Heather felt it and looked his way, but Phil shook his head with a smile, so she went back to what she had been doing.

"I've tasked Nam with managing some portions of the research, so that the locals aren't as likely to get nervous about what new things I invent."

"Terrible weapons?" Samnang asked.

"Perhaps," Phil nodded. "Points where *Aquitaine* technology can be fused with local things to create new systems. Like sensors that can map the Cluster Wall fine enough to find paths suggested by math."

Hollywood had gone a little green. But then, a year ago, she had been a mid-level command centurion, flying the equivalent of a light cruiser in *RAN* terms. Now she was engaging in diplomacy and politics at the topmost levels.

And doing a pretty damned good job of it.

Phil shrugged inside at how dumb it had been around here that so much of the culture was male-dominated, leaving many women only the option of a career with the pirates, if they wanted to go into space and get ahead. Only *Aditi* really balanced those things.

"So what are you proposing, Phil?" *Hollywood* asked next, having caught her breath.

"Three ships, at least at first," he replied. "Running the triangle under an *RAN* flag, and later *Meerut*'s neutrality. Couriers like you do with *Ellariel* or *Ewinhome*, but just making that run, hauling news and mail. No cargo. Occasional diplomats."

"What if more people want to come?" *Hollywood* pressed.

"Like you and I discussed at the beginning then, Captain Ward," he smiled. "Maybe you need to get into the passenger liner business one of these days. Or have such a boat available for charter, because *Belamel* and *Toulouse* are both mature colonies with population excesses. What might it take to induce merchants, artisans, and eventually immigrants to come to *Urwel*?"

"Those are also sector capitals, First Centurion," Samnang pointed out.

He turned to her and smiled.

"So will you be, once everyone gets over themselves," he replied. "One successful colony on this side will cause miners to spread out looking for ores that can make them money. Those people will need food. Eventually you will need farmers and ranchers producing that food. That turns into a second planet, then a third. Meanwhile, *Aditi*, *Ewin*, and *Dalou* are trading on an even footing. News is rapidly disseminating from that triangle, because let's face it, *Meerut* will always be an out-of-the-way place."

"At least until outside merchants start entering the Cluster from our side," *Hollywood* noted.

Phil nodded.

"Decades that, if not generations," he replied. "Though I reserve the right be wrong on both ends."

"What you propose will significantly alter the center of gravity of the Balhee Cluster, First Centurion," Samnang interjected.

"Yes," he agreed. "What's wrong with that?"

"*Gloran* and perhaps *Yaumgan* will wish to participate in such trade," Samnang said. "Lest they be left out."

"Good," he nodded. "Exactly my point. Everyone comes to *Urwel* to trade. Did you think I would forget the man who stood as my shield wall in the face of everything the pirates could throw at me?"

Both women got a little pale. His voice might have risen in volume, but that couldn't be helped.

They were talking about Makara Omarov. *Morninghawk*.

Just because he was no longer flying escort for *Urumchi* didn't mean he couldn't give other places nightmares still, as Iveta had so prophetically noted.

"This is just another reward for turning into the man he is, Samnang," Phil continued. "What he did at *Ellariel* might have permanently altered the trajectory of history for the Balhee Cluster."

"And not *Meerut*?" *Hollywood* asked.

"*Meerut* was merely a battle, *Hollywood*," Phil scowled at her, just a little. "*Ellariel* was an entire war, all by itself."

SEVEN

URWEL COLONY, DALOU HEGEMONY

Kaur had worked hard as part of Phil's squadron, having been there from day one, for all intents and purposes, sailing out to meet him when *Urumchi* came out of jump at *Vilahana*. Time and again, she had expected her Directors back home to issue orders for her and her ship to finally return to base, where supposedly she would be promoted to Director herself, and given command of a Ship of the Line like *Khandoba*. Assuming she wasn't give a Court Martial and thrown in prison for something.

Neither had occurred yet, but something was coming. Hopefully, it would be good.

Phil just kept disrupting everyone else's plans with his history-making missions, first to *Meerut*, then *Ellariel*, then *Ewinhome*. With that in mind, Kaur half expected that she would remain attached for the full run to *Derragon*, and then finally *Kyulle*.

What would her place be in the histories written? She had no idea, but standing on the surface of a *Dalou* world, casually chatting with other captains, felt like a future they all needed to embrace.

So she stood and talked as people came and went, both *Aquitaine* and *Locals*, as Phil liked to group everyone from the Cluster. Like they were one people.

Perhaps they were.

Nam appeared out of the crowd and stepped close.

It was amazing what a year had done for the woman. She looked ready to take command of her own ship now, rather than merely returning to *Aranyani* as a potential First Officer when Kaur left, assuming that Arya Chaudhari got promoted when Kaur did.

They touched glasses of wine silently, just to say hello. Nam was a peer these days in many ways, rather than a subordinate. She had taken the challenge of learning about *Aquitaine* and run with it.

"Holding up?" Kaur asked the woman, noting that Nam was still gorgeous, just too short to have been a fashion model.

"Phil has me on a new project," Nam said quietly, glancing around to make sure nobody was close enough to eavesdrop.

"Oh?" Kaur asked.

"Remember that thing that *Urumchi* did at *Ewinhome*?" Nam asked.

"Iveta called it *Ghost Mode*," Kaur did remember. "Something that Keller invented, back during the war with *Fribourg*, right?"

"Yes," Nam nodded. "Overpower someone with the sensors on a scout by putting out as much interference as they can. Worked then with surprise. It will work here until people upgrade their targeting systems to be able to filter it. Which I think involves a rebuild or a new design."

"Do you know how to do it?" Kaur asked.

"Yes," Nam said calmly. "They've hidden nothing from me there. In fact, I get the impression that they want me knowing these things, and transmitting them home."

"Won't that give us an advantage on everyone else?" Kaur

asked, brow furrowing as she tried to work out all the implications.

Phil Kosnett might be an open book at times, but he was also playing chess on a level nobody else could match, much of the time. Except maybe Heather. Never discount his Command Centurion.

Still, he wanted everyone at peace.

Nam laughed. "They have the impression that spies from everywhere else will steal everything about twelve hours after it makes it to *Aditi* proper," she said.

Kaur couldn't really help but laugh at that point. *Aditi* was notorious for backroom deals and double-crosses, even within the government. If making a rival look bad involved enemy spies, it would happen.

"So what is the new project? What are they building?" Kaur asked, wondering where Phil was leading everyone.

"It is like Ghost Mode, but even more interesting," Nam answered. "At least if it works."

"If what works?"

"Phil tasked a team, including me, with modifying a Shield Projector that they stripped off a Picket that had been nearly destroyed at *Meerut*," Nam replied. "When potentially overwhelmed with missions or torpedoes, an *Aditi* or *Ewin* ship shuts down all their active systems and launches a shuttle designed to mislead firebirds. Usually, it works, too. They want to do something better."

"How?" Kaur asked, wondering if he was about to upend weapons technology again, right as everyone started the process of figuring out what they needed to do to use *Aquitaine* Pulse technology.

"Conceptually, like Ghost Mode," Nam said. "But the projection is out farther away from the ship, off to one side, and designed to mimic the signature of the vessel. Once they get it tuned, firebirds should track the projection. Missiles, too."

"Once they get it tuned?" Kaur asked with dread in her soul. "They've already done it?"

"Mostly, the thing was a question of power, Commander," Nam said. "And they have more power than anything we build right now. The formulae have all been worked out, and they have started building control systems and software to handle it. That's actually my contribution, since I know how those systems work better than *Aquitaine* folks. If Phil hadn't decided to take the whole force with him, I might have been transferred over to a Science Lab on *Meerut*, along with a few dozen others, to keep building the systems while he was gone. Instead, he wanted me with him."

"Why you, though?" Kaur asked.

"Because Markus would have seen it as a punishment detail," Nam laughed brightly. "He still has all ten fingers."

Kaur was lost, but it seemed to make sense to Nam. If she remembered correctly, Markus was the aide who followed Phil everywhere, the burly redneck who was *always* prepared. How smart was the man, anyway?

"It's the *Aquitaine* way, Commander," Nam explained when Kaur fell silent. "Whoever is best suited is put in command, regardless of rank. Markus is only a Senior Chief, but is routinely in charge around Senior Centurions, and not just because he is Phil's man. But the threat to keep him from misbehaving is to send him back to Engineering permanently if he loses a finger blowing something up or machining."

"I see," Kaur did. She knew all this, at an intellectual level. It was odd coming to understand it.

However, this was exactly why she had assigned Namrata Nagarkar to serve aboard *Urumchi*.

To learn their ways.

"So you will build a new weapons system?" Kaur asked.

"Yes, Commander," Nam nodded. "Defensive, but if *Ewin* missiles and *Dalou* firebirds are neutralized, that cuts out two navies, and impacts both *Gloran* and *Aditi* to a lesser degree.

Combined with the Pulse technology that Phil is planning to license to all players, Iveta expects that the entire Cluster has to start from scratch, building new fleets to replace every ship in service now. That disrupts everything for a decade, according to their expectations, while trade ramps up. As a result, everybody hopefully becomes better friends and unwilling to fight as much."

"What about piracy?" Kaur asked, cycling back to the reason that they were headed to *Gloran* right now.

"That, according to Heather, is the wildcard," Nam nodded. "The pirates might cause problems that cause people to overreact."

"Which is why Phil is bringing everyone with him."

Kaur saw the shape of things now. *Gloran* ships weren't as good as *Aditi* or *Dalou*. Frequently, they purchased *Dalou* hulls secondhand, without the weapons, and installed their own, meaning that a *Gloran* squadron was frequently an odd mix of shapes and sizes. *Dalou* and *Ewin* were the ones that would have to rebuild the fastest, limiting them, while *Gloran* retooled or stepped up to build better hulls and *Aditi* intermediaries and corrupt officials took their cuts.

"A decade is ambitious," Kaur noted. "Most will need that decade just to build the prototypes."

"You think so, Commander?" Nam asked.

"Yes," Kaur decided. "Let Heather or Iveta know that, as with everything else, most of us will not move quickly. Might even continue building the old hulls, in spite of their new weaknesses, just because we'll have to study how to build new fleets before we start welding hulls. And work out new deals with the oligarchs who might get cut out if the government back home isn't careful."

Nam nodded and they fell into silence.

Kaur nodded back to the woman and they separated.

Nam had made many friends among the *Aquitaine* folks. That would serve her in this new future, just as Kaur hoped her time with Phil would reflect well when she had to stand before all her Directors.

They were coming to another one of those inflection points where whole nations might suddenly change direction. *Dalou* had done it. *Ewin* had been forced to. *Gloran* was probably next.

Kaur couldn't help but wonder if *Aditi* still had a reckoning in their future that they had not internalized.

EIGHT

DATE OF THE REPUBLIC MARCH 6, 412 URWEL COLONY

Heather no longer growled when Cruiser-Captain Adham Khan stepped close. Partly, that was him getting the savage end of her tongue enough times to shut down some of the casual and possibly unconscious sexism that had come out of his mouth before.

However, he had learned, just as Striker Solo had tamped down his exuberance and flailing hands. Heather had a hard time believing that the man was known as Solo the Quiet at home.

Khan stepped closer. Politely. Diffidently, even, which just showed how far the man had come from the early days.

Heather decided to ambush him anyway. Just to keep the fellow on his toes.

"So tell me about your Penal Fleets, Khan," she requested, even as he opened his mouth to say something else.

Worked. The man's entire conscious being short-circuited and then rebooted. Heather took a long drink of her juice as she waited. Probably didn't help his peace of mind that she was nearly a handspan taller, but Khan never came across as a small man.

Merely compact.

Khan's mouth finally opened a third time before words came out. She smiled to prompt him.

"Warriors are warriors," he said, head tilted a little and eyes still not quite focused. "At times you make a bad decision or such. Too hasty. Too aggressive. But not dishonorable. Not cowardly. So the punishment is to be removed from your current vessel and transferred to the Penal Fleet. After a time, your sentence is complete and you come back to the regular forces. Or you might distinguish yourself in some way. Battle or emergencies or simply exceptional service that causes you to be sent back early."

"Have you ever been?" she asked, a bit intrigued.

Back home, if you messed up that badly, your promotion prospects would be over. Or you might be bounced out of the Navy. Or prosecuted.

The *Republic of Aquitaine* Navy had far more Court Martials than most fleets she knew of, but they also used them as educational tools. Being brought before such a tribunal might be that you had done everything right and just suffered bad luck. Robbie Aeliaes and *RAN BrightOak* had suffered an engine failure at *First Ballard*, but subsequent investigations had praised the man and his crew for overcoming an unknown maintenance failure from a previous drydock and keeping it from destroying the ship in battle. He'd even gotten promoted.

Khan had started to glower, but then cleared his face and waved a hand.

"But of course, you would not know such things," he began.

Heather shook her head.

"My father was a Fleet-Captain before running into a semi-famous *Aditi* Director in a running battle that got out of hand," Khan said mournfully. "Afterwards, he was broken all the way down to Frigate-Captain for many years, outranked by his own Cruiser-Captain son who was not in the Penal Fleet. Later, he made it all the way back to Fleet-Captain, before retiring a few years ago. One of the few men to ever accomplish such a feat."

Heather smiled and nodded. She'd heard rumors that Khan had a famous forebear. Apparently, much more famous than the son generally let on to. At the same time, she could see that, if he had been embarrassed by his father for a time, he was now only proud.

Must make family reunions interesting.

"Are we likely to encounter such ships at *Carinae II*?" Heather pressed.

Khan shrugged. "Who is to say?" he replied. "If the Emperor is angry, he might send a warfleet to remonstrate on *Aditi*'s border. Or he might send a Penal Squadron. I do not think that they would necessarily raid across, because this cowardly act was done by pirates, but we will not know until we arrive and ask."

"Will they let us help?" Heather asked.

For the longest moment, Khan looked at her like she'd asked the question in the Mongolian she still had shards of from the war against *Buran*.

"Help, Command Centurion?" he finally managed.

"Your colony was attacked," Heather pointed out. "Nearly destroyed, save for a few, scattered survivors. Granted, more than a month ago, but we'll be arriving with this entire force. That is a significant tonnage of vessels and crew resources that could be brought to bear."

He blinked too many times, mind obviously racing madly down various channels of thought, explored and discarded at terrible speed.

Heather was pretty sure that Khan was recalibrating everything in his head at her words. Possibly even growing up from the man who reminded her initially of a teenage firebreather rather than an officer.

"I do not know, Command Centurion," he finally admitted, crestfallen. "Others would never make the offer, let alone mean it. We have been at strife with *Aditi* and *Dalou* for centuries, to the point that if they showed up, our forces would immediately open fire on them defensively, assuming some ambush."

Heather nodded. Shoot first, don't ask questions.

The Balhee Cluster way, going back to *Vilahana*.

With the singular exception of *Aranyani* and Commander Kaur Singh.

"Let me pose a different question, then," Heather continued. "Should we fly directly to *Derragon* instead of *Carinae II*?"

Khan started to say something hot and probably rude, but caught himself. He even smiled.

"If we have just arrived to help, the Emperor cannot order the First Centurion to leave without offering insult," Khan said with a grin. "Whereas he might forbid us going, if we got to the capital first. I think *Carinae II* is the wiser choice, because my comrades back home do not understand what the First Centurion really means."

"What does he mean, Khan?" Heather pressed.

Adham Khan had always been loud and aggressive. A Warrior's Warrior, in a squadron composed mostly of professional sailors and diplomats. That was why Heather had put him and Striker Solo on the same wing, then placed that wing closer to any perceived enemy, since they would charge in and attack without much provocation.

"We were recruited to break the pirates, Lau," Khan said with deadly seriousness now. "Kosnett did that at *Meerut*. Then he went to *Ellariel* and broke the Hegemony. Others might not see it, because it will probably be after my lifetime before it really happens, but you have *Morninghawk*, the Crown Prince, and the future Shogun here on this planet, at this party, even. That was unthinkable even a year ago. *Dalou* will never be the same, even before you start selling everyone pulse weapons."

Heather nodded for him to continue. He seemed to be on a roll.

"Then we went to *Ewinhome*." Khan's eyes got big and excited as he spoke further. "Functionally overthrew the King, while breaking two of the biggest troublemakers and rewarding those folks more willing to talk and trade with neighbors like

Dalou. Even *Aditi* has asked for more. I would have, but that is a bridge too far, at least as *Gloran* culture today would see it."

"Today?" Heather asked.

"Kosnett will not be happy until he has infected every nation with *innovation*, Command Centurion," Khan's smile expanded. "With casting off the old ways and embracing a grander, broader galaxy than just the Cluster. Until we are a waystop for you going beyond, and merchants from *Aquitaine* or *Fribourg* make the long run into darkness to trade with us. We will never be the same."

"And your take on all that?" she pressed, wondering if the man had gotten a little drunk to loosen up, and taken it too far. This was the most useful conversation she'd have with him since they had met.

"Long overdue, Command Centurion," he replied sharply, nodding at some internal commentary. "You could have sailed in here with the fleet of destruction that Kosnett occasionally threatens, and swept the skies clear of anywhere but *Yaumgan*. And nobody knows how well the philosopher/kings might have resisted. Instead, Kosnett will cause everyone to destroy themselves, but do it in a way that they might build something better. *Dalou* saw that and immediately took hold with both hands. *Ewin* is broken, but they might not be smart enough to fix it. *Gloran* is next, but I have the advantage of seeing both ends of the possibilities having already unfolded."

"And what would you counsel your Emperor, when he calls you to the carpet for an accounting of the last year?" Heather leaned in. Not towering over him. Focusing the man. Just the two of them.

A duel of words and intellect, which she hadn't previously thought would be a fair fight.

Was Khan just shy?

"The *Dalou* approach," Khan nodded up at her. "Losing missiles won't hurt us as much as *Ewin*. Or *Dalou* and their firebirds. At the same time, we need something larger than a

Main Gun, perhaps equivalent to your Type-4 beams, so that we can sail farther from our home ports and not end up disarmed, like those fools at *Ewin*. Bedrov was a pirate in his time, but has become a businessman. I would challenge the Emperor to send a captain to *Ladaux* or *Petron* to hire the man to design a fleet that *Gloran* could build. Failing that, we need our own Bedrov."

"What about Lady Moirrey?" Heather asked.

The man shuddered.

"Godslayer," he whispered under his breath like a religious injunction before his voice got stronger. "We do not need her. Like you and Kosnett and the others, my hope is that everyone can grow up and our future ships aren't intended for conquest. Perhaps I am a radical, but you radicalized me. We are a century behind *Aquitaine*, and you are not standing still. We will need centuries to reach parity, assuming we wanted to. Better to transform the Cluster into a destination and then spread our singular culture wider. The darkness is not complete around here. It is just that the stars are much thinner between arms."

Heather was shocked. She'd rated the man as *dumb muscle* for a year, and he'd acted it for much of that. Somewhere in the last however long, he had woken up to where *Gloran* stood in the scheme of things. Likely relegated to the same backwardness as *Ewin*, when *Aditi* and *Dalou* walked forward. A second-rate power, third if *Yaumgan* was as advanced as all the whispers suggested, but Heather was still of the opinion that *Li Jing* and the *Eight Immortals* represented a public relations program designed to intimidate the other nations into leaving them alone.

It had worked this long, hadn't it?

What would Phil discover when he finally got to visit *Kyulle*?

But she had Adham Khan in front of her now, standing as if on pins and needles.

He really had gone out onto a precipice, hadn't he?

"Khan, I wouldn't have said this earlier," Heather nodded to the man, "but I'm glad your Emperor chose you to accompany us on the piracy mission. Hopefully, he will listen to you in the future."

Khan nodded back and she could see an internal sigh in the way his shoulders sagged a little. Like maybe he'd been afraid he had been wrong in talking to her, only to find out he'd been right.

"Come," she said, turning him with a hand on his shoulder like drinking buddies. "Let's go get some more juice and talk to folks about what to expect at *Carinae II*."

NINE

MOUNT PENMERTH, DALOU COLONY URWEL

Makara watched the lights of Phil's GunShip recede into the night sky with longing and regret.

Samnang came up behind him and wrapped her arms around his waist, laying her head on his shoulder.

"It's hard," he said aimlessly.

"I know," she replied. "You want to be standing there where Sugawara has taken your place, when Phil strides into his next battle."

All the command centurions and others had only come down for the day, now returning to orbit so that the squadron could continue its run across *Aditi*-claimed sectors to reach *Gloran*. And possibly head off another confrontation, if he'd read the various underlying emotions correctly.

Carinae II had been functionally destroyed. Makara was initially surprised, because he didn't think that there were any Syndicate forces that powerful still in existence, most of them having run as fast as they could from the law and breaking up their crews to take whatever amnesty might be offered.

Phil had been ironclad about letting people walk away from their past, if they did it before a certain date.

"He will need me," Makara grimaced at the night sky, as the GunShip turned into a shooting star.

"He has *Forktail* and *Storm Petrel*," Samnang said, moving around to his side. "But you see more."

It wasn't a question. This woman knew him better than friends of decades. Knew his soul. Truly, completed him in ways he could have never imagined.

"Where would you run, having done such a thing to *Gloran*?" Makara turned inside her arms until they faced each other. "Kosnett and others are likely to offer rich enough bounties to make someone talk, at which point you have both fleets coming for you. In the old days, *Dalou* and others frequently paid pirates under the table to raid and bother other nations."

"Indeed," she chuckled. "As an Imperial Inspector, I occasionally delivered such payments personally. But what do you see?"

What did he see? Many people had taken to asking him that question, convinced that he had developed some magical precognitive ability, when really it was just processing all the present tense and anticipating the shifting tides going forward.

"It is a planet close to the *Aditi* border, which suggests that they might have fled across to hide somewhere," Makara said. "Would *Dalou* still be funding such things?"

"Not when last I knew," Samnang replied. "The Shogun had decided that his contribution to peace was to withdraw such payments, and to offer amnesty to those people who weren't wanted in *Dalou* space, but would not necessarily be welcome elsewhere. At least those that didn't choose *Meerut*."

"So *Dalou* is not funding such an operation," Makara nodded, ticking off points in his head. "*Yaumgan* retains their enforced aloofness, at least until their immovable object encounters Kosnett's irresistible force. We just broke *Ewin*, and I cannot imagine that they came up with such a thing in the time since *Second Meerut*."

"You do not believe the piracy cover story?" Samnang turned serious.

"Red herring, as they say," he replied. "Left in the middle of the trail to distract people with an obvious story to follow."

"So *Aditi*?" she continued.

"Or *Gloran*," he countered. "Who knows what internal pressures have developed? They have had a year to watch Phil and Heather upend our systems. I can only imagine what they said when they heard about *Ground Control*. Then Phil went to *Meerut* and *Ellariel*. *Ewinhome* probably was happening as whoever planned this thing."

"Did you discuss it with Heather or Phil?" she asked.

"Only broadly," he shrugged inside her arms. "I was talking to *Hollywood* about setting up a local circuit of transports hauling news and messengers."

"You should sit down and write him a letter before they depart," she said now, insistent. "They will be in system for several more hours, so you have time, but Phil needs to know. You might not be able to sail on his van, but that's no reason you cannot be there to protect your friends."

He smiled at his wife. His partner. His friend.

"Yes," Makara agreed, turning and taking her hand.

That much he could do, for the man who had made it possible to stand on a hill named for the capital city of the *Republic of Aquitaine*, and gaze out over the future of the Balhee Cluster.

TEN

CLIPPER HOLLYWOOD, URWEL ORBIT

Hollywood scowled at the man on the screen, but he was at least as stubborn as she was.

"Because I said so, Jones," she answered.

"That's a load of sheep shit, *Hollywood*," Esser replied.

Not that she blamed him. She'd brought *Hollywood*, *Tralfa*, and *Varmint* on this mission. She'd even stopped calling her ship a Raider and was telling everyone that the class were Clippers now, intended for long, fast flights, rather than lurking quietly at the edge of the gravity well and pouncing on unsuspecting freighters coming and going.

Legitimate business now. Honest.

The smaller ones used to be called Pickets, because that was what they were used for. Used to be used for. Now, they were Rapid Couriers, designed to run as fast as possible between two points. And if you weren't hauling around a lot of boarding party crew, you could go a long time between resupply runs.

"Kosnett specifically wanted me here because I can represent the old Syndicates when we run into people," she continued. "And I know a lot of those people personally. That leaves me *Tralfa* to run ahead to *Derragon* to let them know we're coming, and you. I need you to haul ass to *Meerut* and tell Dexter to recruit three ships, if he can find them, to set up a triangle run here at *Urwel*. The faster you move, the sooner you'll join us at *Carinae II*."

He growled at that. But that was Esser Jones. The man reminded everyone of a tornado, with long, soot-black hair back in a tail like a comet's, and big muscles. Still something of a pussy cat, when you approached him right, but she didn't have time to flatter the man right now.

"Hey, you want to keep flying an *RAN* transponder, sometimes you get the shit details, Esser," *Hollywood* said, getting a little exasperated at his intransigence. "If you really piss me off, I can transfer you to this job, instead of running around with *Urumchi*."

That got his attention, like an open-handed slap might.

Kosnett had hired her to put together a communications network. And *everyone* else was contracted to her right now. That included Esser Jones and *Varmint*.

And sometimes, a girl's got to pull rank.

Esser understood that, too. He was just being balky. Too long as his own captain, answering only to the board of directors or Enforcers like *Triumphant* or *Glorious*. Not Raiders like *Hollywood*. Or Clippers these days.

"Straight to *Carinae*?" he asked now, voice and mannerisms more subdued.

"With the usual drop outs every few days to make sure everybody arrives at the same time," she nodded. "Since you don't have to do that, you ought to be able to drop out on Dexter, tell him everything he needs, plus give him the packet Lord Morninghawk is sending along, then chase us straight across. We'll handle whatever resupply you need from Kosnett's stores at that point, since you're doing him a major favor by getting all this moving today."

"Why does it have to happen now anyway, *Hollywood*?" Esser asked.

"Because people are lazy, Jones," she retorted. "Prince

Kalidoona will have his hands full with shit over there, but if we start running to *Toulouse* with *RAN* sanction, they won't argue with us. By the time they do get their shit sorted out, it will have become a habit. What?"

He was laughing at her now, great big guffaws and peels of hilarity. It was a good thing both of them were alone in their respective offices, talking on a tight-beam comm.

The galaxy wasn't ready to know just how big a goofball Esser Jones could be.

"What?"

"You," he finally managed to gasp. "*Ewin*. Getting their shit together. Seriously?"

"Kosnett's betting a lot on it," she replied. "So is *Dalou*, in the form of Lady Kugosu, so put that in your pipe and smoke it. *Aditi* wants more trade. Always has, even on their own terms. Lord Morninghawk turns that on its head, because he's the Golden Boy right now with the only person that really matters around here."

"Oh, alright," the man finally admitted, however begrudging. "I suppose I have to go off and save the galaxy again, like I did after *Second Meerut*."

"Exactly, Esser," *Hollywood* agreed, relieved that the man would listen to reason. And threats. "The faster you get gone, the better for you."

"I'm just afraid I'll miss all the fun," Jones said ruefully.

"You think anybody stands a chance, if they start shit with this force?" she challenged the man.

"That's my point, *Hollywood*," Esser laughed. "*Gloran* might be that stubborn. And I won't be there to watch Kosnett hand somebody his head for it. Watching the logs and scans later won't be nearly as much fun as being able to taunt those poxy bastards in real time when they try."

"Then you best haul ass, *Varmint*," she ordered. "Maybe you can get back fast enough, if you'd stop arguing with me."

"Yes, mother," Esser chortled. "Back soon."

And he was gone.

Hollywood cut the line from her end and leaned back to study her office. She spent a lot of time on the stations with Dexter Milose, the Governor of *Meerut*, and his staff.

Current governor, she amended herself. Kosnett had asked her if she wanted to become the next Governor, or the Fleet Admiral/First Centurion of that little fleet, or go into business.

This still felt like the best option, long term. At some point, somebody would try their luck attacking *Meerut* again. Maybe with enough force to actually succeed.

At least until Kosnett brought in a wall of Heavy Dreadnoughts and curb-stomped the responsible parties. Irresponsible parties, because he'd warned everyone.

Yaumgan wasn't dumb enough to challenge him. *Gloran* might. If they could bottle stubborn and sell it, they'd be rich, but in many ways, they were as badly disorganized as the fools at *Ewinhome*, just in a different direction.

The Princes were all about the blood. If you had it, you could be a big-time player. If not, you were a peon.

Gloran was the warrior culture. Aggressive, militant, hardass. Hard work got you promoted, rather than blood like *Ewin* and *Dalou*, or connections like *Aditi*. Any commoner could aspire to become a Fleet-Captain, or even a War-Captain. Historically, a few crazed berserkers had either married into the Imperial Family or been adopted when it made the most sense for them to inherit power.

Better than civil wars. At least for the locals.

Pirates like she'd been, once upon a time, had thrived during periods of instability and chaos, since fleets were too busy chasing each other off to stop and protect every little irrelevant colony.

Which was why some dumbass had hit *Carinae II*. And why it didn't make a damned bit of sense that they had. *Dalou* was stable. *Aditi* was stable. *Gloran* might be next up for crazy, but they were stable now, and would be angry.

Was that the thing? Make the Emperor too angry to listen when Kosnett came along with a new future?

Who came out ahead?

Hollywood Ward didn't have any ideas, but she had a few days to mull it over. Esser and *Varmint* would be hauling ass to catch up. Kosnett might be willing to take a little extra time from here, just to give *Tralfa* a chance to get to *Derragon* with his messages from the First Centurion.

Which suggested that the first major confrontation would occur in *Carinae*'s orbit.

What did they have to look forward to?

CARINAE II

ELEVEN

DATE OF THE REPUBLIC MARCH 14, 412 RAN URUMCHI, WAYPOINT FIFTY-THREE

Iveta had asked Phil to take a longer break at this second-to-last waypoint, just so she could assemble all the Tactical Officers and talk in person. That meant all of the Senior Centurions she needed.

The Tactical Officers off the Corvettes were an even mix. Four men, three woman. What you got in the *RAN*, plus *Auke* Alma off *Viking*, the big genius who reminded everyone of a giant hummingbird.

It also meant Arya Chaudhari of *Aranyani* instead of Kaur Singh. Plus both Right Gunner Ju Tou and Left Gunner Ying Xa-Mu off *Li Jing*, leaving Captain Xue Dao Zhiou minding the ship.

Captain Sugawara off *Forktail*, but only Commander Iyo Takahashi of *Storm Petrel*, a tall Rajput with a fierce, if well-trimmed, beard, instead of Captain Yukimura.

Gunner Holman, the homely redheaded woman off *Hollywood* who had no known first name. And a fierce growl.

Gotzon Solo, Striker of *Shadowbolt* had come, mostly because he had never trained his First Officer to handle combat tasks and now was not the time to start. Even he knew that.

Cruiser-Captain Khan, like Solo, was too much of a control

freak to let someone else shoot things, but competent once you laid down strict rules of engagement. And had Heather yell at the fool a few times to get him to behave.

Everyone seemed to be nervous of Heather. Far more so than Phil. But then, she was the scary one, and Iveta could testify to that.

Phil was a diplomat. Even as a pirate, he'd been the Fleet Centurion of the growing force, staying with the flagship and issuing orders while Heather had been part of the boarding assault team that had captured *Packmule* during a raid that was still studied by marines in training back home.

And the woman had moved an entire planetoid by herself. Everyone else had just been along for the ride at *Vilahana*.

So Iveta had gathered her warriors in the rear conference room aft, about as far away from the Arboretum as you could get and still have space for this many people. She studied them now, a spectrum of uniforms and faces, but each of them hyper-focused, because they were here to talk about warfare.

"Phil is not here to fight," Iveta began, just to remind everyone. "His preference is always to talk, preferably in small groups lubricated with a little wine and finger foods. However, not everyone else is that smart, so he has to have us around."

That got a sound out of them. A little chuff of exhaled breath, multiplied by a dozen mouths. Not an angry growl. Not far from it.

"When we get to *Carinae II*, the *Gloran* Emperor might be there, since we're letting *Tralfa* run ahead with the news, assuming that it isn't already there," Iveta continued. "This was likely to be a touchy situation, though, as someone blew up one of their colonies. Not as bad as those idiots would have done at *Vilahana*, but not good, either. All the men dead. All the old people. An awful lot of young women unaccounted for when the *Gloran* fleet got the message and sent a ship to investigate."

The growl was there this time. Louder. None of these folks were shrinking violets. And everyone was offended at the suggestion of sexual slavery going on. That the pirates had done such things in the past wasn't something anybody was willing to sweep under the rug today, but most of those folks had been hunted down and killed, either by Phil or other folks.

Some lines even the most corrupt folks won't cross. You had to be plain evil.

"At *Ewinhome* the second time, it was necessary to wade in and stomp on things," Iveta continued. "To stomp on people, because they wouldn't listen to reason. *Gloran* is not *Ewin*. They will be aggressive because they are, and because we're technically trespassing here. They will not, however, just open fire without a damned good reason."

She was looking directly at Khan as she said that. He nodded back to her, somewhere between serene and carnivorous. Right where a lot of them were today, when you got down to it.

"What *are* we expecting?" Right Gunner Ju Tou asked.

On *Li Jing*, he was responsible for the right hand super beam, the greatly-upscaled mega Power Tap that fired over six pulses instead of three. The thing they called the *Ōdachi*, or *Greatsword*. It was an impressive weapon, especially compared to the lesser versions that other fleets had in their three-shot Power Taps.

Still paled next to the Type-4. Especially when you had to fire it, and only then could you try to achieve a lock, then hold the lock when the other guy started wriggling on the hook.

"*Gloran* has had time to analyze our force, Right Gunner," Iveta replied. "To count hulls and understand that missiles and firebirds are a waste of time and magazine space when facing the *RAN*. They'll leave those at home, as well as the few carriers they have started to experiment with over the last generation. Instead, we'll be facing off with warships that have a crap-ton of Main Guns and Titan Bolts. They won't disarm themselves as fast as a *Dalou* or *Ewin* fleet would, but we aren't here to fight a pitched battle with them under almost any circumstances. If it looks like that's happening, Phil's orders are to run."

This time, that sound was a gasp. All of them were aggressive. Only half understood how frequently you had to withhold the blade. The other half were learning, to give them credit.

"Run, Iveta?" Arya Chaudhari asked archly. She'd known them all the longest, clear back to *Vilahana*.

"That's right," Iveta acknowledged. "Get backwards out of the gravity well and Jump. There will be waypoints communicated on the final drop into realspace before *Carinae II*, but I expect that we'll jump to one just long enough to round everyone up, then either shift across the *Aditi* border, or make a long run backwards, possibly to *Urwel* again."

"Why?" several voices asked at once.

"Because the damage is already done," Iveta reminded them. "The colony was wasted more than a month ago, so there's nothing useful we can do except show up and offer support for *Gloran* in their time of need. If they order us out, we go. If the Emperor is there and orders us to attend him at *Derragon*, we go. If we go there, however, it will be the same sort of rules of engagement as we had at *Ellariel-jo*, so I want you prepared."

"*Ellariel?*" Makana Christensen confirmed. As Tactical Officer of *CB-502*, and Erle Kuiper's right hand, he would be the third part of any battle, as Phil had frequently assigned *Task Force 502* with operations in hostile situations.

"That's right, Makana," she told him. "I'll have Tactical and Flag for as long as necessary at *Derragon*, sleeping in the ready room while the ship stays at combat alert and Phil tries to defuse things with the Emperor. Again, that might be a run like hell situation, because they'll likely bring in a huge fleet if they decided that they wanted to fight the *RAN*."

Iveta turned to Khan now and nodded to the man.

"*Juvayni* is one hell of a combat vessel," she said, to take the sting out of her next words. "However, *CB-502* could take you one-on-one."

He flinched, opened his mouth, and then closed it without ever making a sound. Shrugged, unconvinced.

So, Heather had been right. The guy was growing up. Might be dangerous if he did that. Less predictable.

"If we had to shoot our way out of orbit to escape, I will expect all of you, with the possible exception of *Juvayni*, to absolutely lay waste to anyone and everyone trying to stop us," Iveta said.

"They do that, and I'll be on your van shooting, like *Shadowbolt* was at *Ewinhome*," Khan snapped angrily. "Or *Morninghawk* at *Meerut*. They will also have to answer to me, personally, Iveta. That is a promise."

Iveta let him have that last word with a sharp nod.

Khan hadn't changed sides by any stretch, but he was part of *this* team until his Emperor ordered him to return home, possibly in disgrace at that point to command some Penal Cruiser or something.

She wondered if he'd go at that point. Or start his own war with the backwards-ass fools who had refused to acknowledge that the future had already arrived.

TWELVE

DATE OF THE REPUBLIC MARCH 16, 412 RAN URUMCHI, WAYPOINT FIFTY-FOUR

Phil had Heather and Iveta in his office. Just the three of them, with Markus keeping everyone else out for now.

Everyone had had their say. Orders and plans had been exchanged, reviewed, polished, and understood.

"And we're taking our time," he said aloud, just as though he'd been speaking all along.

Both women had been with him long enough to follow along without a hymnal, at this point.

"What are you expecting, Phil?" Iveta asked.

He marked that as a point of her personal growth, that such a question, such a personal level to it, had finally become second nature.

"A small squadron that got dispatched from the capital to investigate," he replied. "Maybe a frigate force like they do, three of them as a compact and self-contained team. And then a much larger force got rounded up and is hauling ass when they get the note that we're planning to stop in and offer whatever help we can, en route to *Derragon*. It really all comes down to the emperor himself."

"What do we know about Adric Kerenski?" Heather asked.

"Not much," Phil replied. "Warrior, like they all are.

Adopted by his predecessor when that man had no children hard enough, *militant* enough, to take the throne and hold it. But that's nothing new. Only about one in three or four ever does. Usually, it is much more of a Roman model. I'm hoping we can appeal to them on that level."

"At least he's not known to be an incompetent drunkard, like Doysan IV was at *Ewinhome*," Iveta grumbled under her breath. "More like the Shogun, then?"

"I'd split the difference," Heather interjected. "He's been in power for about fifteen years, so older and presumably more mature and settled. Looking forward to the day he retires, I would guess, and measuring all the young punks around him to see who might measure up. They aren't much better about marriages as a strategic thing, so they're more like *Ewin* that way than *Dalou*. Or rather, being the offspring of somebody important just opens doors. It doesn't guarantee you anything once you get there. Khan's father was demoted, transferred, and eventually worked his way back, but not all of them do. And the old man must have been legendary to do it."

Phil nodded. He'd picked up tidbits from various folks, suggesting that Artak Khan had indeed been a serious, badass tactical and strategic commander in his time. Possibly another genius like Jessica Keller, without the protection of First Lord Kasum at that first Court Martial where she'd defied orders, saved the day, and gotten promoted to the Strike Carrier *Auberon*, initiating her galaxy-shaking legend.

"So what do we want out of *Gloran*?" Heather asked. "We've seen everybody else, excepting *Yaumgan* due to circumstances. What's our best result?"

Phil had given that a lot of thought over the last year.

"On the map, *Vilahana* really isn't claimed by anybody," he said. "Wasn't before we arrived, and I've made it clear that nobody gets to change that if they want trade with *Aquitaine* going forward. From *Vilahana*, you are quickly in *Gloran* or *Dalou* space, depending which flight vector you take, though there are few stars colonized in that region right now. *Aditi* sits mostly at the center of the sphere, which give them the shortest defensive lines in a war, but enemies on all sides, so they are not expansionistic in a manner similar to the old *Fribourg* Empire. However, there are a dozen star systems that could be claimed and developed in the *Vilahana* area, with more than half of them in what we might consider the *Gloran* sphere of influence. Right now, trade from home will have to come through *Vilahana*, so if the Emperor is sharp enough, he'll start leaning this way."

"Can he do that, if pirates are hitting colonies on the other side?" Iveta asked pointedly.

Phil considered his words carefully. Studied the two women as everyone fell into an uncomfortable silence.

"This does not leave this room," he said.

Phil waited for both women to nod before he continued.

"I have extremely strong doubts about the pirate story," he said. "It might have been them, but that looks like a heap of bullshit to me. Iveta, you just spoke the thing that has been niggling at the back of my mind since *Tralfa* first showed up. Who stands to gain?"

"Who does?" she asked now, leaning in predatorially.

"*Dalou* used to fund a lot of pirates, just to keep things stirred up," Phil replied. "As did *Aditi* and everyone else. *Dalou* has a lot of other places to invest now, starting at *Urwel* and working down both frontiers, towards *Meerut* and across the long front with *Aditi*. That's a generation getting started, and a few centuries working out. *Ewin*...let's face it, the Princes couldn't find their own asses with both hands, a map, and a flashlight right now. *Yaumgan* probably has active espionage and insurgency funds, but we're in the wrong place and both *Gloran* and *Ewin* generally leave them alone."

"That leaves *Aditi*, Phil," Heather pointed out with no emotion in her voice whatsoever.

"It does," he agreed. "And I can't prove anything. Plus, Kaur and her folks have been as good as anyone from *Ladaux* on this operation, so I will not cast doubt on them. However…"

He left it dangling there.

"However," Heather took up the thread, "if *Aditi* did get *Gloran* focused inward on them in a military way, they might not be paying attention if some *Aditi* colonies suddenly sprung up on long-ignored planets closer to *Vilahana*, where the *Consensus* might be able to dominate trade coming in from the galactic arm."

"Which, I will point out, includes more than just *Aquitaine*," Phil said. "We happen to be closest. Nothing more. Karl VIII will send ships at some point. She can't not do that. *Corynthe, Lincolnshire*, and even *Salonnia* will likely get in on it as well. Plus whoever else wonders if these new worlds represent an opportunity to get rich as a merchant or pirate. That's one of the reasons First Lord Naoumov authorized me to license and sell Pulse technology. That short-circuits any pirates from our end in a hurry, meaning that nobody can come in here and just run rampant after we leave."

"So we really are building a fortress here?" Iveta asked.

Phil started to speak and Heather waved him to silence, turning to face her First Officer. Her Jessica Keller clone with her own—*earned*—pirate nickname. *The Junkyard Bitch*. Meanest warrior on the block.

Any block.

"More classified information you can never repeat, Iveta," Heather said.

Iveta Beridze had been chosen specifically to sit here in situations like this, so Phil leaned back and watched.

Iveta sobered and nodded.

"*Aquitaine* faces *Fribourg* on the frontier towards the galactic core," Heather began. "*Salonnia* on the galactic east or anti-spinward. *Lincolnshire* towards the edge. Once you get out of the arm itself, stars thin out considerably, to the point that neither us nor *Fribourg* ever really moved west. Established a few bases and forts, but that was it."

Iveta nodded silently, absorbing things. Heather glanced over at Phil.

"Per Phil, and these are matters at and above his level, there are hints and suggestions by historians that study such things," Heather continued, pausing only to give Iveta the untaken chance to speak. "The phrase used in conversation was *Imperial Aquitaine*. Think along the lines of the Imperial Rome that replaced the Republic in the early Common Era that used to be how calendars were measured."

"Imperial?" Iveta confirmed with a shaky voice.

Phil and Heather both nodded.

"Rome transformed over the course of two generations of civil wars," Heather spoke. "Then became radically expansionary, because most empires in history have had that problem. Expand or collapse, without much steady state in between."

"So we're forcibly uplifting the Balhee Cluster to modern technology, to keep future First Lords and First Centurions from being able to just waltz in here and conquer a more backwards people?" Iveta asked penetratingly.

"You will not repeat that, *Junkyard*," Phil said. "Except and only if it comes up at whatever Court Martial brings down both me and Petia Naoumov. These are her orders, working quietly with a few folks in the government. And a few outsiders who understand. Karl VIII is not aware of this, but has advisors who are."

"Denis Jež," Iveta said as her eyes got huge. "Keller's most dangerous commander."

"Most dangerous?" Phil asked, confused.

He had lots of good things to say about the man who had been his squadron and fleet senior command centurion, back in the day, but *most dangerous* wasn't usually among them.

Not in any squadron where Tomas Kigali and Alber' d'Maine served.

"When we came close to both a general and a civil war five years ago," Iveta said. "The *Horvat Affair*. After Keller had effectively won, all the commanders around her gathered together to decide what the future should look like. Jež was the one that laid out the plan that was eventually accepted. *His* plan. Plus, the Red Admiral himself had previously handed an **Aquitaine** commander control of the most dangerous **Imperial** warfleet ever assembled. Again, Jež. Not the most aggressive. That would be Kigali, with d'Maine a close second. Jež is probably the smartest by an arm length, though."

Trust her to have gone that deep into Keller and the Merry Men. And to understand the implications that had caused Jež to retire to *St. Legier* and become a trusted senior advisor to the Emperor. A man Casey Weigand referred to publicly as an uncle.

That Denis Jež.

Phil nodded. She understood where things were, from the terrible awe that was in her eyes now.

It was nice to be able to surprise and maybe frighten a woman like *Junkyard* occasionally. Phil had been concerned that he'd gotten predictable, when so many people had been able to upset his plans. In the end, it had merely been the fog of war, and he'd managed to get inside everyone else's decision curve again, forcing them to respond to him.

Hopefully, the Emperor of *Gloran*, one Adric Kerenski, would take the most predictable route to handle things, and Phil could just be another messenger from afar, bringing trade and development to yet another Balhee Cluster nation.

Without *Kongō* and her sisters coming to the dance.

THIRTEEN

DATE OF THE REPUBLIC MARCH 18, 412 RAN URUMCHI, CARINAE II OUTER ORBIT

Heather had everyone organized like this was a promenade, in spite of Iveta's folks all being prepared to unleash unmitigated mayhem at the drop of a hat.

Juvayni was right ahead of *Forktail*, because this was a *Gloran* world. Captain Sugawara didn't care, and was going to escort *Urumchi* as well as *Morninghawk* ever had. *Li Jing* and *Aranyani* on one wing. *Shadowbolt* and *Storm Petrel* on the other, with *Viking* in the high slot rear above *Hollywood* and the corvettes in a sphere outside that. *Tralfa* had gone ahead to *Derragon*, but *Varmint*, bitching all the way into Jump, had made it back to *Meerut* and then caught up with the squadron at the last waypoint.

Right now, Esser Jones and crew were more or less hiding in *Hollywood*'s shadow, just like she was with *Urumchi*.

Good thing, too, as Phil had called this one.

"Leyla?" Heather asked, turning to look at her Science Officer, currently face down on her screens, typing furiously.

"I got two squadrons, I think," she replied. "Big, gnarly battleship that identifies itself as *Glanthua's Stand* in high orbit, with a handful of cruisers that look like lesser versions of *Juvayni*. Plus a mess of smaller ships."

"Command Cruiser, Heavy Cruiser distinction?" Heather asked, going back to the old way of doing things, before the Expeditionary classes.

"Yeah, Khan's bigger. These guys are showing a smaller power curve, but better shielding, so maybe combat variants," Leyla said. "Other squadron is more interesting. They have flags identifying themselves as a Penal Fleet team. Two *Type Five* frigates and a *Type Five Heavy*. The one Khan said they were building recently as a command variant, because it has a third, big engine, attached directly to the boom instead of the pair on the secondary hull like everyone else. Same as *Glanthua's Stand* does it, but half the size."

Interesting. Frigate wolfpack, probably capable of taking a pirate Raider like *Hollywood* apart at the frames. Even an Enforcer would have gotten the short end of the stick eventually, but probably only after crippling at least one of the Type Fives.

"What about the planet?" Heather asked next.

"I have orbital debris suggesting a station at one point," Leyla replied. "It got smashed, but we knew that already. There is a freighter nearby, so maybe they have the components to build a new one, or are just taking the place for now. The frigates are close to that, but below it, like they have been sending shuttles down regularly, or bringing survivors up. The big force is above them and facing outwards."

"Threatening?" Iveta asked.

"Negative," Leyla said sharply. "Laagering, if anything. Got comm traffic coming in for Phil."

"Route it and keep watch," Heather ordered. "Iveta, you have Tactical. You also have the flag until Phil calls for it."

Iveta nodded.

"*Aquitaine* Squadron, this is Beridze, aboard *Urumchi*, I have the flag," the woman said on the general line. "Standing orders. Standing expectations. *Juvayni*, you have the point as needed. *Forktail*, stay in close escort. Everyone else stand by. If all goes well, we'll step down in two hours and start on long watch at lower alert levels. If not, you have your firing lanes assigned."

Heather nodded. Hopefully, it wouldn't come to that. *Gloran* ships were designed to get up close and duel. Not as close as the sharks half of her force had been designed to maul, but enough to make themselves a pain in the ass.

That was why Iveta had the flag.

FOURTEEN

DATE OF THE REPUBLIC MARCH 18, 412 RAN URUMCHI, CARINAE II OUTER ORBIT

Phil was in his seat on the flag bridge, Harinder across from him, and Kohahu off to one side. She could return to training and qualifications later, but having the young woman handy now meant that she was prepared to answer questions as they came up.

The frontier separating *Gloran* and *Dalou* was much fuzzier and more amorphous than the others, mostly because the big, open mouth of the Cluster itself, pointed straight up when seen from *Ladaux*, ran right across the territory involved and mostly acted as something of a river keeping the sides separate.

Few wars between the two, with both more likely to tangle up with *Aditi* trying to drive wedges into the space. Doubly so now.

Around him, all the main flag bridge crew were on alert and hyped, even though Iveta was controlling things currently. Her orders would route through his people if combat broke out, for as long as it took to extricate himself from this mess.

"I have a call for you, Phil," Harinder notified him. "Channel nine. Light-speed lag about two and a half seconds."

Out a ways, but not impossible. Close enough that they

could sail down to the edge of the gravity well in a few hours, or short hop.

Not close enough to shoot at each other. Even the tightest beams would diffuse after traveling through so much solar wind. Still, all of his ships were defensive, just as the group over there.

Two nervous badgers, waddling up to each other as if for a sniff.

Phil nodded to everyone, checked against last minute messages, and drew a breath before speaking.

"This is War-Captain A.Q. Tanel, speaking for the Emperor," a man said as he faded into existence. "To whom am I communicating?"

Phil only had a bust in the projection, but the man gave the impression of tallness. Perhaps greater than his own. Lean, though, like an athlete who had kept the training up, even as the man himself appeared to be in his mid-fifties, give or take. A decade older than Phil then, for what that might be worth.

Widow's peak hair slicked back, with a handspan at the top still dark brown and both sides white, like racing stripes that just accentuated his sharp prow of a nose and big cheekbones. Predatory bird, maybe.

"This is First Centurion Philip S. Kosnett of the *Republic of Aquitaine* Navy," he replied. "Currently in route to *Derragon* at the Emperor's invitation, but we heard about *Carinae II* and took a short detour to see if we could offer any assistance here."

He waited for the man to react. Just enough lag to make conversation awkward, but Phil preferred it this way. At *Ewinhome*, it had kept his people safe when Doysan IV got drunk. And stupid.

Later, it had put him in a position to control the outcome when Kalidoona needed to run what basically ended up as a soft coup that saw all the other troublemakers brought to heel.

"What kind of assistance could *Aquitaine* offer, First Centurion?" Tanel replied at last, his voice harsh and not quite dismissive as professional diplomats master young, in order to be able to speak without *technically* offering insult.

Phil chose to ignore it. *Gloran* culture was all about the warrior, rather than the Blood Princes. They saw themselves tougher than everybody else.

After a year in the Balhee Cluster, Phil didn't figure he had anything left to prove. At least in a positive way.

There were always bad examples to be made, he supposed.

Still, he smiled. These folks were looking at the tonnage of destructive firepower he'd brought with him, rather than anything else. Almost made Phil wish he could have brought a Construction Legion with him.

Maybe next time.

"What do you need, War-Captain?" Phil asked simply.

No emotional loading on his words or his tone. Simple inquiry, if they chose to take it at face value. Which they should. *Aditi* or the old *Dalou* would have parsed for esoteric meaning, but they were all about that sort of thing. *Ewin*? Ass, map, flashlight, still lost.

Phil was rewarded by the screen freezing at the far end. Somebody pausing things, likely so they could argue with each other without the company listening. The joys of electronic diplomacy. And another one of the reasons he liked cocktail parties instead.

Got people talking. In a good way.

"How long do you intend to remain at *Carinae*, First Centurion?" Tanel came back now, having hopped over several intervening conversations to land on this one.

"If the Emperor is here with you, we will let him determine our schedule," Phil replied. "We can remain on station while being resupplied, or depart for *Derragon*. As you prefer."

"We are investigating the attack that functionally destroyed this colony," Tanel said baldly, finally showing some emotion.

Good ones, too. The warrior who is upset that he wasn't able to protect people counting on him, rather than an aggrieved

Prince or *Dalou* nobleman who had all his investments in a planetary development scheme destroyed.

"Understood, War-Captain," Phil said. "As noted, I am happy to place my resources at your disposal to assist. Or, if that would be better, we can withdraw to *Derragon* and await the Emperor's pleasure there."

It was informative, watching the man's face cycle through several emotional states. Tanel had obviously never really spent time as a formal diplomat, where folks learned to lie with their eyes and keep their own counsel at all times.

"Just like that?" Tanel demanded, like he didn't believe.

"Just like that," Phil agreed. "Cruiser-Captain Khan extended the Emperor's invitation to visit *Derragon* as part of our tour of Balhee Cluster capital worlds. My only regret is that we were unable to do it sooner, such that the Emperor has a small situation on his hands here, at the same time as he has guests. However, it would not offend us if we should need to delay such festivities, given the serious nature of things below us. A crime has been committed, War-Captain. Those responsible need to be brought to justice."

Tanel's eyes started big, then got hot, then got icy as he listened. A nod as Phil's speech finished. An agreement, however unspoken at present.

Warriors, speaking a language that civilians and others might not understand. If they had done their research, Phil knew that his past as both a pirate and a squadron commander facing off against the most dangerous Imperial Task Force *ever assembled* would come up.

That ought to open some doors and smooth some egos.

The line froze again. As Phil had expected. Like him, there were probably several people silently off screen, listening and offering advice.

Phil had literally spent years preparing for this sort of conversation.

A.Q. Tanel came back after a few moments.

"Your understanding is most commendable, First Centurion," he said firmly. "The Emperor would gladly host you and your captains. I am given to understand that you would prefer a simple reception, rather than the grand formality of a State Dinner and Reception?"

"It makes it easier to talk to people, War-Captain," Phil said. "To make friends because you have done the work of understanding one another, rather than spending time listening to formal speeches that obscure as much as they communicate. But that is me. What would best serve the Emperor of *Gloran*?"

More pause. This wasn't *Ewin*'s First Minister Bereoa, a smooth diplomat used to maneuvering around fragile egos. If Phil understood *Gloran*, this War-Captain might be the senior-most active duty officer in their fleet, or such a man recently retired to take up a position as an advisor to Kerenski. One of the Lords of the Fleet back home, rather than a mere First Centurion like Phil was.

Good thing Phil was Ambassador-Plenipotentiary as well, so he could talk turkey with such people.

"Your understanding is appreciated, Kosnett," Tanel said, relaxing as he spoke. "I am instructed that our respective staffs will be able to engage and work out all the details. It is late in our working day at present. Would a period twenty hours from now suit your personal clocks?"

Interesting way to put it, but it made sense. Phil had adjusted the squadron to *Meerut* time since they'd been there doing repairs. And kept it, even after *Urwel*. The Imperial squadron was probably operating on the time zone of the Palace at *Derragon*.

"That would be most admirable, War-Captain," Phil replied. "I will have my Command Flag Centurion contact your folks and let them arrange things. I look forward to meeting you in person, as well as calling politely upon the Emperor. Thank you."

The line cut from the other end, but that was fine. The

important parts had been covered. Harinder could handle *Gloran* bureaucrats, because that was what was coming next. Less rigid than *Dalou*. More organized than *Ewin*.

He turned to Kohahu Kugosu, silent through all this.

"Thoughts?" Phil asked the young woman.

FIFTEEN

DATE OF THE REPUBLIC MARCH 18, 412 RAN URUMCHI, CARINAE II OUTER ORBIT

Kohahu knew that her *Aquitaine* rank was more honorary than not. At the same time, it fit her into their system, so that they could deal with her as a person, rather than an Ambassador or *Important Personage*. It let her be like Nam Nagarkar. And it let her see things that no outsider would ever truly understand.

Phil Kosnett was an avalanche, however polite and friendly he presented to most viewers. Social, political, intellectual. The death and destruction of the Balhee Cluster as it had been two years ago, hopefully only from a social perspective, thus to be replaced by something better.

Aditi and *Dalou* were on their way. *Ewin* had, perhaps, stopped backsliding.

Gloran would be an issue.

But Phil had asked her a question. An open-ended one, at that. Like her father might have on the dojo floor, when it was just them and whatever silent bodyguards gargoyled around the edges of the room.

Nothing simple there. Phil Kosnett was not a simple man, for all he took a direct and easy-to-understand approach to many things.

It was the natives of the Balhee Cluster who had to make things complicated. Herself included.

Hopefully, the act of joining the *RAN* squadron as an observer, then actually enlisting enough to become one of them for a time, would put her on a radically different path than she might have otherwise.

"No *Gloran* personage can admit to fear," Kohahu replied to Phil's initial question, falling back on something her father liked to repeat. "That is the backbone of their entire society."

Phil nodded and watched, so Kohahu decided to expand. He had asked her an *open-ended* question.

"They will see the terrible firepower you command, and have to bring something roughly equivalent, or perhaps just slightly less, because to bring more would suggest to an outside witness that they are afraid of your fleet," Kohahu expanded. "That they would fight you anyway from weakness just meant that their destruction would be recorded in one of the great oral poems for which they are known, harking back to primitive warriors around a fire recounting tales of glory and lost friends."

"And if we aren't here to fight?" Phil pressed.

"They might not be sure how to react," Kohahu said. "Everything for them is seen through that lens. We do not wish to be seen as menials or servants, but the act of offering to help can be taken that way, if they chose. Or it can be an acknowledgment of peers assisting one another because both happened to be present. Warrior comrades in the field, as it were."

She had said *We*. Interesting choice of unconscious vocabulary, though it was likely never to emerge from this room, so she would be safe later when others accused her of being seduced by the power and glory of *Aquitaine*.

They would be right in the outcome, and wrong in the reasons, though she might have to formally raise Morninghawk to one of the Great Houses in another few decades, just to make that point clear to the fools not paying attention.

"*Dalou* had a…*concern* that I would decide to attack them at *Ellariel*," Phil shared a ghost of a grin with her. "They had to bring home three battleships, just to establish my place in their hierarchy."

"At the time, I think the Shogun's Advisors probably thought it would be sufficient," Kohahu noted dryly. "Today, they are probably offering extra blessings at their family altars, having read the reports from *Ewinhome*."

They all had a smile at that. *Dalou* would have only attacked out of panicked fear, and Phil Kosnett had offered no hint of treachery, even when *Dalou* nearly turned itself inside out anyway.

Kohahu could at least put that down to a frustrated Emperor testing his leash.

How would the history of the Balhee Cluster have turned out, without Lord Morninghawk there to guide everyone? To literally save *Dalou* from imploding at one of the most critical moments in their entire history? Captain Sugawara aboard *Forktail* had been at pains to live up to that standard, that legend, but Kohahu was mature enough to understand that *nobody* could, with the exceptions of Phil and Heather.

Kohahu slipped backwards to some of the histories she had read of Kosnett's adventures in *Buran*. Neither he nor Heather had written a definitive treatise, letting their reports speak for them, but others had been privy to enough material and witnesses to piece together some kind of truth.

Having met Markus, *Stunt Dude*, and Sam Au, Kohahu was certain that the writers had never been told the really good parts.

And Kohahu needed to lean on *Stunt Dude* and Sam to write down their story. Too often, it started with her sailing away aboard a returned hospital ship, *Stunt Dude* retiring from active duty, and then showing up on her doorstep with roses, two years later.

Nobody had ever gotten the rest from the man.

"You were a pirate," Kohahu said after a short break.

She couldn't help that her voice had turned authoritative. Side effect of dealing with most of Father's previous advisors. The Stodgy Old Farts, as she had taken to thinking of them.

Kosnett nodded, eyes sober and focused on her.

"What do pirates do, when they want to attack some isolated colony?" Kohahu asked.

She looked purposefully over at Markus Dunklin, including him in the conversation by force of will. The man sat up straighter, then actually stood up from his chair, though he didn't yet approach the command table.

Phil noticed and nodded the man over. Then he opened a channel and Heather's face appeared in the projection.

"What's up?" Heather asked.

"Kohahu just asked me a most interesting question," Phil said. "It offers us an in with the Imperial Suite that they might not have seen coming. What do pirates do, when they want to attack some colony?"

"Scout the damned place secretly," Heather replied instantly. "Stay off scanners and make sure nobody sees you coming."

"Where?" Phil asked.

"*Mansi-D*," Markus replied instantly.

Heather had been an officer serving aboard *CS-405*. Markus had been an actual pirate marine, boarding and capturing several enemy warships, if you could call those vessels warships. A freighter, a mega-freighter, a hospital ship, and a rescued police cutter stolen out of a boneyard on the surface of a moon.

A moon. *Mansi-D-3*.

Persephone.

Kohahu had an idea.

"I need Nam," she said simply.

No one else in this room could answer effectively. Kohahu didn't have the experience. The others had the background, but maybe the *RAN* did things differently that Cluster pirates. Well, of course they did, but how differently?

Phil did something and Nam's face appeared next to Heather's.

"First Centurion?" Nam asked.

"Need you on the flag bridge, Nam," he said simply. "Please drop whatever you are doing and haul ass this way. Heather, you too."

He cut the line and looked at Markus now.

"*Lady Blackbeard*," Phil said in an almost reverent tone.

"Miss her," Markus replied. "We'll get you close, though."

Kohahu had no idea what message had been communicated, but Nam and Heather arrived quickly and took up spots.

"*Mansi-D*, the first time," Phil set the stage as Kohahu watched, the man surrounded by many decades of hard-won naval experience Kohahu could only imagine.

And now use.

"Piracy," Kohahu said to start things.

"So we set ourselves up in scanner shadows from our target," Heather said. "Then Evan Brinich, or maybe *West* Lovisone slipped us up over the edge of the planet, blacked out and listening. Passive sensors only, but when you are a scout, that's a lot of electronic firepower and processing capabilities. Stay put for a bit, pretending to be an anomaly or a moon, then drop back down. Stay hiding, and drive backwards in such a way as to remain hidden before hitting JumpSpace."

Kohahu nodded. Just as she'd read about. *CS-405*'s legend had come with so many important members of her crew aboard *Urumchi*.

She turned to Nam now.

"Pirates," Kohahu said simply, waiting for the woman to nod. "Let's assume that they've done the same thing. Let us assume sufficient competence to actually pull it off against a halfway competent defender. At least until they know that *Carinae II* doesn't have any warships in orbit to worry about. Do they dump their trash, just before launching the attack, so they have that much extra space to store whatever valuables they intend to steal?"

Kohahu could tell she'd hit on something from the way everyone around the table rocked backwards. Along with several people who still sat around the edges of the room listening with one ear.

"Shit." Nam seemed to sum it up nicely with that word. "We probably would have. No reason to suspect that whoever hit this place didn't. Won't say standard operating procedure, but yeah, maybe we don't keep things as clean and formal as we should. It all burns up in the atmosphere anyway, eventually."

"Assuming atmosphere," Markus said. "Or simple gravity wells without messy multi-lunar attendants with some big planet."

He stopped and did something on the console in front of him. Leyla Ekmekçi, *Urumchi*'s Science Officer, appeared suddenly.

"Leyla, I need the orbital layout of the local system, as it was on the day of the attack, with vectors and known moons," he said simply.

Kohahu was still getting used to a place where a burly redneck Senior Chief could just give a Senior Centurion orders. And have them followed without question.

"Stand by," Leyla replied. "Rewinding. Transmitting. Want it in the projection?"

"Please," Markus said.

The image appeared. Star off to one side, not to scale. *Carinae II* in the center.

Kohahu had to get used to the *Aquitaine* method of lettering planets from closest to farthest, instead of numbering them. *Carinae II*, one of three rocky worlds relatively close in, with three more gas and ice giants beyond that, before you got out to comets and iceballs in the distant darkness.

"Four?" she asked Markus.

"That's where I would hide right now," he nodded. "Angle is

good. Three is too far off on the other side of the star to be any use. Five and Six are resonant, but not particularly well placed. I'm a pirate, so I'm a lazy-ass punk who bullies people because it is easier than working for a living."

"Don't tell *Hollywood* that," Heather snapped.

"She's a woman, in a place where the folks around here are too dumbass to admit that she's smarter than they are," he snapped back. "And works three times as hard."

Neither of them had spoken harshly, but Kohahu was still amazed at the openness of their conversation. Nothing at all like *Dalou*.

Old *Dalou*. The sclerotic nation that had been slowly sliding into senescence.

She needed to change a lot of things when she got home and started building her own networks to take over, one of these days.

"I agree," Phil spoke anyway. "I'd look at Four. Leyla, we're going to stay over here for now, but I want you and Sunan Bunnag from *Viking* studying Four like I expect a doctoral dissertation on the planet at a later date. Throw Arkan Bobrov on *CM-507* in as well, but keep everything generally quiet and passive for now. I'll talk to the locals about sending a task force over to investigate it later, once we know how they will likely respond to us meddling in an internal *Gloran* thing. Questions?"

Nobody had any, but that was to be expected. Still, Phil turned to her with a broad smile.

"Extremely well done, Kohahu," he said.

She found that she could blush, after all. It felt weird, but good.

Like she belonged.

SIXTEEN

DATE OF THE REPUBLIC MARCH 19, 412 RAN URUMCHI, CARINAE II ORBIT

Iveta was in charge. Primed. Armed.
Poised.
And wishing that absolutely nothing at all happened today.

Urumchi had sailed down closer to the *Gloran* squadron. The three Penal Frigates had sailed up, so now there was a massive constellation of ships in close proximity, at least on her scanners. Even packed tight, you were still kilometers apart. And operating on different planes of motion.

It just looked like a traffic jam on her screen.

"Science Officer, what's our status?" Iveta asked the room.

Nam and Kohahu had traveled with Phil and Heather, so Iveta had the main team on duty today, fortified with coffee and snacks tucked into drawers against need.

"GunShip is approaching *Glanthua's Stand* now," Leyla replied. "Everyone else is behaving."

Iveta let a small sigh go. Silent. There were any number of things that could go wrong yet. Phil had left sets of orders in his safe in his office and his personal quarters, for Heather to read. Or Iveta if something happened and she was suddenly filling a Fleet Centurion's slot until they could get messages home.

"How's *Viking* doing?" Iveta followed up.

"We could probably find a couple of astronautical engineering post-docs and give them all the data they ever wanted to write papers on this solar system," Leyla chuckled. "I think Sunan is training folks, because she's been busy pinging everything that moves around here and recording the responses. Mostly ignoring the *Gloran* ships, but we could easily update the meteorological records of the planet below if you found me some students there."

Iveta joined her in the chuckle. You got a job on a survey vessel, *Urumchi* notwithstanding, because you were at heart a science nerd. Phil ordering you to *indulge* such nerdiness just meant that they would.

Because it's there. That was what they would always say.

All they needed.

But *Urumchi* was a flagship. A warship, for all they called themselves a Survey Dreadnought. That was because Bedrov's plans had identified this variant of a Heavy Dreadnought thus. They could still kick ass and take names in a place like this.

"Talk to me about the frigate leader," Iveta said next. "*Arteshbo.*"

"Named for an ancient Persian warrior queen from way back in history," Leyla said. "I'm guessing that the same records that got saved at Alexandria Station got disseminated here, because they seem to be the source of what's really known about Earth. Frigate-Captain Kira Zaman, a woman, is in command right now, but Khan's records suggest that nobody serves on Penal ships that long. Either they get their shit together or they finish their contract and retire in semi-disgrace."

"Semi?" Iveta asked.

"Folks earn a monthly stipend based on many things, just like back home," Leyla said, raising her voice into lecturing mode so that everyone on the bridge or listening in could hear. "Retirement money tops that in an even more complicated manner."

Nerds. Audiences. A story as old as stories.

"If you are an officer, you can make up to about four times what an equivalent enlisted sailor makes in retirement," she continued. "Except that if you are in the Penal Fleet when you retire then it is only about twice as much. Still not bad, but not that great. They have a General Basic Income which means nobody starves. For a lot of warriors, it lets them train much harder than they would if they had to hold down some kind of a job somewhere. Also keeps the peace with the general population, because the artists have the same option to commit art."

"Interesting," Iveta noted. "They don't talk about that much."

"Warriors first, last, and in between," Leyla laughed. "Spartans, maybe, without the massive underclass of slaves. Renaissance Europe, if you had enough money floating around that you didn't need a formal patron, but could scrape by just playing."

"What about the vessel itself?" Iveta asked now. "Talk to me about *Arteshbo*."

"So, somebody got weird a while back," Leyla turned serious. "I don't have the right books to consult, but maybe we could check something out of a library when we get to *Derragon*. Most *Gloran* ships have that standard flat hull with big engine pods out both sides and curved down, kind of like a goose might fly. *Dalou* just does them straight out and keeps the entire naval architecture flat. Similarly, *Dalou* booms tend to be bigger on the front. Bulbs. Native *Gloran* designs make them more like lighthouses sticking out."

"With you so far."

"Since the booms separate in order to land, most of the crew of a *Gloran* ship is in the rear section," Leyla continued. "Along with most of the power systems and weapons, though they have Mains forward. The new Battleship design like *Glanthua's Stand* added a third engine, above like a crest or a Mohawk. Means that they can actually go to Jump while separated, as they have small JumpSails in the boom. And have enough power to keep fighting if the secondary section is lost. It worked out so well that somebody else decided to try something similar with the Type Five Frigate, creating a new thing that they sometimes call a Type Five Heavy, or maybe a Type Six. I might get rude and call it a Frignought. Dangerous vessel. The Type Five is fragile all by itself, but they were designed to operate as part of a wolfpack of three or five. The Frignought has the firepower and shielding to stand toe-to-toe with a destroyer, or even a light cruiser for a short time. Any of our Guardian corvettes could take her, but it would be brutal and messy."

"*Rajput*," Iveta nodded. "Alber' d'Maine's original Heavy Destroyer when he got assigned to Keller, back at the beginning. They were a crappy design and fleet never built a second one, because they were desperately overpowered and overgunned while sacrificing sailing comfort to get it. But he took on an Imperial Light Cruiser named *SturmTeufel* and killed it in single combat before they took him down at *First Ballard*."

Nods all the way around. Everybody studied Keller's many battles at the Academy.

Iveta had gone well beyond merely understanding how Keller had fought. She'd wanted to know how the woman had won, time and again, against seemingly impossible odds. Kigali, d'Maine, Aeliaes, and Jež had all played outsized roles, but Keller had been the genius who'd elevated them.

Who had taken the same tools everybody else had and won three wars with them.

"How good is a penal frigate squadron?" Hào Boyadjiev asked from his Gunnery station.

"Depends on the commander," Iveta replied with a shrug in her voice. She'd studied those sorts of things from Khan's notes while Leyla had been studying hulls and planets. "Only about ten percent or so of *Gloran* officers are female, either AFAB or in presentation. That we have such a Frigate-Captain in *Arteshbo* means she had to be good, because she must have come from a regular frigate, or been demoted into this position."

"What about something like *Dalou*?" Hào asked. "One of the Great Houses on the outs with the Emperor. Unwelcome daughter, but maybe as good as Keller?"

"If she's served in the Penal Fleet for long, that might be the reason," Iveta noted. "Make a note to ask Phil or Heather that when they get back. Not particularly relevant to the current situation, but it would make one hell of an interesting story, if so."

He nodded and Iveta checked her scans again. Not that she had stopped staring intently, waiting for anyone to step wrong.

Urumchi and *Viking* were in a position to punish most of the *Gloran* fleet if the worst happened.

She'd be thrilled when nothing did.

SEVENTEEN

DATE OF THE REPUBLIC MARCH 19, 412
GLORAN BATTLESHIP GLANTHUA'S STAND, CARINAE II ORBIT

Phil noted the marine honor guard drawn up as they exited the airlock. His GuSship was too big to enter their small shuttle bay, which was why he'd chosen it as his chariot.

All Balhee Cluster ships tended to follow the boom and secondary design. *Buran*'s Energiya Module logic. Excepting, of course, *Yaumgan*, who just landed an entire ship on the surface like a giant statue.

As a result, nobody but *Ewin* really did shuttle bays of a size like *Urumchi*. Or carried GunShips. *Gloran* did have older vessels that they might now call Light Battleships, converted over into something like *Aquitaine*'s old Fleet Carriers, but Emperor Adric hadn't brought one with him.

Probably rightly understanding how irrelevant they suddenly were, against Expeditionary forces. Jež had suggested in one of his letters that the era of the snubfighter was definitively over, at least until technology advanced enough to make them pocket warships with enough shielding to withstand a spread of Pulse-Two beams and a Type-3-Pulse. Plus maybe a small JumpSail.

Which rather well described his GunShip.

Phil made a note to talk to Iveta about something Keller had once done, putting a squadron of GunShips on a converted freighter the size of *Packmule*, where it acted like a mothership. Fast, heavy, and rude. *Junkyard* would have all those details at her immediate command.

But for now, Phil was following his people out into a reception bay. Security Centurion Xochitl Dar had gone first, because she was like that. Harinder and Fleet Ambassador Aliza Babatunde followed closely behind.

Phil could see Command Diplomatic Centurion Miliya Gavraba standing over next to War-Captain Tanel. Aliza had assigned the woman to *Gloran* after *Vilahana*, partly to reinforce with these folks that *Aquitaine* was more like *Aditi* in gender balance.

Nobody had complained here, where they might have at *Dalou*. *Ewin* should have thrown a temper tantrum. *Yaumgan* would have welcomed her with open arms.

Gloran was still the wild card, in too many ways.

Adham Khan, Cruiser-Captain of *Juvayni*, was second to last, standing to one side with his chest puffed out proudly. Phil took them all in and smiled.

He turned to the War-Captain and bowed his head.

"Thank you for taking time out of your busy schedule, War-Captain," Phil said. "I understand how stressful such situations can be, having been there myself in the past."

That caught the man off-guard. But then, Phil didn't talk much about *St. Legier*. He had been part of Keller's squadron when the news arrived. And had later walked on the surface, in one of the places left destroyed as a reminder that some crimes were simply too evil to exist.

Buran had been executed as a result of giving that order. And only two *Sentiences* were currently allowed to exist. The Librarian at Alexandria Station. The Bartender at *Petron*.

Phil had never met the latter, but he had had a chance to correspond with the former during his time teaching. And to ask her questions about the galaxy that had been before.

"Welcome to *Carinae II*, First Centurion," Tanel replied after a beat so short that people might have missed it.

And pigs might fly.

Quickly, Phil got introduced to the many Cruiser-Captains and Frigate-Captains around them, all dressed in close variants of Khan's black leather with chain mail and a belt knife.

Fleet-Captain Kiri Povoloi was commander of *Glanthua's Stand*. He reminded Phil in many ways of a tightly coiled spring. Large brown eyes and brown skin that didn't go at all with thick, wavy, lemon-yellow hair worn back from a high forehead in a style that reminded Phil of a rooster's crest. He was as tall as Phil, but still shorter than Tanel, and had an elegance to him that belied the martialness of his costume.

"Fleet-Captain Povoloi, this is Command Centurion Heather Lau, commander of my flagship," Phil made a point to introduce them directly, after everyone had been named. "Your rough equivalent, given the differences in how the two navies handle rank and command."

"*Ground Control*," the man nodded almost reverently. "A pleasure to finally meet you in the flesh."

Phil could almost hear Heather's hackles rise, but she'd done it to herself. Apparently, like *Ewin*, they were going to see her as a war goddess around here, because they were still a little backwards in gender roles.

At least it gave him an opening to the woman standing somewhat off to one side, with two men guarding her flanks.

"Frigate-Captain Zaman?" Phil confirmed, drawing everyone off to one side before Heather replied to the Fleet-Captain. "Did I have that correct?"

"You do, First Centurion," Zaman bowed much deeper now. "Commander of the Penal Frigate *Arteshbo*."

Phil nodded sagely, then turned it into something of a matching bow. He might be the visitor here, but he also represented a much bigger political power, however far off to their east *Aquitaine* might be.

"We do not have a similar structure in the *Republic of Aquitaine* Navy, Frigate-Captain," he replied. "I would be most interested in hearing how it works at *Gloran*, since it obviously does."

All those light-centuries had just shrunk, now that he was sending home physical and social maps of the Balhee Cluster.

Phil turned back to Tanel with a smile.

"How best to proceed?" he asked simply, allowing the man to drive the conversation and the evening forward.

It helped that Phil had done this many other places. And that *Gloran* officers and diplomats beyond Khan had been able to participate. To learn a more relaxed way of doing things, when everybody always wanted to set out the long tables and argue across them.

Almost as bad as giving speeches to try to impress someone.

"The Emperor has commanded a cocktail party," Tanel said with a hint of grin that suggested the original order probably would have been a banquet fit for kings.

Big, loud, formal, useless.

Phil nodded and followed as the tall man led him to the various mobs out of the airlock reception area and deeper into the ship.

EIGHTEEN

DATE OF THE REPUBLIC MARCH 19, 412
GLORAN BATTLESHIP GLANTHUA'S STAND,
CARINAE II OUTER ORBIT

Heather had noted the appraising eyes as they made their way forward to what looked like a training deck converted to host a party. The sort of place where *Gloran* marines might set up boxes and tactical situations while training to clear a building or enemy warship.

Ewin had idolized her in ways that made Heather's skin crawl, but that was every single one of them seeing her naked and lusting after her to provide them better sons than some other woman might.

At least *Gloran* saw her as a warrior. They were a warrior culture.

The ship around them reminded her of Khan's *Juvayni*, which she had toured a few times. Every culture handled welds differently. Built to slightly different scales and dimensions. Different alloys and interior paint schemes.

Gloran ships weren't as compact or dim as *Dalou* could be, but they lacked the open brightness of *Urumchi* or any of the others. And this was a *Gloran* design that had come out of a *Gloran* yard. There were a few frigates that had originated in *Dalou*, escorting.

Like most such parties, Heather had gotten herself a can of

cold juice from Markus's stash and moved off to one side of the noisy crowd, where people could watch her and be seen. Let Phil, Harinder, and Aliza handle the heavy lifting of *talking*. She was here because she was senior Command Centurion. Even Barnaby Silver off *Viking* hadn't been invited to this event, though he would come on some later date, when it turned into an open buffet invite. Probably at *Derragon* where they might invite several hundred worthies and show the visitors off.

For now, everybody had done the thing and said the words. Formality had started to dissolve after an hour of chatting with *RAN* officers on the social offensive.

Kira Zaman emerged from the crowd after a time. Frigate-Captain off *Arteshbo*. She even had her two male counterparts with her, Frigate-Captains Nadim Tikka and Zeenat Vaishya, off *Mardonius* and *Darius* respectively.

Penal vessels. Meaning that the officers had been sent here for some infraction large enough to be punished, but not large enough to be cashiered or executed.

The woman paused at a formal distance and looked expectantly at Heather. Heather studied her for a moment. Medium height, strong build. Black hair and dark skin more suited to *Aditi* than most around here. Sharp eyes.

Zaman was dressed in black, like they did, but her pants were cut to remind you that she was a woman, where most of the men wore whatever you got when you took jodhpurs and made them long shorts to the top of the knee. Her top similarly covered everything but didn't let you forget she was a woman.

Heather compared that to her own dress tunic, the one with the epaulets and buttons up the front. It even had extra pockets to go with the ones in her pants. Occasionally, Heather would jam her hands into those tunic pockets, just to establish her body language, but that wasn't necessary.

Heather nodded. Might as well get it over.

"You two go spy on people," Zaman said now, shooing off her companions.

As the only other penal ship commanders present, they didn't separate much, but did wander off. Heather caught Harinder's eye and nodded for the woman to find someone to talk to the men.

More things she could learn.

"Frigate-Captain Zaman," Heather nodded as the woman stepped close enough to have a personal conversation.

"Command Centurion," Zaman replied.

Like Heather, she had a drink in one hand. A dark red wine in a clear goblet, similar to everyone else, though Heather had her doubts about people with booze when long belt knives were readily accessible.

Of course, unlike *Ewin*, these people were probably highly skilled with such edged weapons, so people wouldn't push as hard or as long.

"What news from *Carinae II*?" Heather asked. "Has your investigation turned up anything?"

"Hints of the *Hamath Syndicate*," Zaman replied. "I am no longer central to such things, now that more senior officers are on station."

That was a nice way to put it. The Emperor of *Gloran* and much of his senior military staff, leaving most of the civil-side bureaucrats at home.

"Will you stay then, or be sent to some other station?" Heather pressed.

Zaman was starting to relax. Heather was as relaxed as she was going to get until she got back on her own ship.

"It depends, Command Centurion," Zaman said.

"Call me Heather."

Zaman blinked in surprise. "Truly?"

"This is only semi-formal, Frigate-Captain Zaman," Heather nodded to the room. "Phil's goal is for everybody to be friends."

"Phil?"

"First Centurion Phil Kosnett," Heather grinned, watching

the woman across from her freeze up a little. Not how *Gloran* did things, obviously.

"And you are on a first name basis with your commanding officer?" Zaman asked, blinking too rapidly, her breath kind of gaspy with shock.

"Indeed," Heather said. "That is the *Aquitaine* way, once the team is formed and working well. Not always, but Phil and I served together in a previous war, where I was his First Officer on *CS-405*."

"The pirates," Zaman said, nodding as if to some internal monologue.

"The pirates," Heather agreed. "This time around, he asked for me specifically to take command of his flagship on this mission."

"In that case, I am Kira," the woman replied, pronouncing it KEE-rah, rather than how Heather would have guessed, having seen it only on a screen before now.

"Kira," Heather nodded. "Circling back, will you stay at *Carinae* or be sent elsewhere?"

"That is for the Emperor and the War-Captain to decide," Kira replied. "If they intend to remain here for some time, I might be reassigned. If the investigation turns up actionable intelligence, they may depart and order my squadron to guard the colony while it is being rebuilt."

"And they will rebuild it?" Heather pressed. "From the bits I have seen, it was nearly wiped out."

"The criminals cannot be seen to have won, Comm… Heather," Kira nodded angrily. "If they can attack one of our colonies, wipe it out, and leave an abandoned planet behind, others will be emboldened. So we must rebuild, even as those responsible will be hunted down and killed."

"Phil is likely to place ships from my squadron at the emperor's disposal, to assist in the hunting part," Heather said. "Probably discussing that in vague terms with Tanel or someone, making such an offer tonight."

"Why would he do that?" Kira asked, shocked to her core from the way her eyes got big for a moment.

"Phil hates pirates," Heather said, waving the woman off when Kira started to say something. "That was war against a formal foe, with recognized rules, however insane *Buran* was. We were in uniform and subject to military justice for everything we did. All of the senior officers went through a full Court Martial process when we got home, and were judged by those standards. These people attacked a civilian target and annihilated the local population. We never did that. In fact, Phil bought a new freighter for those first folks we captured when it was all said and done, just because they'd put up with everything we'd done to them and we'd beaten their ship into the scrap pile by the end."

"I was not aware of that," Kira said blankly.

Heather nodded. Public relations folks back home had taken that idea and run with it, but at the time it had been the right thing to do. And *Fribourg* had rated *Queen Anne's Revenge* as a captured warship by tonnage, so the amount of credit offered was enough to set Lan and Kiel up with a full bay of cargo and the ability to trade at *Fribourg* worlds. And they had.

"There are always rules, Kira," Heather said darkly. "That's what separates us from the pirates out there. Phil will crush those fools without mercy."

More was cut short when Adham Khan emerged from the crowd, saw the two of them, and balked so short he almost fell over.

Kira Zaman turned, identified the man, and flinched as well.

"Heather, thank you," she said simply. "I must go."

"I would happily host you on a tour of *Urumchi* soon," Heather replied before the woman got more than a step. "My staff will contact yours."

Kira nodded and fled.

Khan at least had the decency to look abashed as he approached.

Heather gave him the sort of scowl normally reserved for

bugs she found in her storage lockers, whenever she was home from a long sail and wanting to dig out her civilian clothes for a little while.

"I take it you and Frigate-Captain Zaman know each other?" she not-quite-snarled at the man as he stepped nervously close.

Khan was grinding his teeth in a manner probably intended to keep him from speaking the first words that came to mind. Possibly aware that she might backhand him if they were the wrong ones.

She had a good enough opinion of Khan as a warship commander. Adequate on the little things and aggressive in battle.

It was the personality that got her hackles up. Sexist punk. Even more so than *Ewin*, though Striker Solo had corrected himself pretty quickly.

Still, he bowed his head.

"She served with my father in his darker days," Khan finally replied, probably sanding off some of the sharper edges first. "Afterwards, there were…misunderstandings."

Heather felt her scowl deepen. Junior Centurions back home might be wetting themselves right now, if it was aimed in their direction.

"You should probably explain, then," she said in a voice just this side of a growl. "Before there are any other…*misunderstandings*."

In the background, Xochitl Dar popped out of the crowd, like she'd smelled trouble and wandered over to double-check. Heather shook her head. If Khan wanted to get feisty, Heather had other tools at her disposal.

Like having Phil order him out of the squadron and asking the Emperor to replace *Juvayni* with *Arteshbo*. Or something equally *mean*.

Something must have appeared in Heather's eyes, because Khan flinched at her look and obviously wanted to snap around, but that would put him too close to Heather. And turn his back on her as well.

At least he had the decency to come to rest, like a man expecting a knife in the kidneys and unwilling to flinch.

Khan's lips were pressed so tightly together that they turned white. Then he drew a heavy breath.

"Fortunes of war, Command Centurion," Khan said in a much quieter voice than Heather expected. Almost musingly so. "Sometimes, the very gods themselves decide to play dark practical jokes on us."

"What happened with your father and Kira Zaman?" Heather asked point blank.

Khan's head went back and forth, his eyes down and focusing on something nowhere within a thousand light-years of this room.

"She was his first officer on the penal frigate *Dark Victory*," Khan began, storytelling now rather than explaining, at least in the way his voice went up and down without pause. "When he was reinstated to the main fleet, Artak Khan attempted to convince the powers that be that she should also be transferred. It caused a tremendous scandal, as there were unsubstantiated rumors that the two had been intimate. Plus, her background…"

He stopped there like an emergency bulkhead slamming shut in a vacuum alert. His normally swarthy face had gotten almost Anglo-pale now, lighter-skinned than even Phil.

"Let me back up more, Command Centurion," Khan apologized. "Then I can admit my own failings and sins once you are in a position to adequately judge them."

Heather nodded. She would need to see Sam later for some painkillers, because right now she had her jaws clenched so hard that she could feel a headache in the offing.

It was that or bite the man.

"Kira Zaman may, or may not, be a cousin to the Emperor," Khan said so quietly she barely heard him. "I mean, she is.

Genetic testing has proven that, tracing back to Adric Kerenski's grandfather with certainty. But the woman's own mother refused to ever acknowledge who the father was. And that woman tragically took her own life when her only daughter was relatively young, leaving Kira Zaman to be raised by distant relatives with no knowledge at all."

"Why was that a problem, Khan?" Heather growled at the man.

He flinched under her tone. Give the man credit for understanding just how thin the ice had gotten under his feet in the last thirty seconds.

"Because all of the men who could have been her father were married at the time the child would have been conceived," he said. "*Gloran* culture…"

He stopped. Closed his mouth without ever making eye contact with her.

"A year ago, Command Centurion, I would have said that our culture was the highest expression of social order," Khan said, finally glancing up. "But that was before…"

Heather was shocked to hear the man's voice crack now, suppressed emotions fighting to breathe through and almost succeeding. Then he crushed them down and stared up at her with hard eyes.

"And then I met a man named Makara Omarov, Commander," Khan said, pain etched into the backs of his eyeballs. "*Morninghawk*. And I came to understand that not only are we all a little backwards compared to the rest of the galaxy, but that we didn't have to be. That we could change. That an unacknowledged bastard like Kira Zaman was a source of embarrassment to the Imperial House unnecessarily, which was probably why her mother took those secrets to the grave with her. Possibly because someone was trying to blackmail her to ruin lives. That is how we work. *Gloran*. Militant society. Rigid. *Aquitaine* doesn't give a rat's ass about your lineage. They only care about your abilities. But I didn't know that then. And so I did things that I didn't regret at the time, because that was what a *Gloran* son was supposed to do. And I was wrong, Commander."

"What did you do, Khan?" Heather asked, softening her tone from homicidal because Adham Khan was doing a good enough job of punishing himself as she watched.

Which shocked the living shit out of her.

First, that he could. Second, that he would.

"I denounced her, Commander," Khan sighed heavily. "As my father was not yet reinstated, I was the acknowledged patriarch of the family. If he had been intimate with the woman, knowing who she was, he would bring dishonor down upon his own kin. The Emperor did reinstate Artak Khan, and left Kira Zaman in the Penal Fleet as a result of my actions, where she has served for her entire career, because she is that good, but unable to escape her own past. That caused a rift between myself and my father that has never healed."

"Is he still alive?" Heather asked simply.

"What?"

"Your father," she ground on. "Artak Khan. Is he still alive?"

"Yes, Command Centurion."

"Then you will go back to your ship tonight after this event and write him a letter of apology," Heather ordered the man. "That much you can do. Obviously, Kira Zaman is frightened of what you might do to her now, as you are possibly the Emperor's Golden Boy for serving with Phil's squadron. You will remain utterly aloof from her and her squadron. No communications beyond standard station-keeping and navigation. *Am I clear, Cruiser-Captain?*"

"Yes, Commander."

Heather nodded, anger somewhat assuaged. She didn't think she needed to break the son of a bitch right now, but it was oh so tempting. He probably saw that in her eyes, from the way he stood at rigid attention.

"Will Zaman ever be promoted out of the Penal Fleets,

Khan?" she asked now as the silence stretched. "Or has her birth doomed her to the second-class citizenship of political and social unreliability?"

His mouth opened to say something with great emotion, saw her eyes, and slammed shut again without making a sound.

"I don't know, Commander," he finally admitted. "Before, it didn't matter."

"But that was before," she completed the thought.

Khan simply nodded, mute.

"You have done nothing recently to anger me, Cruiser-Captain," Heather finally let him down off the ledge. "Keep it that way."

"On my honor, Command Centurion," he said, bowing and backing away with the sort of precision that they all learned when marching in squares.

Aquitaine's Academy didn't teach you to walk with precision. It taught you to take orders without question, at least until you were senior enough to understand the nature of doubt.

Heather found herself alone, wondering at the aspects of *Gloran* culture that had been hidden by those martial façades before now.

NINETEEN

DATE OF THE REPUBLIC MARCH 19, 412
GLORAN BATTLESHIP GLANTHUA'S STAND,
CARINAE II OUTER ORBIT

P hil had finally met the man in person.
Emperor Adric Kerenski of the *Gloran* reminded Phil of a cobra waiting to strike.

His hair was the color of obsidian, shoulder-length and worn in a practical, severe style that went with his beard and mustache, both graying. He had a lean, muscular build that reminded Phil of Jirou Kugosu, the *Dalou* Shogun and the kind of tanned skin you usually only got from working under real sunlight.

The preeminent warrior of an entire culture of warriors.

At the same time, he didn't give off the same vibes as the Shogun. Partly, Phil put that down to age, as Kerenski was nearly twenty years older than Kugosu, and had been in power for long enough to be secure. He didn't even carry a blade on his hip other than the short one that everyone from *Gloran* seemed to be issued on their twelfth birthday. Not that Phil intended to ask.

True to his word, they were standing around, chatting. Heather had wandered off like she would. Aliza was working the crowd on the other side of the room, where important locals wishing to get on her list could make appointments. *Gloran* understood that a lot of trade was due to be flowing into and through *Vilahana* soon. They didn't want to miss out. Harinder had even wandered off somewhere.

Phil and Dar, standing at a polite distance from Kerenski and Miliya Gavraba. Phil's Command Diplomatic Centurion for *Gloran* had been one of the first delivered and credentialed. Mostly because Heather's work at *Vilahana* had impressed the hell out of folks.

As a result, Miliya was dressed more like a local than an *Aquitaine* diplomat. Still in black pants and shoes, but her tunic had been redone in leather, with the ubiquitous chain mail mesh added to make her fit in more with *Gloran* folks.

She was not, presently, wearing a knife. Visibly.

Markus had vanished like he did after delivering a can of juice. It was really the three of them, as Dar was merely present because that was her job.

"I have read many reports, Kosnett," Kerenski began during one of those lulls in conversation that happened when interesting topics ranged wide enough.

And the *Gloran* Emperor wasn't some dull warrior who only talked forms and battles. He had a good working understanding of literature and music, however limited it was to mostly *Gloran* sources. Still, Phil had some notes for orchestral recording that he might send to *St. Legier*, where Casey would have a chance to listen.

She was all about music as a diplomatic tool. One of the most powerful in the universe.

Phil waited for the Emperor to complete his thought.

"What was it that made you decide to come to *Carinae II* before *Derragon*?" Kerenski asked.

"The need to solve a crime," Phil said, treating the man as something of an equal.

It was messy, trying to figure things out, but *Gloran* didn't maintain mathematically-precise gradations of rank, like *Dalou* did. Or used to.

"A crime?"

"The colony below us was attacked," Phil gestured to the floor plates. "Functionally destroyed. The perpetrators got away. For now."

"For now?" Kerenski asked, one eyebrow going up.

"For now," Phil agreed. "One of the reports I received suggested that almost all of the men accounted for were dead. Women between the ages of about twelve and forty were not. That suggests things that I find so distasteful that *Aquitaine* wanted to offer you the services of my squadron and my officers to help. Someone needs to pay an exceedingly painful bill for that behavior."

Kerenski blinked, possibly surprised at the vehemence in Phil's voice, but it couldn't be helped.

"I might add," Phil said. "If you look at my senior officers, the gender balance leans slightly towards the female in overall squadron numbers, but especially so aboard my flagship. Capturing women for whatever nefarious purposes as the evidence might suggest…"

He left it hanging. They had circumstantial evidence already. Nothing sufficient to hang someone from a yardarm. Enough, perhaps, to suggest who needed to be talked to.

"And what would *Aquitaine* do to such personages?" Kerenski asked.

"Put them to death," Phil said simply. "We don't have a large number of capital crimes. Slavery and treason make up most of them. Attacking unarmed planets as well."

"*St. Legier*," the Emperor of *Gloran* nodded.

"I've walked the surface in the aftermath of that attack, Your Majesty," Phil nodded back. "There are places where they will permanently leave the damage to slowly decay over time. There are a few memorials where entire buildings were constructed over them as hollow shells, just so the ruins do not weather and decay. In the ancient times, *Sentient* warfleets bombarded undefended worlds and came very close to annihilating the species. *Aquitaine* sees itself as a civilizing force, but we never forget where we came from. Even the Librarian at *Alexandria Station* is a songbird in a gilded cage, for all the assistance she had rendered in helping humanity rebuild in the modern age."

"My advisors suggest that you travel with a warship of the *Hamath Syndicate*," Kerenski offered obliquely, showing Phil just how subtle and dangerous the man could be, if they somehow got things so turned around as to be on opposite sides of the table.

"Former *Hamath Syndicate*, Emperor Kerenski," Phil emphasized with just a little steel in his voice. "I personally asked Captain Ward to form a new company dedicated to communication between capitals, because I felt that such a thing was both lacking and necessary. Many of the ships she has subsequently hired might have worked for *Hamath* in the past, but all have sworn off their piratical past and accepted citizenship of *Meerut* and the general amnesty that all the major nations agreed to."

"And you brought her here, why?" Kerenski asked, answering steel with steel.

"Because she knows all the players in *Hamath*, Your Majesty," Phil smiled coldly. "And assures me that all of them are accounted for. That, in fact, none of the known *Hamath* warships could have done such a thing, at least in the timeframe indicated."

The man rocked back, a bit confused.

"Who, then?" Kerenski asked.

"That, Your Majesty, is exactly what I desire to know," Phil answered. "If we discount *Hamath*, and I am willing at first approximation to do such a thing, then it might still be one of the other Syndicates, as not all of them melted in the aftermath of *First Meerut*. Or someone else."

"Oh?" Kerenski perked right up.

Ambassador Gavraba had been silent until now. She leaned forward enough to draw eyes her direction. Phil wondered if she had managed to charm the War-Captain into being elsewhere, or if the Emperor had ordered it, as the man had made initial introductions, then left to talk to others.

Phil hadn't had a chance to prep the woman. Nor work with her all that much because she had been on station for much of the last year, making connections and smoothing things.

"Would the eyes of relative outsiders make it easier, Your Majesty?" Miliya asked now.

He turned to her and Phil saw the trust and communications that had built up over her time.

"You suspect a trap?" he asked. "Something designed to appear as a thing, because *Gloran* could be counted on to open fire first, and maybe forget to ask questions later?"

"Not how I would have phrased it, Your Majesty," she answered with a sly grin. "At the same time, most outsiders have a limited understanding of *Gloran* culture upon which to make such calculations. They might be counting on the fact that you are not primarily recognized for your guile and subtlety."

Kerenski grinned.

"Muscle-headed punks, Ambassador?" he asked.

"I'm sure you have a few in your fleet, Emperor," she nodded. "And perhaps among your advisors. More the fools for the rest of the galaxy to underestimate you."

Phil was impressed. *Gloran* wasn't as utterly chauvinistic as *Ewin* or even *Dalou*, but sending a female ambassador had been a calculated risk on his part. That ten percent of their officers meant that the warriors of *Gloran* did recognize capability.

Miliya was playing to the man's vanity and intellect, but doing so in an obvious way that was flattering without condescending. And it seemed to be just the right touch.

Kerenski smiled at her, then extended it to Phil.

"What do you know or suspect, that you have not been able or willing to communicate generally, First Centurion?" he asked.

That took Phil's breath away. Very few politicians he'd ever met could make such an immediate, intuitive leap. And when they did, it was usually the paranoia speaking.

Phil couldn't help but glance both directions, but nobody was close. Dar and Markus assured that.

Still…

"My senior staff contains a variety of experts, Your Majesty," Phil understated. "During a discussion of piracy, we posited a set of theories about their potential behavior, primarily before the raid on *Carinae II*. Based on those, we suspect that it might be possible to find more concrete evidence about the identity of the attackers, presuming that, as you noted, things left on the ground might be planted in order to cast suspicion on *Hamath*."

"Go on," Kerenski had gotten perfectly still. His voice had taken on the kinds of menace that Phil recognized from Khan, when the Cruiser-Captain got focused down on the job of killing things.

"I would like to move a portion of my squadron over to the fourth world in this system," Phil said. "From there, I have three vessels with extremely sensitive survey capabilities, far beyond anything anyone in the Cluster is currently fielding. We intend to look there."

"You think they hid in the shadow of Four while scouting?" Kerenski asked. "I wondered why your scanners were paying such close attention, when the reports came in."

Phil nodded. Truly, a dangerous player, if he'd seen what everyone else had, and gotten that close to figuring it out.

Good thing they were all on the same side here. *Gloran* might not have the reputation for military capabilities that some of the others did, but they had a sharper leader than anybody else Phil had met so far.

Even the Shogun. While Kugosu was a capable leader, he had previously been surrounded by a cadre of older advisors that hadn't generally impressed Phil. Excepting Tane Eiton, Consigliere and generally scary badass, even into his seventies.

Adric Kerenski was smarter. And had the patience of an

ambush predator. Phil upgraded the man in his estimations, just on that one observation.

"We believe they might have hid there, Your Majesty," Phil said. "However, we couldn't be sure of anything until we visited. And didn't necessarily want everyone traipsing over there, where they might destroy evidence, however accidentally."

"Or intentionally?" Kerenski growled.

"My exposure to the *Gloran* fleet is largely limited to Cruiser-Captain Adham Khan, who has done an exceptional job as part of the force," Phil replied. "But somebody attacked this world. Tried to destroy it. Planted evidence suggesting *Hamath Syndicate* did it. That is not a task I would personally undertake without first gaining significant useful intelligence on the target. In layman's terms, I would suspect a leak, at the very minimum."

"Or a traitor?" Kerenski pressed.

"There is a new Cluster being born, Your Majesty," Phil reminded the man. "Many of the people it has been my pleasure to meet have embraced that potential with both arms. A few have resisted, violently twice at *Meerut*. I do not know your culture or your Imperium well enough to accurately judge if the attackers might have had inside help. Nor do I discount it. We intend to follow the clues and find the pirates. They might tell us even more."

Another lull in conversation. Kerenski watching. Ambassador Gavraba watching. Phil watching.

"*Urumchi* is a Survey Dreadnought, correct?" the Emperor finally asked. "The one with the best sensors to find whatever it is you expect?"

"That is correct," Phil agreed. "We might list it as a training exercise. Or merely me pulling all of my ships out of orbit of Two so that you are free to focus your efforts on the ground and orbit. What would be of the most assistance to the *Gloran Empire*?"

"Find me the truth, First Centurion," Kerenski ordered.

"I will do what I can," Phil offered.

TWENTY

GLORAN EMPIRE HEAVY BATTLECRUISER JUVAYNI, CARINAE II

Adham found himself in his personal quarters, still reeling from the events of the evening. He'd known going into the event that Kira Zaman commanded *Arteshbo*, though that had been a surprise when he'd first arrived with the *Aquitaine* force and took a quick poll of the defending forces.

That the woman had met with Lau was to be expected. Women at the command rank were rare enough for her to find Command Centurion Lau fascinating. Worse, he did as well, having spent a year serving under her command.

Previously, Adham Khan would have been appalled at the thought of serving under a woman. It was unnatural.

And yet...

Yaumgan and *Aditi* had sent such commanders when Kosnett had asked. *Ewin* had none. *Dalou* so few as to be functionally unicorns.

That left *Gloran*.

Didn't that describe so many things? *"And then there was Gloran."*

He was in his quarters. Lau had ordered him to do a thing. Two things, really, but only one of those was difficult. He could remain far and away from Zaman and her consorts, as the frigates were a local force. Kosnett would remain aloof from the Emperor, and Khan's place was guarding and guiding *Urumchi*.

But he dithered.

Adham recognized it for what it was.

Fear.

Artak Khan had been reinstated to his previous glory, but the gap between father and son had never been closed. And Kira Zaman had been the reason.

She might have been transferred to the main fleet as a result of Artak's word, but for Adham's denunciations. Might have moved on to command a ship as powerful as *Glanthua's Stand*.

Might be *Gloran*'s answer to Heather Lau.

But for him.

Adham looked at the piece of paper he had drawn from a drawer. At the pen in one hand. He set the latter down and crumbled the former into a ball that was dumped blank into the incinerator chute with a quick puff of light.

He could not say the words. Mostly because he had no idea what they should be.

Artak Khan had been a widower then, so there would have been no dishonor suggesting adultery had there been any physical relationship. At the same time, Kira Zaman was an outcast in every sense of the word, and Adham had objected to sharing the glory of the Khan name with her in even the slightest manner.

And he had been wrong. Nobody but Heather Lau could have shown him that.

Bizarre, really.

He moved from his desk to the comm panel next to the door, pressing a button.

"First Officer Stasny," he said, identifying the man for the computers to locate.

"Stasny here," Wolf replied a moment later. "What can I do for you, Captain?"

"Join me in my quarters, Wolf," Adham said. "I need to brief you on a few things and get briefed in turn. Much has happened tonight. None of it appears bad, but we will be in motion again shortly."

"On my way."

The line went silent. Adham keyed the switch to unlock his cabin door and moved to sit on the bed.

The immense sleeping space on *Urumchi* had always left him a little sour. Adham had been raised in compact quarters. Even now, he had a single room five meters long, four wide, and ceilings high enough that most crew members could fit.

It was all a captain needed, to say nothing of his crew. *Urumchi* had entire suites dedicated to hosting people in luxury unknown to most of *Gloran*. Space for a small athletic event to be held, if you took out the furniture.

Adham had a bed, a dresser, a desk, and a footlocker.

What more did a warrior need?

He sat at the foot of the bed, meditating on the vast span of his sins. The man he had been a year ago would have been shocked to even have these thoughts, let alone contemplate acting on them.

Thus, must all of Gloran *change.* Morninghawk *showed us that, but most people were too blinkered to understand. Most would fail.*

I cannot fail, because Gloran *fails with me.*

The hatch slid open and Wolf Stasny entered.

Tall. Just barely short enough to serve on starships, where there was an absolute height limit. Wolf even wore custom boots with almost no heel, out of the reverse of vanity.

Perhaps merely the need to serve. As all of them did.

Lean and rangy. Lighter complexion more like *Aquitaine*, though not as reddish. Possibly the scion of some merchant who had come to the Cluster in the semi-distant past.

First Officer on a Heavy Battlecruiser. A noble position, and one that would see him promoted to Frigate-Captain, or possibly even Cruiser-Captain, assuming Adham didn't manage to piss Heather Lau off.

Then, they might all be doomed to a service segment aboard a ship like *Arteshbo*.

"Sit," Adham gestured to the desk.

Wolf didn't sit so much as turn the chair around and conquer it in straddling the thing. But he was like that.

"Did all go well with the Imperial reception?" Wolf asked.

They'd had this conversation an hour ago when he'd returned, but in front of many of their officers, all hopeful that the glory of *Juvayni* would reflect well on their future careers.

If their captain didn't fuck it all up in the next few days.

Adham had never been subject to doubt before now, either.

"It did," Adham reassured his First Officer, thinking about Iveta Beridze and what role that woman played in all this as well.

She had held the flag for the entire *Aquitaine* force while the First Centurion and Lau had been away.

Was Wolf Stasny ready for that sort of thing? And when he wasn't, whose fault was that?

"I expect movement orders shortly," Adham said. "Kosnett spoke with the powers that be and something is up, but in a good way. The squadron will shift, but not depart the system. Now might be a good time to put in for a resupply from stores intended for the Imperial squadron, if there was anything you wanted to sneak in that we couldn't get before."

"Understood, Captain," Wolf nodded. "What did you need to know?"

"The two other squadrons," Adham said. "The Imperial force was expecting to meet Kosnett here. What kinds of pods are they carrying?"

"I noted an odd discrepancy, Captain," Wolf said with a hard smile. "All of them were deployed with combat pods, just as we were. Extra Point Guns for the flanks and the one Main Gun aft, in addition to a slew of extra generators. Nobody brought missile pods or a carrier with fighters."

"You saw how effective such things might be at *Ewinhome*, Wolf," Adham grimaced. "Not even the Princes could threaten Kosnett, though really it was Beridze. And the Type Five Heavy?"

"The two Type Fives do not handle mission pods, as you know," Wolf confirmed. "*Arteshbo* has a defense pod in place for this mission. Two Point Guns forward and a whole series of short-range defensive missile launchers. What I would have equipped them with, were I ordering that squadron to investigate the rumors we heard. Sufficient to thwart any mass missile launch by a Raider or even an Enforcer, while letting the squadron maneuver in close for a kill."

Adham nodded. Warrior thinking. Make sure your shield arm is stable and solid so you can lean in with the sword hacking. *Ewin* would just launch missiles and laugh.

They wouldn't laugh long. *Dalou* would have firebirds, when a frigate squadron with a Five Heavy Leader could hold the line against them.

"Is everything okay, Captain?" Wolf asked.

"I need to brief you on a few topics that you will never repeat outside these quarters, Wolf," Adham said. "If something happens to me, this space will become yours, so you might have to repeat them to your new First Officer later. Our careers might hinge on mistakes I made years ago and am trying to salvage now. I might not be able to, and thus may have to fall on my sword, metaphorically *if not literally*. I will shield the rest of you as much as I can, but the dishonor might be too much for one man to claim."

"*Arteshbo*," Wolf said.

"Kira Zaman," Adham nodded. "You must take this to your grave, unless the Emperor himself commands. Am I clear?"

"On my honor, Captain."

"Let us start at the beginning, Wolf…"

TWENTY-ONE

IMPERIAL FLAGSHIP GLANTHUA'S STAND, CARINAE II

Adric, Emperor of *Gloran*, sat in his personal quarters and stewed.

When he'd been a mere Cruiser-Captain, he'd had a space like all officers, but Emperors were busier men, so he'd taken a triple suite instead. Five meters long, twelve wide, and ceilings higher than most ships allowed.

Decadence, but he understood that most leaders of nations might have a bedroom this large, plus several more rooms for various entertainment and business functions.

The outer hatch pinged with a visitor, though Adric had left all his bodyguards outside. Such was his prerogative, to rise now and answer his own door. Six men stood in the hallway, escorting A.Q. Tanel.

"Come," Adric nodded, motioning the man inside. He turned to the guard in charge. "Unless *Aquitaine* opens fire on one of our vessels, I am not to be disturbed."

The man saluted and Adric pushed the button to shut the hatch. A lock was not necessary, as those six men would hold it at any and all costs in the face of such an order.

"Sit," Adric motioned Tanel to a worktable near the door.

One square meter of light wood, with four chairs. Sufficient for tea and not much more.

Adric Kerenski didn't need much more.

"Was there a problem?" Adric asked Tanel as he joined the man.

Tanel might be a candidate to be the next *Gloran* Emperor, except that Adric was still going strong and Tanel was only three years younger at fifty-five.

Adric suspected that the Empire might need a younger man next. Perhaps forty and full of the fire and fury to accomplish the sorts of radical changes that *Aquitaine* threatened.

Tanel's mouth moved like he'd sucked on a lemon.

"Zaman sought out Lau and spoke extensively with the woman," A.Q. replied. "At one point, Khan almost blundered into the conversation, but Zaman fled immediately. Lau proceeded to dress Khan down harshly, but quietly. If I could not read lips, I would have missed it all, as did everyone else. As it was, I only got parts, but even those parts were somewhat damning."

"Dressed him down?" Adric asked, feeling a twinge of rage niggle at his belly that a foreigner might have the audacity.

But it was Command Centurion Lau. *Ground Control*. Perhaps the most dangerous starship commander in the entire Balhee Cluster, though Adric wouldn't say that out loud around his own men. They would be offended, however wrong they were.

"I got the impression that Khan gave Lau a good deal of the history of himself and Kira Zaman, Adric," A.Q. said.

He could use the Emperor's given name in private. They'd been friends for decades, after decades previous as rivals.

"Did he now?" Adric was surprised. Not many outsiders were privy to those secrets.

But he supposed that Lau would need to know.

"How angry was she?" he asked now.

"Chewing nails and spitting iron, Your Majesty," A.Q.

laughed. "I thought Khan might wet himself by the time she was done."

Adric nodded. Considered his options. As Emperor of *Gloran*, he could order just about anything and have it done. Such was the executive authority vested in each emperor.

However, his predecessor had shared one of the most important tidbits Adric had ever heard, there at the end.

Never issue an order that might make people question the wisdom of following you. Often, you will have to lead them, rather than shoving them to a place, which can be dangerous if you guess wrong. That is why the Imperial Robes are so heavy.

Adric had never forgotten that. Most of his important decisions had come through that lens.

"What of my cousin?" he asked. "How is she?"

"Well, from what I can gather," A.Q. nodded. "Her squadron continues to earn top marks, though looking at the careers of the other Frigate-Captains that cycle through, it is obvious that the glory is hers. Little though she can bask in it."

"She serves, regardless of the rest of us," Adric said sternly. "Remember that. She is tougher than you are, because you never had those headwinds. Nor did I. I would move her to a cruiser if I thought the old farts in charge of the Penal Fleet would not piss and moan over such a thing. My only current issue is that I never imagined that Kosnett would come here first instead of *Derragon*. Else I would never have sent my cousin's squadron to *Carinae*."

"Dare we order her home?" A.Q. asked.

"No more than I dare dishonor Khan by ordering him elsewhere," Adric said. "However, Kosnett offers me a solution that, while it is not my first choice, handles the situation with Khan and Zaman well enough."

"Oh?"

"His people posit that the raiders who hit *Carinae* might have approached via Four, hiding in the sensor shadow," Adric said. "And that they have the scanner power to perhaps locate signs of the ship that attacked the colony."

"After so long?" A.Q. recoiled.

"Remember the thing that *Urumchi*'s First Officer did at *Ewinhome*," Adric reminded the man.

"Beridze," A.Q. nodded. "Blinded everyone. Well, there is a so-called Survey Dreadnought and an Expeditionary Survey Cruiser there. Send them all to Four for now, keeping *Arteshbo*'s squadron here?"

"Indeed," Adric said. "That should keep my two problem children apart."

"Is there a way to reconcile them?" A.Q. asked. "Ever?"

"That would solve many other problems, my friend," Adric said. "But you and I both know what a stiff-necked man Adham Khan can be."

TWENTY-TWO

DATE OF THE REPUBLIC MARCH 21, 412 RAN URUMCHI, CARINAE IV ORBIT

Phil studied the projection as the squadron settled. All the ships in a ring facing outward, rather than the usual defensive formation. All the command centurions as small faces, projected from their own bridges.

Below them, metaphorically, the north pole of *Carinae IV*, a green and red gas giant with a massive collection of moons. In many ways, it reminded him of the great planet *Jupiter*, part of Earth's system and the largest planet of the many there.

The records didn't indicate any significant destruction in the *Jupiter* region, but he supposed that any number of small stations and colonies on various moons might have been attacked when the *Sentient* Fleets destroyed *Earth* itself.

Or not. They might have been ignored and allowed to wither, without supplies. That had been the whole point of the war those machines had fought. Without factories making parts, or ships carrying food, many places had been too inhospitable for people to survive.

And the machines had slammed asteroids into planets elsewhere, though even then *Earth* had gotten the special treatment of being rendered entirely uninhabitable, even today. That took a massive amount of rocks. And infinite patience.

Phil shook off the image and returned to the work at hand. He opened the squadron line and drew a breath.

"This is Kosnett, aboard *Urumchi*," he said solemnly, still caught up in the edges of those emotions. "Markus, you have the flag."

He turned to the man sitting ninety degrees off from himself and Harinder. Markus had even gone to the barber and gotten his hair trimmed short. And put on a nice uniform, rather than one of the ones that might have stains from *something*.

But Markus had long-since proven that his technical redneckery went far beyond making grenade launchers.

"All hands, this is Dunklin, I have the flag," the man said. "You've got your zones of observation calculated, which is why I have you all spread out in a flat ring for this. *Urumchi* will ping. *Viking* and *CM-507* will sit on their corners and listen. Everybody else will do the same, cataloging anything that comes up with any sort of reflection, regardless of size. Nobody will move until ordered by me or Heather, because we need to triangulate anything that looks interesting, and will probably deploy administrative shuttles with EVA teams, depending on the size for recovery. Are there any questions?"

He paused there and Phil studied everyone. Noted the seriousness on those faces, even for something so exotic and unusual as this. But then, Markus had started inventing new weapons and defensive systems that might be installed on warships soon.

And supervised the astronomical team that was calculating how to find sailable gaps in the Cluster walls. They existed, but short of finding one at random, they were usually more trouble than they were worth.

Unless you already knew exactly where to look.

"*Urumchi*. Science Officer Ekmekçi," Markus called Leyla specifically. "First hard ping."

Phil listened as the computers played a note. The sort of thing you could identify, even in the middle of a battle, just as each beam emplacement was aurally coded, to the point that you could follow a battle blindfolded if you needed to. Or were too busy with your own station to follow everyone else.

They waited a significant period of time. Markus and a small team had calculated the optimal position for a raider to be sitting on approach, in the days before the attack itself. That was all just mathematics and patience. Two things Markus didn't like to admit he was good at.

Like many other things.

On the screen, signals started showing up as the pulse reflected. Four had an equatorial ring, as a result of a moon that had been mortally wounded by some collision in the last hundred thousand years, to the point that it had bled off parts and continued to do so in the complicated gravitational dance of so many other moons around it. Fortunately, all of that helped to mark an area to avoid, as the impacts of rocks on shields might cause enough of a flash that some distant scanner might notice.

Thus, they were high. People tended to act as if the galactic plane was up and down, and maintained that rough general orientation.

Orbital space around Four was a mess. But, as Leyla and Heather had noted previously, they could probably hand all this data to an Imperial Astronomer at some point, looking to publish papers. They had a lot of data already.

"Okay, Leyla, I have adjusted the focus of your ping," Markus said after some twenty seconds had passed. "Put the second one down this corridor, please."

Again, the note. Markus had shifted the target up, over, and out a shade, which seemed to be useful, because the clutter in that area got denser as the signal penetrated.

"Hey, that's interesting," Sunan Bunnag, Science Officer on *Viking*, said over the general line. "Markus, I've got a signal that doesn't wash out. Extremely high reflective value. Way above the albedo of everything else we should see. Here."

Phil noticed a targeting point appear in the mess. Markus dialed the magnification much tighter and Phil watched something grow to visibility. Impossible to identify from here, but they were at astronomical distances, and the target read as only a few meters across.

"*Viking*, hammer it with your targeting scanners now," Markus ordered. "Send me an updated feed while everyone else watches everything else move around."

"Coming up."

Phil saw the calculated wavefront of lightspeed wash over the signal, reflect, and return to *Viking*. A few moments later, a still image appeared in a side projection, washing as the scanning systems depixelated it.

"Shit, that's a box," Harinder said. "Small shipping container that they kicked overboard rather than take the time to break down."

Phil didn't see it, but he trusted Harinder's instincts. He turned to Markus. That man was in charge.

Markus pursed his lips.

"*Li Jing*, you are closest," Markus said after a moment. "Send Guardian Ma with a team to recover it. *Stunt Dude* is not allowed to accompany them."

"Why not?" *Stunt Dude* demanded from the bridge of *Li Jing*.

"Because you're management now," Markus laughed. "Ambassadors aren't supposed to get their hands dirty, piratical raids on enemy platforms notwithstanding."

"You were there, too, you know," *Stunt Dude* snarked.

"And I don't get to go today, so you don't either," Markus grinned. "Ma and his folks can handle it just fine."

"Dunklin, would you like us to recover it, or transport it to *Urumchi* directly?" Captain Xue asked now on the same line.

Markus looked his way, so Phil shrugged. It was Markus's operation. He got to decide.

"Bring it here," Markus said. "Now, everyone else, we'll keep pinging while that's happening, so you might need to adjust your orbits for better parallax around the blind spots that the shuttle is likely to introduce. Let your Science Officers and Pilots handle that part. You hired them for a reason."

Phil grinned. Markus refused to become a centurion, but he'd have been quite good at it. Look at how he handled flag operations today.

Already they had found something. Hopefully, something good.

TWENTY-THREE

ASSAULT SHUTTLE ONE, INDEPENDENT EVA, SKYCRUISER LI JING

Guardian Ma knew he had a problem. He'd brought four troopers with him, plus the pilot, after measurements told them how much of the aft cargo bay was going to be filled by the hidden treasure *Urumchi* had found.

They were closed up now, with the life support system slowly refilling the entire shuttle and everyone staying bottled up in their suits.

He was just glad that he had been ordered directly to the flagship. Still, Ma Jianhong Ping shifted over to the short-range band that wouldn't leave this shuttle.

"All of you will remain silent about this," he ordered. "The First Centurion and the Command Centurion will make any decisions about what we found. You will not discuss it with your mates, your bunk buddies, or even letters to your mother without first clearing it with one of them or me. Not even Captain Xue can override that, nor does she get to know until someone is cleared to tell her. Am I clear?"

He turned in place as heads nodded, nobody even wanting to speak at this point.

Ma nodded to himself, feeling the grimness of it all working its way into his bones.

The box was a standard shipping container, alright. Previously filled with life support spare parts and such. That was all well and good, except that Ma understood things about such systems that the others probably missed.

The old Syndicates had used vessels that weren't really warships. Instead, the designs tended to be extremely durable civilian hulls with weapons added. Sure, you could add armor plate and such, but warships like *Li Jing* and others had been designed from the welds in to be able to take a lot of damage, torque, stress, and wear. As such, all those systems were usually custom designed.

That included life support systems. Civilians didn't put nearly as much effort into them, because of an expectation that you could slip into a softsuit if you had a vacuum breach, until such time as you could either slap a patch over it, or set up portable airlocks on a frame hatch and escape to a safe environment.

So civilian systems were pretty basic. *Commercial, off-the-shelf* was a term Ma had picked up from *Stunt Dude*.

This box had not been commercial.

It had come from an *Aditi* vessel. Which, as far as Ma knew, none were supposed to be in this system.

Ever. And the box had not been exposed to solar wind and radiation from the gas giant for all that long, either, so it wasn't some relic from generations ago. Too many parts were still polished and clean.

Shit.

"Pilot, what's our ETA?" Ma asked, wishing, yet again, that Dunklin had allowed *Stunt Dude* to accompany them.

"Final approach to *Urumchi* now, Guardian," the woman replied.

Ma kept his thoughts to himself. Then thought better of it. He switched channels to a specific one.

"*Urumchi*, this Guardian Ma, on final approach," he said. "Command Centurion, could you meet us in the landing bay?"

TWENTY-FOUR

DATE OF THE REPUBLIC MARCH 21, 412 RAN
URUMCHI, CARINAE IV ORBIT

Heather hadn't been able to get anything more out of *Li Jing*'s Dragoon. Or Guardian, as they called them. So she'd left Iveta in charge on the bridge and headed aft. Markus was already there when she reached the lounge on this side of the airlock, so Heather stepped close.

He was surprised to see her.

"Ma asked me specifically to meet him here," she said simply to his unvoiced question.

Markus had a team of engineers handy, though no officer, she noted with a grin. All enlisted folks who liked to get their hands dirty. Troublemakers, the lot of them.

Beyond the bay window, the shuttle from *Li Jing* was settling, with all of *Urumchi*'s craft stored off to one side on racks to make space for the bigger vessel.

The bay got sealed and atmosphere was pumped in. Lights turned green. The airlock door unsealed.

"Ma wanted you specifically?" Markus asked after having been silent for several minutes.

Heather nodded.

"You lead, then." He stopped and thought about it, then

turned to the others. "In fact, all of you remain here while I go with Heather and scope it out."

Groans and profanities greeted him, but that was normal. The man was going to go have an adventure and leave them behind.

Heather went through the door with him a step back and to her right. The side hatch of the shuttle had opened, but not the big cargo door. Ma stood in it, his name clear on his helmet.

What was so bad that he didn't want anybody to see it?

He gestured her in and stepped back. She and Markus followed.

Shit.

"I've ordered my people to remain silent, Command Centurion," Ma began. "You, me, and the First Centurion are the only ones that can override that with my people."

"Probably wise," Heather replied.

There was no doubt where that box had come from. Markus moved past her and knelt, inspecting things with his gloved fingertips, close enough to breath on it. The metal was so cold that ice had formed.

Then Markus stood up and pointed to two of the troopers in armor.

"You two get that side," he said simply. "I need to rotate it ninety degrees on this axis to get at the shipping code information currently face down on the deck."

Heather got out of the way, as the box nearly filled the space. Light, though. Strong metal that didn't weigh much, so mostly the four of them were dealing with the awkward shape.

They got it turned quickly and settled. Markus pulled out a comm and started taking pictures of things. He started to do something more, paused, and looked at Heather.

"How tight do we keep this?" he asked sharply. Nervously.

After all, if an *Aditi* warship had been here, they probably had been the ones to attack the colony, while leaving an awful lot of evidence on the surface implicating pirates instead. Had this box been used to store all the fake evidence until it got loaded onto an assault shuttle?

Heather studied the folks around her.

"Guardian Ma, as you will likely not be surprised, I need you to remain aboard *Urumchi* for a bit while Phil sorts things out," she said.

That man nodded.

"Everybody, out of your suits and into uniforms," he said now, popping his helmet off.

Heather nodded to Markus and they withdrew to give people space. And time.

She moved to a wall comm.

"Flag bridge," she said, pressing the button.

"Harinder here, Heather," came the quick response.

"I need you and Phil aft," she said, not commenting where others might hear.

Her crew were exceptional, but sailors were sailors, and would gossip. Even the rumors that would start from the current secrecy would be interesting, but she doubted that they would be as bad as the truth.

"Inbound," Harinder replied and cut the line.

Heather moved to the airlock door and gestured one of the Chiefs closer. The woman came with a hint of trepidation.

"Six sailors off *Li Jing*," Heather said simply. "You need to get them accounted for with the Quartermaster and anyone else. They'll need bunks, food, entertainment, and possibly training space while they are here."

"Got it," the woman nodded.

Heather moved back to the shuttle and waited. Ma and his crew emerged in regular uniforms about the time that Phil and Harinder came through from forward. The Chief fell in with them as they crossed the bay.

"All of you but Ma can go with the Chief here," Heather gestured. "She'll get you taken care of for now and I'll let

Captain Xue know you're staying aboard *Urumchi* for a few days."

Glum looks, but not surprise. That box was an explosive surprise. A Cluster-wide incident just waiting to trigger a war.

On the one hand, she was glad they'd found it, and could attribute the attack to someone. On the other hand, chasing pirates down and blowing them up was a much better outcome than sailing back to *Aditi* proper right now and demanding answers.

Assuming Kerenski wanted answers and didn't just sail to the nearest *Aditi* colony and bombard it in retribution. Heather might argue against that, but she couldn't say the man was wrong.

Hammurabi had etched this into stone, several thousand years ago.

Ma had come to attention. He wasn't much taller than *Stunt Dude*, but slender. And fast. *Stunt Dude* had compared sparring with the man with trying to catch a greased chicken in the rain.

But he was the Guardian of *Li Jing*. The Dragoon. Those two men had formed a close relationship, though Ma was probably wishing that *Stunt Dude* had gone instead and he'd remained back with his ship.

"First Centurion, if you would accompany me?" Ma said now, turning and marching into the empty shuttle.

Heather and Markus accompanied, until it was just the four of them inside the smaller space.

"Oh, fuck," Phil grumbled. He turned to her. "You were right."

"It was a guess, based on random evidence and a little paranoia, Phil," she countered. "And you'd been guiding the conversation that way."

"True," he nodded. "Ma, thank you for not broadcasting this, even over a secured line with squadron encryption."

The man nodded, but otherwise fell into parade rest and remained silent.

"I'll need to talk to Kaur Singh," Phil mused aloud. "And *Hollywood*. And probably Khan. Ma can brief Captain Xue, though I suppose that it would be better coming from me. That leaves Solo as the only person here without an axe to grind, but if I invited everyone else over for something and didn't include him, he'd find an axe after all. So I need to bring all my captains together. And quickly."

"Phil, I had invited Captain Zaman to join us aboard *Urumchi* for a tour and an overnight stay," Heather reminded him. "She's due in about fourteen hours. Can this wait that long, or do you need to jam it in and get it resolved before then?"

He fell into thought. Heather and the others watched and waited.

This might be the single biggest threat to the overall mission since *Vilahana*. Letting the truth be known could start a war. The exact sort of thing he'd been trying to avoid. Her, too.

"Just Zaman?" he asked her now.

"Her consort captains are more sidekicks than anything," Heather admitted. "Both assigned to Penal Fleet over infractions that they can clear with two years' service, after which they transfer back out."

"But not her," Phil growled.

"Not her, correct," Heather acknowledged. "Khan's story ruffles things, but uninviting her now sends a powerfully wrong message at this point."

"Agreed," Phil said. "In fact, there are probably no right answers, as I'll need to have Kugosu involved. She should meet with Zaman and hopefully those two can bond. The young woman has good instincts, but this might be the situation where I get ordered to *Derragon* to await the return of an angry and vengeful emperor."

"How do we prevent a war from breaking out?" Ma asked quietly, having obviously done the math ahead of time.

"I don't know that we can," Phil nodded to the man. "We would like to; however *Aditi*—if they did this—might be counting on us stopping *Gloran* from making them have to pay any particularly egregious price for such shenanigans. At which point, I might decide to be extremely pissed off and walk away from *Aditi*."

Ma shuddered. Heather understood. Phil had warned everyone, time and again, that his patience wasn't infinite. Somebody might have finally miscalculated where that fine line was when they went to dance along it.

"Do we need to host the Emperor?" Harinder asked. "Not deliver this thing to his doorstep, but bring him here and talk in circumstances where we might have a chance to shape outcomes before he goes off?"

Phil paused. Studied the four of them. Her, Harinder, Markus, and Ma stared back.

"We owe the man a reception," he said. "If we draw in all my command centurions, we can invite all of his as well. However, I need to crack heads together around here first, because that situation will be rough with ugly emotions when this comes out. None of these people are shrinking violets like me, after all."

Heather chuckled with the others. Phil was just nice enough to let you throw the first punch. Before he returned the favor with interest, then maybe curb-stomped you afterwards.

"I'm not sure that's wise, First Centurion," Ma spoke up. "Yes, a reception is necessary. You've gotten great mileage out of such things. But Kerenski has a reputation for a thinking warrior, so maybe you need to bring him in for something small. After all, to date you haven't really done that with the other leaders, beyond working meetings. Maybe a small, private Tea? You and Heather. Him and…crap, who's the Fleet-Captain in command of *Glanthua's Stand*? My brain has gone blank."

"Fleet-Captain Kiri Povoloi," Phil filled in. "He was at the first reception, though I really didn't talk to him all that much. And yes, your idea has merit, Guardian Ma. Let's break now and I will order the shuttle isolated while we figure out how we want to approach this. Please, join me for dinner tonight. The five of us, I think, alone."

Ma nodded. Phil glanced over at her and Heather understood a wide, unspoken raft of various orders from the man, all of which were things she'd have done anyway. Too many years as partners in this endeavor. They could read each other's minds.

Now, what would they say to the *Gloran* Emperor?

TWENTY-FIVE

AQUITAINE FLAGSHIP URUMCHI, CARINAE IV

Kira Zaman, decorated Frigate-Captain of the Type Five Heavy *Arteshbo*, sat and fidgeted nervously as the shuttle docked with an airlock and connected. Command Centurion Lau—*Heather*—had immediately set her staff to working out arrangements to host Kira aboard the flagship. That had turned out to be a large shuttle they called a GunShip making a short jump over to pick her up and bring Kira out to Four.

She felt a little naked without security troops, but there were no criminals on *Urumchi*. Nobody sentenced to penal service in the fleet, doing time either aboard a penal ship or demoted and left on a main vessel while security watched them like hawks.

What would it be like to live in a place without the paranoia of the Security Ministry watching?

She let the sour grapes of her life wash over her in a private fit of might-have-beens and focused on the thing at hand. At thirty-four, she was already a Frigate-Captain and squadron commander, which most of her peers would not achieve ever; and those that did not until they were much older.

Artak had taken charge and made sure she was the best officer, the best First Officer he could make her, but even Artak

Khan could not lift the stain of her birth from her soul and get Kira transferred to the real fleet.

So she served as best she could. Did what she was allowed.

Her cousin the Emperor didn't seem to have a problem, as her team was frequently the one dispatched to trouble spots. And not just because they were less worthy than main fleet.

Kira Zaman got things done. She could just never be rewarded as even a commoner might.

The jostling stopped.

"Frigate-Captain, we've arrived," the pilot said from forward. "Docking complete shortly."

She'd gotten so wrapped up in her own thoughts that Kira hadn't paid that much attention to the vessel she'd ridden.

Huge. She understood that it was armed and had a JumpSail. It might qualify as a small Type four patrol vessel in *Gloran* service, but that in itself was rather impressive as it was carried inside the flagship. It might also be more dangerous than such Type Four ships she had known.

This one was apparently configured as Kosnett's personal transport, with a small lounge designed to carry a dozen in relative comfort. Perhaps a little nicer than *Gloran* would have done it, but utterly plain and devoid of luxury compared to other nations, at least according to the rumors she'd heard.

Kira comforted herself with imagining *Aquitaine* as something more similar to *Gloran* than the others, though that was likely wishful thinking. *Aditi* was the closest to them in form of government. And *Dalou* had a Crown Prince and possibly the next Shogun operating with this force, if rumors were true.

Truly, Kosnett had done the impossible, bringing the Five Nations together as equals.

As she unbuckled and rose, Kira wondered if it would be possible for her to be saved as well.

She moved to the hatch as it opened, having ridden alone watching screens showing stars.

Heather was standing on the other side. Again, without

security troops. Kosnett had that one dangerous woman Centurion with him, but that was because he was irreplaceable, and everybody else wasn't.

Heather smiled.

"Welcome aboard, Kira," she said as Kira crossed the airlock line and took the outstretched hand.

It was all a little strange.

For one, the ceilings were impossibly high in here. And the lights were much brighter. The walls painted either an off-white or dark green, rather than the heavy gray she was used to.

It almost felt like a civilian passenger liner, but Kira knew that *Urumchi* was likely the match of *Glanthua's Stand* in single combat. Perhaps its better.

"How goes your mission?" Kira asked innocently, but noted the short break of restraint in Heather's eyes before the woman answered.

"We're looking and charting," Heather replied brightly, but Kira wasn't fooled.

She'd spent twenty years trying to overcome her past. To move beyond the limits her unfortunate birth had cast upon her.

Decades spent hearing the slightest false note in a voice. Or in an eye. Perhaps the way a hand was moved.

Heather was good at lying, but not good enough.

They found something. And whatever it was is explosive. So terrible that they haven't figured out how to tell everyone else. What could be so bad?

Kira smiled and accepted the lie for a face-saving gesture. For now. *Gloran* was a closed book to outsiders. And Kira Zaman was a prime example of the ways that they differed from *Aquitaine*, where a poor, commoner girl named Keller had risen to the grand heights and saved the galaxy so many times that she would probably end up being deified on enough planets to matter when she died.

They would not know the best way to share whatever it was

they had found. Worse, they had only been here a few days, so they would need time to sort it out.

Kira fell in next to Heather as they walked. *Urumchi* was simply staggering, from the inside as well as the outside. Wide corridors. Bright and cheery in ways Kira had never considered. Smiling crew members walking the other direction, instead of firm glares or scowls.

Kira was, however, going to requisition new shades of paint when she back got to her home base after this mission. What were they going to do, sentence her to a Penal Frigate?

Then they passed through an airlock and entered…a forest. Trees? BIRDS? Was that a bee?

"Wha…?!?!"

Heather smiled.

"On a standard Heavy Dreadnought, this space is the generator and launcher for the *Reversed Field, Pinch, Plasma Implosion Generator*," Heather said. "But you'll probably only ever hear it called a Bubble Gun."

"Bubble Gun," Kira repeated slowly, brain still rebooting as they walked down a game trail **on a starship!**

"Taking it out frees up a tremendous amount of volume," Heather laughed. "So Phil has space for ambassadorial suites and a functional conference center with kitchen, plus an arboretum that lets him trade plants. Oh, hello, Sergey."

A man had appeared out of the underbrush. Short, about Kira's height. Muscular when she settled for athletic. Rough hands, like he literally dug in the soil all day. The man's hair was a little long, and a shade of orange that looked utterly alien, but Kira knew that to be her own upbringing, around folks so much darker than the red-brown of most of *Aquitaine*.

"Master Gardener Sergey Cummins, allow me to introduce you to Frigate-Captain Kira Zaman, of the Penal Frigate Leader *Arteshbo*," Heather said.

Kira watched the man study her like a wild animal deciding

whether to flee or attack. And this was a gardener? On a spaceship?

He grunted. Nodded. Possibly smiled, though Kira might have imagined it.

"Pears are ripe forward," he said simply. "Don't tell Phil. Planning a surprise."

Then he was gone.

Kira blinked.

"Wow, he likes you," Heather said approvingly. "We just got permission to steal two pears from his orchard and munch on them while nobody is around."

"Okay?" Kira replied, even more off-centered than she had been two minutes ago. "Real pears?"

"This way," Heather said, taking Kira by the hand and guiding her off the main trail through brush the same direction the gardener had appeared from.

Pear trees, though she would have only known that from the fruits growing.

"Aren't they normally taller?" Kira asked.

"These are grafted *espalier*," Heather replied, like that explained it all. Kira's face communicated something else. "So the root is allowed to grow to a certain height. Here. You can see where the vertical shaft was grafted on. Then each of these branches was grafted on to that. We have nearly a dozen, identically built, each with six flavors of pears growing."

"And bees?"

"You need Mason bees to pollinate much of what's in here," Heather nodded. "Natural ecosystem. Here, we're taking a pair of the boscs."

She proceeded to pull a pair of impossibly lovely brown fruits and handed Kira one.

Kira had served on starships from the earliest she had been allowed to enlist. Even then, that had only been the Penal Fleet, but they took her at fourteen when the main fleet had a minimum cutoff of sixteen. Greenery left her utterly confused. *Aquitaine* took it for granted?

Was that decadence, or wealth? Could you have one without the other?

Heather took them deeper into the brush, until they emerged in a clearing that was tiny. Maybe three meters across the widest part, but facing a round portal that looked out over stars and Carinae IV.

"I asked Iveta to give us a good view for our picnic," Heather said.

Picnic. There was a basket from which Heather began extracting containers. A bench that they sat on. Food and drink.

And stars and gas giant.

Kira sat in shock. No other term could encompass it.

Heather smiled and began to unpack food in various small bins and boxes. Again, some dried fruit. Freshly baked bread by the texture. Salad.

There had been a legend of a girl who fell through a mirror into a magical otherworld and had adventures. Kira began to wonder if the GunShip had done that to her when it deposited her on this deck.

More than once, she opened her mouth and closed it again when nothing useful came out. Heather just nodded, like she understood. How could she possibly?

Except that it was there in her eyes.

So they ate. Dessert was a bosc pear picked from a tree thirty minutes ago and still juicy with ripeness in the firm flesh.

Heather was watching her.

Finally, Kira found words.

"I would ask what I have done that rated this, but that opens whole other cans of worms, doesn't it?" she asked.

"I had a chat with Khan," Heather replied in a heavy, sour voice that suggested so much more than *chatting*. "He's been ordered to remain away from you while we're in squadron. Not to so much as transmit anything to *Arteshbo* beyond navigational necessity."

"But why?" Kira asked. "He is a Cruiser-Captain. And a favored of the Emperor, to have been sent to join Kosnett's jihad against the pirates. I am…"

"I also got some of that story from him," Heather interrupted. "Not all of it, but enough. He understands that he's on dangerous ground with me right now."

Kira was back to hollow silence, unable to form words.

"Why?" she finally managed.

"I've had to deal with *Dalou* and *Ewin*," Heather said. "And all the bull-headed sexist bullshit that they need to get over if they want to be considered adults by the rest of the galaxy. *Dalou* is on their way. *Ewin* might just have to implode for a generation and emerge as something else. *Gloran* is an odd duck, in that they allow women, but they make it almost impossibly hard. From what I've been able to determine, you must be one of the best officers they have, to have risen to where you are, as young. And yet…"

Kira nodded.

"And yet," she agreed. "*Gloran* will not allow me to advance further, for reasons that are not worth rehashing now, though I do understand that *Aquitaine* would be different."

"Which is what pissed me off about Khan," Heather agreed. "*Aquitaine* is different. *Gloran* will need to get over that shit one of these days."

"And if they don't?" Kira asked, intrigued by the forthrightness of Heather's words.

"Then they end up being no better than *Ewin*, at a time when *Aditi* and *Dalou* might be joining the future."

"Such a thing is beyond my power, Heather," Kira reminded her. "I am the bastard daughter no one is willing to acknowledge. A threat to the Imperial House by my mere existence."

"Doubly so because you are more competent than most of them," Heather nodded.

Kira let that go. It wouldn't do her any good.

Still, Heather was trying to be an ally. Had gone to great lengths to impress her. Even the small talk had made it clear that Heather saw her as a peer, something nobody but other Penal Fleet officers would acknowledge.

"What is your game, Heather?" Kira asked. She might as well have that confrontation now, while things were friendly. "Why all this?"

"To show you a different way, Kira," Heather replied. "The *Aquitaine* way."

"It's not like I could quit the *Gloran* and join your navy, Heather," Kira replied sharply.

"As you wish," Heather said ambiguously. "I have other officers that were born in the Cluster."

Kira had to replay those words to fully understand that. She blinked too many times.

"Senior Centurion Nam Nagarkar was, until a year ago, a Senior Officer on the *Aditi* Cruiser *Aranyani*," Heather said. "Now, she is qualified to sit bridge watches on *Urumchi*. Cornet Kugosu is in training, and making great strides, though she is coming from a much smaller start, being only fourteen years old."

Kira flashed back to those days. Young, yes. Hungry for what glory she could achieve. Able to enlist in the penal fleet—practically required to, in fact—but good enough to learn fast. And advance fast.

It helped when all other officers above her would eventually transfer out, returning to the main fleet at the end of their sentence. Only Kira had the institutional knowledge at that point.

It had made her indispensable. Or something.

"Wait," Kira stuttered. "She was born in the Cluster, and is only fourteen? Who?"

"The daughter of the current Shogun of the *Dalou Hegemony*," Heather said. "The middle daughter, but the one intent on rising to power when her father retires."

As if it was just that simple.

"*Dalou?*" Kira demanded, shocked out of her wits.

"*Dalou*," Heather nodded. "She had been traveling with us as a personal representative of the Shogun, but decided that she needed to learn our ways, so Phil allowed her to enlist as an officer-trainee. And at least as good as any new Cornet I've gotten fresh out of the Academy, on any of the ships I've served on or commanded."

Kira leaned back and felt the whole galaxy twist somewhat, forming into a new pattern she had never considered.

"Careful," Kira laughed brittlely. "You might be accused of instigating revolution with your words."

"Good," Heather said so calmly that Kira's head snapped around to study the woman. "That's my intent with all of *Balhee*. *Dalou* is getting over themselves. *Ewin* had to get their teeth kicked in first, but we might have done a sufficient job there. *Gloran* has…*attachments* to…*more primitive beliefs* that have no place in a modern galaxy."

Kira was having a hard time breathing. Just saying those words on the deck of her own ship would get her a visit from the Security Ministry troops. If not arrested and transported somewhere.

Gloran had a structure, and it would not change.

Could not change.

Could it?

Kira took a deep breath to settle her racing heart. Some. Considered what Heather must have learned from Khan, and how that peasant would have spun things. She remembered the words. The hostility.

In another universe, she might have even had grounds to challenge the man. But her kind had no rights to object to the ways of men like Adham Khan. Even Artak had been unable to move his own son, and that had caused a rift in the family that might never heal.

Kira Zaman didn't need to aggravate things.

"I thank you for your words and your intent, Heather," Kira said, speaking from her soul. "I doubt that it will change anything. At least in time to help me. Perhaps your revolution can help our daughters thrive in soil too barren for us."

"I have no children, Kira," Heather replied. "I have officers I have nurtured. They will change the future in their own way. In their own time. That is my legacy. To leave behind a better galaxy than I found."

Again, the words shocked Kira. She was used to such complicated circumnavigations around certain topics that it might take ten minutes to actually say something.

That wasn't Heather's way, obviously. Direct. Forthright.

Possibly brutal.

But this same woman had moved a world, literally. There might not be anything she could not achieve, were she to set her mind to it.

"Can I ask a question then?" Kira posed. "In the circumstances of openness and communication as you've laid them out?"

Heather nodded, eyes shrouded now, like a curtain had suddenly been drawn across them.

"Go ahead," Heather replied, her tone making no promises.

"I promise that I won't discuss the matter with others, but what did you find when *Urumchi* arrived at Four?" Kira asked.

"What makes you think we found anything?" Heather asked.

Again, she sounded perfectly normal, but Kira had spent thirty-four years hanging on the words of others. The charity of strangers for her mother, later for the kin that had taken the orphan Kira in.

She could hear the doubt in Heather's words.

"Because whatever it was, it has frightened a dangerous warrior like you with its implications, Heather," Kira said simply. "I have been wracking my brain trying to encompass something that bad and frankly haven't been able to come up with a scenario that covers it."

Heather studied her carefully. Kira tried to project calm intent.

Perhaps not the best way to approach it, but at the same time, there weren't many people Kira could tell. Or who would even listen to her.

Heather seemed to be doing those same calculations.

"Knowing locks you into something bigger and more dangerous, Kira," the woman warned her. "Phil knows, and is gathering all his command centurions together to inform them, as a prelude to inviting the Emperor to come aboard and learn."

"That bad?" Kira gasped in spite of how tough she thought she was.

That it could frighten the same people who were disrupting the entire Cluster with equanimity took things to a whole new layer.

"Would it be better for you, then, if I didn't know?" Kira pressed. "If I simply returned to *Arteshbo* in ignorance until the Emperor told everyone?"

"Is he really your cousin?" Heather asked, shifting things a new direction.

"We share a grandfather," Kira nodded soberly. "But that man had a dozen sons, including various mistresses pensioned off quietly for their secrecy, so it is impossible to confirm which of them might have been my father, short of testing each individually, which nobody is willing to suggest. And none have volunteered the truth."

"Do they know?" Heather pressed.

Kira shrugged. Unknowns stacked atop unknowns. The man responsible had abandoned her mother, if he had known. And he had to know by now. But her mother had been a nobody. Not a great player whose life mattered to the Lord of the Empire.

Not even her daughter mattered. Except when she had gotten involved in such politics.

"Why did he send you to *Carinae*?" Heather shifted the conversation yet another direction, but Kira assumed it all made sense.

"My squadron are penal frigates," Kira replied. "Not as valuable as main line cruisers. At the same time, I get things done, where other officers might fail because…"

"Because they fear making the sort of mistake that punishes them by transfer to the Penal Fleet," Heather filled in the words when Kira fell short.

Kira nodded.

That was quite possibly the story of her career. Of her entire life.

What did she have to lose at this point? At any point?

"As I said, it would initiate you into a space that might grow uncomfortable, if others discovered that you knew the truth before they did," Heather said. "Before the Emperor did."

Kira found that she really didn't mind whatever opprobrium might accompany such a thing.

What would they do, sentence her to the Penal Fleet?

She smiled grimly at Heather.

"Do your damnedest," Kira challenged the woman with more bravado than she really felt.

So Heather told her the truth.

TWENTY-SIX

DATE OF THE REPUBLIC MARCH 22, 412 RAN
URUMCHI, CARINAE IV ORBIT

Phil looked at the officers around him. Barnaby Silver was here, but none of the Corvette Command Centurions. They were all busy on their own bridges, against whatever happened next.

That left Phil with his six locals, plus Heather, Barnaby, and Guardian Ma at the table and Markus in the corner like normal. At least for now.

Even Lady Kohahu and the Crown Prince were not invited to this meeting, though both might be able to make exceptional cases to the contrary. Nor was Nam Nagarkar. That woman might have to remove her new green and black uniform and depart with Kaur Singh after this, though she didn't know it.

Too much unknown.

He had gathered everyone aft in one of the smaller conference rooms. It was a compact space, because he wanted to keep all the emotional explosions isolated.

Phil rapped his knuckles on the table top to still the side conversations and draw all eyes to him.

Cruiser-Captain Khan. Striker Solo. Captain Xue. Commander Singh. Captain Yukimura. Captain Ward. Not even Captain Sugawara, off *Forktail*. Just the cruiser commanders.

He nodded first to Gotzon Solo.

"Striker Solo, representing *Ewin*, has no real purpose to be here today, save that not inviting the man would be an undeserving insult, especially in light of the service he has given," Phil announced. "Gotzon, thank you for everything you have done to date."

The man had twitched hard. Wanted to say something, probably with his hands, but he refrained. Nodded compactly instead, a little at sea. For a moment more.

"Captain Ward, the original reports from *Carinae II* produced evidence that the colony was attacked and functionally destroyed by pirates associated with the *Hamath Syndicate*," Phil continued. "The former Syndicate."

Hollywood nodded. She'd been at great pains to produce all her private records accounting for anyone important enough to matter. A great many of those ships, or at least crews, had made it to *Meerut* in the last six months, accepting Phil's parole. Not everyone knew how many because neither he nor Governor Milose had made any public announcements.

Phil turned to Xue next.

"*Yaumgan* is isolated from everyone, but does share a long border with *Gloran*," he said, then nodded to Yukimura. "*Dalou* as well, but that border is less peaceful. And includes *Vilahana* at the main access point to the outside galaxy. Still, *Gloran* is not generally aggressive in those two directions."

He paused then nodded to both Khan and Singh.

"That leaves the long, messy frontier that the *Gloran Empire* and the *Aditi Consensus* have maintained for some time, with *Gloran* slowly losing ground over the last few centuries as various colonies have either declared neutrality, or turned their favor towards *Aditi* merchants," Phil said. "We're going to operate under complete secrecy until I say otherwise, because I have a problem. Guardian Ma, what did your team recover from orbit when we identified refuse that wasn't natural?"

All eyes snapped around to Ma Jianhong Ping, Guardian of *Li Jing*. Phil would have called the man the ship's *Dragoon*.

"We were dispatched when *Urumchi* and *Viking* identified an object in orbit that did not fit with other debris characteristics," the man replied, voice gone hard and formal, as though typing out a report. Or testifying at a Court Martial. "Upon recovery, the item was determined to be a shipping container that was in exceptionally good shape and an unstable orbit."

"Define exceptional, Guardian," Phil ordered the man.

"It had hardly any exposure to either solar wind, or the damage you commonly get from micrometeorite impacts," Ma nodded. "Almost pristine."

"Thank you," Phil said. "And now define unstable."

"According to calculations by the Science Officers off *Urumchi* and *Viking*, it would have degraded and fallen into the gas giant in another year, or been thrown longways up and out of local orbit by the complicated motion of several nearby moons in only a few months. We did not observe it long enough to determine which would be more likely."

Phil nodded. He turned and made eye contact with each of the six captains at the table, ignoring Ma and Heather.

"Not there for long," Phil reminded them. "So we can assume not an ancient relic we accidentally stumbled across. And wouldn't have remained for long had it not been recovered, therefore, we can generally assume that it was not planted in that orbit, as a great deal of supposed evidence was on the planetary surface. Furthermore, the type of container—or rather, the contents—also lead us to believe that it was exactly what it purported to be, which was various boxes of spare parts for a ship's life support system."

If any of them were breathing right now, it was probably through their eyeballs, because they had fallen silent and utterly still. Like students confronted in class by *The Professor*.

"As you know, everybody builds their life support systems

differently," Phil continued. "In spite of the unnecessity of such an action. Autarky, where everyone has to do it their own way. At least the former Syndicates didn't do that, as they didn't have purpose-built warships like the rest of you. We can eliminate *Hamath* and the others for that reason."

"Whose box was it, Phil?" Kaur asked now, eyes already acknowledging where he was headed.

"The Light Strike Cruiser *Kartikeya*," Phil replied. "An *Aditi* vessel."

He leaned back and let the explosion of sound and shouts of anger erupt for a few moments, like a boil that has been lanced.

Then he nodded at Heather.

She slammed her open palm down on the table top so loudly that everybody not expecting it jumped. Sounded a great deal like a knife boning a hunk of steak for dinner. Only louder.

Shocked silence fell. Phil felt his glower step up a notch and used it to cow everyone into leaning back in their chairs again.

Mouths opened and then shut when he snapped around to scowl at someone.

Finally, Khan leaned forward and nodded. Phil nodded back.

"Is it sufficient evidence upon which to recommend a course of action, First Centurion?" the man asked, never once so much as glancing at Commander Singh.

And surprising the hell out of Phil, who had been expecting the man to be a death or glory kind of warrior demanding immediate retaliation against *Aditi*. Probably shocked everyone else by being so in control of himself.

No, check that. Heather nodded serenely. Phil made a mental note to ask her what the hell had just happened.

Adham Khan acting like a rational commander was actually a wild card in Phil's planning. And not in a good way.

Then he acknowledged that he didn't have as high an opinion of the man as he did most of the others, for no legitimate reason at all. Other than everyone else had had their opportunity to step into the gap and prove their loyalty to their teammates around the table.

Including *Hollywood*, weird as that was.

"Recommend?" Phil asked, pausing for the man to nod. "Certainly. Will anybody listen?"

Khan's face showed a sudden pain like someone had just stomped on his foot under the table.

Every head turned to Kaur now. She looked stricken, utterly pale and pupils huge.

"I have been with this squadron, this team, since Day One," she reminded them. Longer than anyone else here not in black and green. "If it is as you say, and I assume so simply because you brought us here now to tell us, then *Aditi* may have committed an intentional act of war against *Gloran*."

Phil nodded. Everybody else had been cowed, so they didn't scream any insults or invective, but he could see it in their eyes.

Even Barnaby was grinding his teeth from the way his jaw muscles clenched.

"What does that entail, First Centurion?" Dao Zhiou Xue asked from her spot between Solo and Singh.

"A year ago, it would have meant an escalating series of reprisals and attacks up and down that frontier," Captain Yukimura offered in a scholarly tone. "Possibly the kind of local war that we've all fallen into the unfortunate habit of pursuing from time to time, *Yaumgan* excluded because everyone else is smart enough to generally leave you alone."

Xue nodded to acknowledge that, then turned to Khan.

"Honor makes nonnegotiable demands?" she asked that man.

Whatever Heather had said to Adham Khan—and Phil had only gotten pieces because she hadn't wanted to go into detail—it had apparently transformed him into something of a stranger. Calmer than before. Almost introspective.

Adham KHAN?

"Honor always makes such demands, Captain," Khan replied

in a hard, quiet voice. "Sometimes, we allow ourselves to be blinded by such things. However, I am not the man who will make that decision."

He turned his attention to Phil instead.

"I presume that you will need to tell the Emperor shortly," Khan said simply.

"Indeed," Phil nodded. "Immediately after this meeting is concluded and I know the state of this squadron, I intend to contact him for a private meeting aboard *Urumchi*, where he can see for himself."

"What will he do?" Striker Solo asked carefully, the odd person out of this group because he had no shared borders with *Gloran* and little interaction with them other than Khan.

"He has many options," Phil said. "Kerenski can order us out of his space, and we will go. He can order us to attend him at *Derragon*, though I might not accept his hospitality. Or at least, not bring the entire squadron with me."

"Not, First Centurion?" Solo pressed.

"If he's about to start a war with *Aditi*, or at least escalate one that they started, I will not subject one of my ships to the risk of an attack. And if *Aranyani* is not welcome, then none of you will be brought along, and Kerenski will be dealing directly and exclusively with the *Republic of Aquitaine*. That will change his thinking, I suspect."

"Oh," Solo observed.

"Finally, I might be able to keep harsher emotions from running out of control, to the point that we could go demand answers from the *Consensus*," Phil said. "The entire point of this squadron maneuvering together for so long was that you have started to break down the old barriers to communication that had grown over the decades. I am loathe to give that up when we are so close to completing that element of our mission."

"First Centurion, could this be the act of someone desperate to retain the old ways that they were willing to take such risks?"

Khan asked, looking for an out for reasons Phil did not understand.

"Who stands to benefit?" Barnaby leaned in and scowled mightily at everyone like a bear roused mid-winter.

"We can leave *Ewin* and *Yaumgan* out," Yukimura interjected without emotion. "They don't gain anything at all, one way or the other."

"Unless someone at *Ewinhome* wanted *Aditi* facing the other direction when they launched attacks like that idiot baron did," Solo countered. "I don't wish to be a troublemaker here, but we've all got to admit that our various governments have funded the pirates extensively in the past, whatever politeness they share with the general public. This feels deeper than just some greedy schmuck trying to score a few new trade routes. Someone doesn't want peace. Simple as that. Who?"

Phil wondered if he'd fallen into some fairy tale, where his two most aggressive warrior command centurions had flipped inside out. But Solo had been there when he tried to save *Ewin* from imploding. Khan was there now.

All eyes roved around. Captain Xue cleared her throat.

"I suspect, like the rest of you, I could be removed and court martialed for what I am about to say, so just nod and save your own careers," she spoke clearly. "*Yaumgan* has worked extensively over the centuries to keep the rest of you weak and at bay by paying pirates to harass you. That budget, to the best of my understanding, was almost as big as the one for our fleet, just because we saw the Syndicates as our front line defense. *Aditi* was kept surrounded on all sides, not just by your fleets, but by *Hollywood*'s people, specifically so you were never a threat to the *Domain*. As were each of the others. I have no doubt that all of you could tell a similar story."

She paused and looked around. Phil counted the nods. All of them. It had been an open secret before.

Someone didn't want peace.

"So we're facing a new divide, Phil?" *Hollywood* asked. "Those looking to the future against those demanding the past?"

He considered her words. Phil wasn't sure he could speak it more concisely without a speechwriter.

"Yes," Khan broke in. "At *Meerut*, it was thus. The pirates under Utkin saw that the future had arrived and they sought to carve out a new place, rather than simply fade away. Since *First Meerut*, they have shifted over to the future. *Hollywood* and her network of ships are testimony to that. *Dalou* sent the Crown Prince and the future Shogun because *Morninghawk* showed them that the past could not be sustained. *Ewin* had to be broken, but the men in charge now have seen where all of their neighbors will be in a generation, and hopefully learn."

He fell silent there.

"*Gloran* has yet to be tested," Heather spoke up for the first time here. "And *Aditi* as well, because we simply sailed in and were welcomed as another republic. They never had to confront their past."

"They are aware of it, though," Kaur replied. She sat a little straighter. "At the time Phil opened his invitation to hunt pirates, I had a meeting with one of the top politicians in the *Consensus*. She basically offered me the bribe of another year in charge of *Aranyani*, after which I would be promoted to Director and given command of a Ship of the Line. All I had to do was be something of a spy."

Phil wasn't as surprised as the rest. All of them were functionally here for the same reason, sent as favored children to see how much of a threat the outsiders would be.

Worse than any of them imagined, he smiled to himself.

"We are all spies," Xue acknowledged. The men grunted assent to that, now that it was in the open.

"So to answer the original question, yes, it might be a trap designed to draw *Gloran* and *Aditi* into a war that saps all their time, energy, and focus, while somebody else commits mischief," Phil said. "Short of confronting the Directors of the *Aditi*

Consensus fleet, we can't know if *Kartikeya* was really here, or was framed in an elaborately staged triple-cross. You are here because you were assigned to my squadron, under my command. Originally, that was to hunt and break the pirates of the various Syndicates, but we have transcended far beyond that, my friends. We have so far visited four of the six capitals, including that new thing at *Meerut*. We were poised to travel to a fifth at *Derragon*, but that depends on how Kerenski reacts to this news. I do not wish to break this force up before we have the chance to travel to distant *Kyulle*, but that might be out of my hands. You are specifically ordered, however, not to discuss this matter with anybody outside of this room, until such time as I rescind that order. Am I clear?"

He went face to face now, making sure everyone understood that this was a line from which there was no redemption if crossed.

Someone had set him up. Someone who didn't want the kinds of peace that *Aquitaine* threatened, where trade and diplomacy replaced autarky and piracy.

Where the Balhee Cluster might finally decide to grow up.

Phil was pretty sure he'd be cracking heads together, before this was all done.

He just needed an address.

TWENTY-SEVEN
RAN FLAGSHIP URUMCHI

Kohahu wasn't acting as a representative of the *RAN* today. Heather had asked her to entertain Frigate-Captain Zaman while an emergency meeting of only the local cruiser captains took place. And to do so as the Personal Representative of the Shogun.

So she had on the crimson and gold of Kugosu instead of the black and green of *Aquitaine*. Just changing uniforms had put her mind in a different place. Almost back to when Lord Morninghawk had stepped onto the deck at *Ellariel-jo* and saved the entire *Hegemony* from imploding. Or being swept away by the tides of history.

She wondered if Heather appreciated that. Worse, if the woman had planned it. Little got past Heather Lau.

Kohahu waited in a small, private lounge forward. Two comfortable chairs and a table with a tea set between them. Not all that far from the arboretum where Heather had met earlier with Zaman. Kohahu was alone, but a marine guarded the door outside, as she was here in an official capacity, rather than an officer-trainee like Shingo, over on *Storm Petrel*.

Knuckles rapped smartly on the hatch, a moment before it opened. Kohahu rose as Frigate-Captain Zaman entered. She had seen the woman officer at the first reception, but not spoken with her. At the time, it hadn't seemed important, as Zaman was part of *Gloran*'s Penal Fleet.

Only later had Kohahu learned some facet of the truth. From Heather. Which was why, Kohahu suspected, Heather had insisted that they meet.

Kohahu was tall. Almost as tall as Heather. Frigate-Captain Zaman was shorter. Medium height for a *Gloran* woman. They both had broad shoulders and muscles, even more so than Heather did.

Was every comparison Kohahu would make centered on Heather Lau? So it seemed.

At the same time, Heather set a high bar. People meeting that were worthy of knowing.

Kohahu bowed her head in welcome as Zaman entered, the various marines remaining outside to give them their illusion of privacy. Kohahu had no doubts that the room was monitored. Maybe not every word spoken, but a cry for help or a scream would set off some alarm.

But they were alone.

"Frigate-Captain Zaman, it is a pleasure to meet you," Kohahu said. "I am technically Lady Kugosu in formal company, but please, call me Kohahu."

They shook hands across the table where Kohahu had tea steeping. The timing was perfect.

"Kohahu," Zaman replied, nervous for reasons that Kohahu could not identify as yet. "I am Frigate-Captain Kira Zaman. Kira, please."

"Kira," Kohahu nodded again. She gestured. "Please, sit. The tea is ready."

They sat. Tea was poured and began to cool as it warmed fine, porcelain mugs that Phil and Heather had supplied, with the *RAN* logo on one side and the patch of *Urumchi* on the other, a square tower with a wall to one side and an open gate, signifying the start of the ancient, fabled Silk Road and the

Great Wall of China that had once spanned the entire northern frontier.

Kira noted that and studied it.

"Heather told me that you had temporarily enlisted as an officer in the *Aquitaine* fleet," Kira said. "And yet today you wear the Shogun's colors?"

"She asked me to meet you in that official capacity," Kohahu replied. "It allows a *Gloran* captain to meet a *Dalou* official in such a manner. The First Centurion is confident that more people making friends across formerly enemy lines can only bode well for the future of the Cluster."

"Normally, I would say he was correct..." Kira trailed off.

Kohahu nodded.

"I was also given some tidbits of your past, Kira," she said. "Enough to understand who you were and why you commanded *Arteshbo*, when a...*more lenient* Emperor might have you commanding his flagship instead."

"His flagship?" Kira asked, shocked.

"Heather's opinion, when I asked," Kohahu replied.

They sipped tea and fell into silence. Kohahu watching. Kira seemingly lost in thoughts that she didn't want to share. Not yet, anyway.

"Where does *Dalou* see the future taking us?" Kira asked abruptly.

Kohahu wondered if Heather had primed the woman to ask such questions, or if they arose naturally when a victim of *Gloran*'s rigid legal system encountered someone in the process of overcoming *Dalou*'s caste.

"When Phil arrived at *Ellariel*, it was to honor a *Dalou* captain that had served with his force when they attacked *Meerut* to root out the pirates," Kohahu said. "The other nations had sent cruisers, but Kosnett had already met Makara Omarov, so he requested that man, and *Morninghawk*, his Heavy Escort, by name."

Kohahu paused there, trying to find the words to contain

everything that had happened in those two days. How they had forever altered the arc of history, as it would remember *Dalou*.

Morninghawk.

Kira seemed poised to listen.

"Omarov was a herald," Kohahu continued as Kira watched intently. "We did not understand it at the time, and history might deify the man as some messenger from the gods themselves, though he was really just the ultimate expression of honor and duty as *Dalou* sees itself on its very best days."

"What message did he bring?" Kira asked, eyes locking in now.

Kohahu began to understand why Heather had insisted on the crimson and gold, but wasn't in a position to ask either woman what had happened before, save that Heather said they had enjoyed a picnic forward.

"Morninghawk spoke of an avalanche, already roaring down the mountainside, preparing to sweep away everything before it, willing or not," Kohahu said, falling into the sorts of fanciful language that her younger sister Ema might have chosen. Ema was the artist of the family, just as older sister Kokoro was the scholar.

Only Kohahu was politician enough—*warrior* enough—to follow in Father's footsteps and try for the Shogunate itself, rather than settling for a dynastic marriage to one of the Great Houses.

But then, she already had her eyes on such a match. One that would either heal *Dalou*, or destroy it entirely.

"Avalanche?" Kira asked.

"Phil Kosnett," Kohahu said simply, gesturing to the ship around them. "He will change everything he touches. And not even destructively, because we are all already poised to do that to ourselves, caught up in our old ways. Those who will not change will fall by the wayside as those who do move into an irresistible future."

"Why have there been no wars as a result of Kosnett's meddling?" Kira asked.

Kohahu laughed in spite of the seriousness of their situation.

"*Ewin* tried, Kira," she said. "The first time, Phil merely withdrew to summon assistance from Duke Kalidoona, Prince of the Eastern Fleets. The second time, when *Ewin* and *Dalou* had signed a new treaty that established rules for neutral trade and friendly communications, Phil had to step in and utterly crush the forces of Duke Bertrand Farouk and Fleet Admiral Duke Michelle Agrimond in order to get them to listen. Well, Iveta did that. Nobody will ever forget that woman."

"Iveta?" Kira asked.

"Heather's First Officer, here on *Urumchi*," Kohahu said. "Certain favored officers have been awarded pirate nicknames in service, dating back to Phil's adventures on *CS-405*. Heather is known as *Ground Control*, but only a select few are allowed to call her that to her face. Iveta earned the nickname *Junkyard Bitch* at *First Meerut*. She showed everybody why at *Second Ewinhome*."

"Second?" Kira asked.

"*Aquitaine* numbers such battles, presuming that there might be more in the future," Kohahu said. "The pirates were routed at *First Meerut*. *Second Meerut* was when Baron Russand attacked the moorage, leading to *First Jacoby* where Phil paid him back by capturing his flagship and his drydock, hauling them off to *Meerut* and selling them to the Governor there, Dexter Milose, for one Lev each. The *Aquitaine* currency."

"So Kosnett does bring strife?" Kira asked.

"And bends over backwards to keep it from happening, Kira," Kohahu said. "We saw that at *Ellariel*, when the situation was incredibly tense and could have gone many directions. We saw that at *Ewinhome*, when he withdrew without firing a shot. If you look at their records, his first encounter with the pirates of *Ingham Syndicate* at *Vilahana* began when *Tango* and its consorts opened fire on *Aranyani* and *Urumchi* unprovoked.

Phil could have annihilated them all, but withheld the blade after showing them what they could have suffered. Why? What has happened at *Carinae II* that you find such knowledge critical?"

Kohahu had been watching the woman. Something about the conversation with Heather earlier had left Kira concerned for a war about to break out. A big one.

Kohahu knew that the squadron had found something here at Four. Had recovered *something* that caused Phil to immediately shut down a lot of things and summon only his cruiser captains to a meeting, that thing happening aft even as Kira and Kohahu spoke.

"Has Heather told you?" Kira asked, jumping to that same spot.

Rumors were only rumors, as nobody but a select inner few knew. But that alone promised that it was big. And troubling.

"She has not," Kohahu replied. "When I wear the black and green, I am junior to every centurion on this vessel, an officer trainee ranked a mere Cornet in *Aquitaine* service. I am not important enough as such to be told."

"You are not wearing the black and green, Kohahu," Kira noted.

"Heather insisted that I revert to my formal attire to meet you," Kohahu replied, then fell sharply short. "That this meeting take on formal overtones as a thing between *Gloran* and *Dalou*, even though neither of us represent our superiors formally."

"Formally," Kira replied. "Has she told you my past?"

"Some of it," Kohahu said. "Enough to fill in the blanks with higher probability than Heather could."

"I do not speak for the Emperor, even though many secretly acknowledge that I am a cousin," Kira said.

"And I am the daughter of a Shogunate that has only ever been held by men," Kohahu countered. "But that was the past, and Phil Kosnett has already arrived to deliver the future that the rest of us must shape ourselves to understand."

"Some fools will seek to blame Kosnett for what is about to happen," Kira explained.

"Then they are fools indeed," Kohahu growled.

Stranger this woman might be, Kohahu found herself warming to the woman, a victim of a system rigged against her, even before her birth. Before Kosnett, there would be no opportunity for redemption, which also described things from Kohahu's perspective. Maybe that was why Heather had wanted this meeting to happen this way.

Red and gold.

Kira grew uncomfortable as Kohahu watched. Stewed with indecision, which did not begin to describe any commanding officer of a successful naval vessel.

"I am breaking a vow to Heather to tell you this," Kira finally announced. "At the same time, I feel as though she intended it, because neither of us would find out the truth immediately. This First Centurion Kosnett will have to dance with the Emperor, and I do not know how that will go. As much as I might represent some facet of *Gloran*, I would ask you to represent *Dalou*, and accept that this is a powerful secret that needs to go beyond military commanders. As the personal representative of the Shogun, you may have to meet with the Emperor over this."

"I negotiated and signed a treaty with *Ewin*," Kohahu said. "It was Phil's idea to help Prince Kalidoona secure his rear flank against *Dalou* attacks while he worked to shore up the crown itself. I appreciate that you cannot do such things, but I can make this official. What do you need?"

"For you to do nothing," Kira said now. "Specifically nothing, for the exact same reasons. What they found was evidence that confirms that *Aditi* launched the attack, rather than pirates."

"Confirms?" Kohahu gasped in spite of herself. "Why would they do that? No, I understand why. As you noted, my treaty with Kalidoona allowed him to turn inward and handle that problem. Is there a war pending with *Aditi* when the Emperor finds out?"

"I don't know," Kira admitted. "I only known what Heather told me an hour ago. Right now, the First Centurion is telling all of his captains, I presume because of how much friction and difficulty it will create."

"And you want *Dalou* to stay neutral," Kohahu confirmed.

"If this is to be a war between *Gloran* and *Aditi*, they have provoked it intentionally," Kira replied with a nod. "Attacked a *Gloran* colony and destroyed it. Then tried to frame pirates who don't exist anymore. Speaking as a Frigate-Captain of the *Gloran Empire*, I would ask *Dalou* not to interfere. And also not to let this situation cloud the possibility that we might actually have peace and trade between *our* nations, even if *Aditi* has finally decided to start the war that everyone has been expecting for so long."

"Are they counting on Phil to save them?" Kohahu asked.

"Would he?" Kira countered.

Kohahu leaned back and considered that. Noticed that her mug was empty. Kira's too, lost in the emotions. She paused to refill both while weighing the odds.

"Time and again, Phil has tried to do what was right, in spite of having overwhelming firepower to simply dictate terms to people," Kohahu said finally. "I've watched it, both remotely and firsthand, sitting on Heather's bridge or in meetings with the man. If *Aditi* did this on purpose, assuming that he would try to talk everyone out of retaliating, they might have guessed wrong this time. He might side with *Gloran* as the aggrieved party and issue demands to *Aditi*."

"Would they back down?" Kira asked. "*Gloran* is more honor-bound. And hidebound."

"And Phil will recognize that," Kohahu replied. "*Aditi* has chosen a dishonorable action. *Dalou* would not side with them. We do not often interact with *Gloran*, given the wide gap the runs down much of our border where the mouth of the Cluster opens. None of that real estate was particularly valuable until now. Oh, shit."

"What?" Kira demanded.

"That real estate is now extremely precious," Kohahu noted. "*Dalou* maintains an entire wall of systems that were uncolonized, but could be developed. We didn't because that gave us a physical barrier to our neighbors, including *Gloran*. Lord Morninghawk is in the process of creating *Urwel* as a trade station on the corner where *Dalou*, *Ewin*, and *Aditi* connect. And he will be successful, because the Shogun has commanded it, and his daughter has signed a trade treaty with *Ewin*. Is this action *Aditi* trying to start enough of a war that they could claim many of these stars and take command of trade coming from the east? From *Aquitaine* and later *Fribourg*?"

"JumpSails mean that physical location is irrelevant," Kira noted dryly.

"Physical, yes," Kohahu agreed. "But what about social or mechanical? If you could trade with colonies just inside the mouth of the Cluster, and didn't have to sail deeper, would you? Many such freighters will likely choose the easier route, with others forced to go deeper for better profits, but at a cost of time. *Vilahana* stands to become immensely wealthy, but Phil has told everyone that that system will remain entirely neutral. He is even negotiating treaties to base *Aquitaine* warships there to enforce that, just as *Meerut* on that corner."

"Will all worlds become neutral at some point?" Kira asked sourly.

"Wouldn't it be better if all of the Balhee Cluster were one great nation instead?" Kohahu fired back.

She felt a little bad to be lecturing a woman more than twice her age, old enough perhaps to be her mother, but Kohahu had sat on the dojo floor and in meetings with her father the Shogun, while Kira Zaman had been forced to scrape hard and outwork everyone else in the Penal Fleet to advance.

That she had was testament to how good Kira Zaman must

be. And why Heather wanted this to be more of a formal meeting between nations rather than a friendly thing between fellow officers.

"Is that Kosnett's mission?" Kira asked, still a little angry.

"No," Kohahu said. "His mission was to see who lived here, and talk to them, so that trade could occur. He's trying to prevent wars. Possibly trying to save us from ourselves, assuming we want to."

"And if we don't?" Kira pressed.

"Then we are probably on the verge of a major war between *Aditi* and *Gloran*," Kohahu replied. "One that might draw in the other players simply because *Aditi* has antagonized all of us at one time or another. Never enough to be genuinely punished for it, but how much provocation would it take right now for *Dalou* or *Ewin* to find common cause to join *Gloran*? Or just pounce on *Aditi* if Phil wasn't going to protect them?"

They both fell silent again. Shocked at where the conversation had gone, if Kohahu had to guess. She certainly was.

Father had appointed her as his personal representative to Kosnett's squadron, that she might speak in his name.

Was she about to drag him into a Cluster-wide war?

TWENTY-EIGHT

IMPERIAL FLAGSHIP GLANTHUA'S STAND, CARINAE II

Adric, Emperor of *Gloran*, glowered at A.Q. Tanel as the man stood just inside the door to Adric's personal quarters and nodded.

"All three of them?" Adric asked.

"Almost simultaneously, My Lord," A.Q. said. "The formal message from Kosnett was expected, though we were a bit surprised that he summoned all his Cruiser-Captains to a meeting first. That both Khan and Zaman sent messages in code at almost the same time can be chalked up to both of those officers being aboard *Urumchi* and not being able to send a coded message until they returned to their own decks."

"And none say anything useful?" Adric demanded.

"Correct," A.Q. replied. "Kosnett asks for a formal, private meeting with you, separate from a large event similar to you hosting him here. Khan and Zaman each simply say they have information critical to your decision-making."

Adric ground his teeth at that. It suggested that *Aquitaine* had found or manufactured evidence at odds with the story of piracy. Badly at odds. That Emperor Kerenski would be moved to a predictable course of action. Were Khan and his cousin both trying to dissuade him, having found the truth?

Khan he could see finding something out. No doubt Kosnett had summoned his Cruiser-Captains in order to tell them. To prepare them.

Kira Zaman had been invited aboard *Urumchi* by Command Centurion Lau, so *Arteshbo* was close by the flagship right now, with *Mardonius* and *Darius* remaining in protective orbit of Two. Presumably she had found something as well, and intently contacted her cousin and emperor at first opportunity.

"How formal?" Adric asked. "How private?"

"Kosnett suggested you and Fleet-Captain Povoloi, meeting with him and Command Centurion Lau," A.Q. replied. "Nobody else. Not even Ambassadors Gavraba or Babatunde. That suggests a heavily military conversation, rather than a diplomatic one."

"He expects me to start shooting immediately," Adric concluded.

"*Gloran* does have that reputation," A.Q. pointed out helpfully with a wry smile. "Khan is an aggressive commander, which was why you sent him. He would be their baseline example of a *Gloran* Cruiser-Captain. Kosnett would have expectations thus set."

"And he wants to prevent a war," Adric concluded. "Something has come up so ugly that he expects me to gather up my fleet and go hit someone. Talk to me about *Ewin* again."

"While he was visiting *Dalou*, a supposedly-rogue *Ewin* Baron attacked the former pirate base at *Meerut*, getting his ass utterly handed to him in the process," A.Q. laughed. "Rather than take a diplomatic approach, or even sail home to survey the damage, Kosnett immediately pounced on the Baron's home base and finished him off as a threat, capturing the man's flagship and only drydock right out from under his nose with security troops."

"And *Ewinhome*?" Adric pressed.

He'd read all the reports composed by Khan and various spies, both aboard Khan's ship and embedded in *Ewin* society at various levels. A smart emperor spent a lot of money on his external espionage services. Almost as much as his Security Ministry efforts.

"The first time, Kosnett's mere presence seems to have triggered a meltdown between various unstable personalities, wherein they attempted to settle decades-old differences with orbital combat, however ill thought out in the moment. Kosnett withdrew, hauling the First Minister with him to their Eastern Frontier, where a plan was organized to sail back and do something about a bad drunkard of a king."

"Only after Kalidoona had signed a treaty of trade and peaceful intentions with *Dalou* to secure his border while he was gone," Adric pointed out. "Kosnett's idea."

"And the daughter of the Shogun signed it," A.Q. nodded. "She travels with Kosnett in both official and unofficial capacities."

"Unofficial?" Adric sat up straighter.

"She has temporarily enlisted in the *Aquitaine* fleet for training, Adric," A.Q. replied. "Junior officer, but I get the impression from reports that she is competent and Kosnett appears to be grooming her for something big."

"Or giving her the training she needs to actually become Shogun, when other Cruiser-Captains would balk," Adric replied. "Making sure that his preferred candidate can ascend when she's ready."

"Would they allow it?" A.Q. gasped.

"Kosnett must think so," Adric replied. "Imagine if I just cast aside Khan's various denunciations and accepted Kira Zaman openly as a cousin and possible heir. My gut instinct is that Kosnett is about to change *Dalou* that much."

"*Morninghawk?*" A.Q. asked.

"Indubitably," Adric agreed. "They stopped at *Urwel* while coming here, just to show support for the man and his efforts to generate trade on that triangular section of space. Do we have anything similar here?"

"Only *Vilahana*," A.Q. replied. "It has never mattered before this, because everybody pretty much accepted the gap leading outward as something of a natural boundary between *Aditi*, *Dalou*, and *Gloran*. That was before Kosnett, however."

"Indeed, before Kosnett," Adric agreed. "What changes now?"

"There are any number of petty worlds out there," A.Q. shrugged. "Most are neutral to some degree, because nobody cared."

"We need to care," Adric ordered. "Find the right people to find the right maps. And maybe I need to also have a meeting with this young woman as a formal thing while we're all here. If she can get those stupid punk chauvinistic drunks at *Ewin* to deal with her as an equal, then she is not a pushover."

"Do we respect what Kosnett's trying to do?" A.Q. asked, scowling now.

"Look at what he has accomplished in a single year, Tanel," Adric pointed out. "And if he intends this daughter to be Shogun, it is in our best interests to know who she is now. Isn't that what Kosnett is about? Meeting one another and talking?"

"Should we look to sign a similar treaty with *Dalou* as they did with *Ewin*?" A.Q. asked.

"Get a copy of it and run it past all the legal officers you can find," Adric decided. "Send home for some if we didn't bring the right minds, and have them delivered here as soon as possible. Maybe we propose to *Dalou* a copy of the exact same thing they signed with *Ewin*, scratching out only the names."

"Why?" A.Q. asked, not seeing it.

Adric wasn't sure he saw it, but he also saw the vast scope of changes that had occurred since Kosnett's first encounters at *Vilahana*. The *Zen-Mekyo Syndicates* utterly broken and swept onto the tailings pile of history, *Carinae II* notwithstanding. A joint squadron representing every nation, including former pirates now, operating together to capture *Meerut* and turn it into a thorn in both *Ewin* and *Dalou*'s sides simultaneously.

Dalou possibly looking at a Crown Prince sailor and a woman Shogun. *Ewin* maybe broken to the bit and halter for once by the superior firepower of *Aquitaine*. Trade at *Urwel*.

And now Kosnett had turned his eyes to *Gloran*.

"Because Kosnett gets things done," Adric said simply. "And everyone else has been unsettled by his arrival. This might represent a once in a generation opportunity to change things. Or lock things in. Best we do them on our terms."

Adric paused and let his eyes unfocus a little, seeing something ten thousand light-years away on a dim horizon.

"Change is coming, A.Q.," he pronounced. "We need to be in control of it when it does, or it will sweep us under and wash *Gloran* away. *Ewin* is probably grappling with that every day. We must not let it overtake us."

A.Q. nodded and accepted that as the dismissal it was, departing quickly and leaving Adric alone.

A possible future Shogun was here, empowered to make deals. Each of the Five Nations—six now with *Meerut* if Kosnett was as serious as he seemed—was present, and could also offer connections, which seemed to be Kosnett's purpose.

Trade, as he loudly proclaimed. Diplomacy.

As well as change at a fundamental, dangerous level.

TWENTY-NINE

GLORAN EMPIRE HEAVY BATTLECRUISER JUVAYNI, CARINAE IV

Adham was back aboard his ship. Surrounded by his crew. Kira Zaman had been aboard *Urumchi* at the same time he had been, but he had scrupulously avoided her, as Lau had ordered.

Even now, *Arteshbo* was sailing in close formation with the squadron, just ahead of the tiny escort *Forktail*, Sugawara taking his responsibilities to *Urumchi* serious enough to be ready to fire into the larger Type Five Heavy, probably at a moment's notice. Like *Morninghawk*.

Like even *Juvayni*, if Khan was being honest. Warriors, all of them.

He was on the bridge now, seated atop his command station, above and behind his officers. The dimness of the space struck him today, in ways he had never noticed before this. Every ship had set the lighting to this level, and yet today it felt wrong.

Urumchi. Lau kept things much brighter. Not softer, because there was nothing soft about that woman, but not as grim. Not as dark. She had proven to anybody who was willing to listen that such things were unnecessary.

What else was unnecessary?

Adham found his eyes wandering over to the two Security

stations, where intent Security troopers kept a random watch on the rest of the crew, lest anybody aft foment revolution. *Urumchi* had their marines, but Kosnett was beloved by his crew, all of whom were utterly loyal to the man and the ship. Kosnett's warriors were for external combat, not controlling the others.

What would it be like to live in a place that had such patriotism? Too many of Adham's crew members were draftees, each planet having an annual number of men selected to serve three years in the fleet before they returned to their other lives. Only a few enlisted voluntarily, though many of the officers were here of their own free will.

His eyes moved to *Arteshbo*, displayed on the main screen at the front of the bridge. Free will did not encompass everybody. Kira Zaman would be elsewhere if she could. Possibly a fellow Cruiser-Captain bringing glory and honor to the Empire.

If she were allowed.

How does a proud man admit he made a mistake? How does honor allow him to retract the insults and accusations that destroyed so many lives, when he finds that in retrospect that they were unnecessary?

That he might have been in the wrong?

Wolf Stasny entered the bridge from the side hatch just then, coming on duty to relieve Adham, who insisted on standing watches whenever possible. Best to remain visible to his officers and crew, that they could see him. After all, wasn't Adham Khan going to bring them all glory in service?

He knew doubt. It was an ugly, unforgiving thing.

"Wolf, join me in the ready room," Adham said abruptly, rising suddenly and catching his tall First Officer off balance. "Flight Officer, you have the bridge. Contact us if anything arises."

Adham didn't wait for a reply, but strode directly aft into the space where the Officer in Command could do paperwork while remaining close. It had to be part of the bridge, rather than in one of the spaces down the two main corridors, in case a security incident required the bridge to be isolated and locked down.

What did that say about the glories of the Empire, when even a well-regarded ship like *Juvayni* maintained a level of paranoia like that?

He went into the small space and gestured Wolf to sit behind the desk. That felt right. More natural. Like Wolf might end up in command when Adham was cashiered in disgrace.

Especially if he brought it upon himself.

Adham reached up and triggered the lock from this side. Only Security could override it now.

"Captain?" Wolf asked nervously as Adham turned back.

"Take a normal coin, Wolf," Adham began, no doubt confusing the man by starting somewhere in the middle of a conversation Adham had been having with himself in the hours since he got back from *Urumchi*. "Flip it in the air so that the face that appears when it lands is entirely random. One of two outcomes."

"Are we limited to only two at this point, Captain?" Wolf asked, perhaps leaping far enough intuitively to understand.

"I would like to think that we were, in fact, facing infinite possibilities," Adham shrugged. "But I fear that it will come down to only a few. Possibly only two."

"What outcomes do you predict then, in your new guise as an oracle?" Wolf asked, only halfway kidding. The man had served with him long enough to make those kinds of jokes.

At the same time, ancient literature had touched on a woman who married prophetic visions to a world where nobody would believe her until it was too late.

Adham Khan found himself better understanding such a thing. Worse, he had brought it on himself.

"Kosnett has found a thing, Wolf," Adham replied. "I will not tell you what, so you cannot be accused of hiding information later when the authorities interrogate everyone involved. Suffice it to say that when our inspired emperor hears it, there will be trouble. I may be dishonored to the point that you are ordered to arrest me."

"I would never…"

"You will do as you are told," Adham snapped angrily, overriding the man's genuine loyalty. "It will be that important. That critical. And the Emperor himself may be ordering it. Your career is more important than my failures of command, Wolf."

"Failures, Captain?" Wolf asked.

"Circle back to the conversation we had earlier, Wolf," Adham said. "What happened with Kira Zaman and my father. She was aboard *Urumchi* at the same time I was, though Lau kept us entirely separate. I have no doubt that Zaman knows the same thing I do right now, which is explosive in many ways."

"Sir?" Wolf asked hesitantly.

"I have sent a message to the Fleet-Captain and the War-Captain, Wolf," Adham shrugged eloquently. "Nothing in the message contained what they need to know, because I must to tell them in person. To communicate it to the Emperor. I presume Zaman did the same. She would be that honorable, even where she serves."

Wolf nodded, remaining silent, watching.

"Is Zaman a threat to us, Captain?" Wolf asked.

Adham laughed.

"Exactly the opposite, Wolf," he said. "We are a threat to her, but she poses no threat at all to *Juvayni*, or to Adham Khan. The only threat to me is myself. That I might make a mistake in what's coming, because I find my loyalties stretched in new ways that hopefully you never have to face when you command this vessel after me."

"Are you expecting to be relieved?" Wolf asked.

"I might be assigned to *Mardonius* as a Frigate-Captain tomorrow, Wolf," Adham replied. "That depends on what our dread Emperor decides. Kira Zaman might be assigned as my superior officer, because someone would be in a position to make that decision binding. And they would be right."

"Right?" Wolf surged upright. "To remove one of the top Cruiser-Captains in the fleet and demote him to a penal frigate?"

"Wolf, if it wasn't for me, she might be my peer now," Adham replied with a grimace he felt all the way to his toes. "Perhaps my legitimate superior, because if she was part of the Imperial Household like she deserves, they might have been smart enough to promote her to Fleet-Captain and put her in charge of *Glanthua's Stand*, or one of that class. Lau has ordered me not to communicate with Zaman, under threat of her idea of punishment, which would mean dishonor for me all the way across the board."

"Are you well, Captain?" Wolf asked.

"No, Wolf," Adham finally admitted. "I am not. It is called a crisis of conscience. Hope to all the gods you know that you never have to face something similar, because that would mean you have lived an entirely honorable life."

"What you did was honorable, sir," Wolf decried.

"Was it?" Adham fired back. "It was *appropriate*. That doesn't make it *right*."

Adham paused and drew a heavy breath.

"You cannot save me, so do not try if it comes to that," Adham said. "I will establish one order that I hope you will honor, if necessary."

"Sir."

"Treat Kira Zaman as she should be, Wolf," Adham said. "If not for me, she would be at least a Cruiser-Captain in the main fleet. She deserves it. Remember that."

"And you, Captain?" Wolf asked, concerned.

"It might be necessary for me to be removed from the game board, in order for an opening to be made for her, Wolf," he said. "And that might be the best outcome for everyone. Do you understand?"

"No, sir."

"That coin has been tossed into the air, rotating in a blur that will be random when it lands," Adham nodded, rising.

"Ruminate on it for a time, but remember my orders. All of them, if I end up being dishonored and cast down. You serve the *Gloran* Emperor and the fleet first and foremost. Adham Khan is a distant afterthought, if those two end up being at odds."

He unlocked the hatch and stepped out onto the bridge, nodding at the heads that turned to look back but moving quickly to the side hatch. He needed some time to process the implications of what Kosnett had found.

And whether or not it was going to start a war.

THIRTY

ADITI CRUISER ARANYANI

Kaur had returned to her ship in a state of utter shock. Nothing in her career had prepared her for something like this. And yet, she seriously doubted the theories put forth by the other Commanders that one of their own governments might have faked such a thing in order to cast *Aditi* and *Gloran* into a wide and ugly war.

Nice as it might be to blame someone else, Kaur suspected that none of them really understood just how underhanded and devious the folks atop the *Aditi Consensus* could be.

She had summoned Arya to her personal quarters, where they had sat in the front room with mugs of hot chocolate as Kaur walked through all the details Phil had discovered, and all the theories her squadron mates had come up with to try to explain it all away.

"Shit," Arya said when Kaur finally stuttered down into silence like a generator that had broken internally.

"Yup," Kaur agreed.

That did kind of sum it all up, didn't it?

"They really don't know *Aditi* at all, do they?" Arya asked, concern on her face. "Even after all this?"

"You will not tell them what we are really like, young lady,"

Kaur snapped with a smile. "Phil and the others think of us in good terms because they had the luck to encounter *Aranyani* first. The greatest fear I have right now is that he's right and we did it. Well, we didn't, but that an *Aditi* warship was tasked with making it look like a pirate raid. *Kartikeya* is a Light Strike Cruiser. They might have been designed for exactly that sort of thing."

Arya perked right up, but she'd gone from Moat ships to *Aranyani* instead of serving a stint on some of the…*more interesting corners* of the fleet.

"Oh?" Arya asked.

"Arya, if it becomes important, you are allowed to tell Phil," Kaur said now. "Or Heather. Nobody else."

"What mud puddle have I just stepped in?" her Sub-Commander asked carefully.

"The *Consensus* is all about the Echelon, Arya," Kaur reminded the woman. "Ships of the Line in the rear. Stronghold cruisers in the middle. Moat ships up front, either combat or escort variants. If it's just a small squadron, then a cruiser or Leader aft and two forward forming an inverted triangle."

"Sure," Arya noted dryly. "That's how we keep all the missile-happy folks at bay. Too many Point Guns covering the approaches."

"There are other classes that don't get discussed much," Kaur explained next. "Light Strike Cruisers and long-sailing Moat ships that are generally not part of normal operating squadrons. On paper, they are often classified as diplomatic couriers, because they are used that way, when you need to haul important people somewhere and don't want to risk pirates or anyone kidnapping them. At least in the old days."

"But they do other things?" Arya asked sharply.

"I am not legally at liberty to discuss certain things with you, Arya," Kaur said in a knowing manner that got the woman nodding. "However, it is not outside the realm of things that I might and might not have been part of such shenanigans, when I was a much younger officer."

"Oh," Arya replied, eyes huge now. "Phil's going to be pissed when he finds out the truth."

"He is already pissed," Kaur replied. "The problem now is that, like *Juvayni*, our superiors might order us to break ranks with the squadron, if Phil really sails into an *Aditi* harbor somewhere and demands answers."

"What would you do?" Arya asked in a small, uncertain voice.

The woman was only a Sub-Commander, but everything Kaur had done and trained had been geared towards stepping Arya Chaudhari into command of *Aranyani* when Kaur left. Whether that was promotion to a Ship of the Line or being cashiered in disgrace hadn't yet been determined.

"I need to play you a section of tape that you are not to admit exists, unless something suspicious happens to me and you suddenly find yourself in at least temporary command of *Aranyani*," Kaur said. She rose from her comfy couch and held out a hand to Arya. "Come."

She led the woman back deeper into her quarters, to her desk, where Kaur located a book on a shelf nearby and pulled out a data chip with no markings. Kaur set Arya down at her desk and plugged the chip into her usual book reader. She powered it on and the face of Director Narang, on that fateful day aboard *Khandoba* as Heather attempted to move an entire planet out of the way at *Vilahana*. Kaur's own face filled the other side of the split screen.

"Listen and learn," Kaur ordered her First Officer. "You will know where this chip is located if you have to take over my quarters for some reason. Make sure you take it with you later if a new Commander comes aboard."

Arya had gone gray and wide-eyed, which said something big considering everything the woman had seen from the bridge of *Aranyani* over the last year.

Kaur hit play and listened to that same conversation as *Urumchi* and her escorts prepared to sail out and intercept the planetary missile. The discussion of whether or not the man would order Kaur to walk away from Kosnett's force at the critical moment. The possibility that Kaur Singh would have to mutiny against a direct order from her superior to attack *Urumchi*, in the middle of everything else, until such time as she could return to *Aditi* proper, broadcast this conversation over every available circuit in the clear, and then wait for her own officers to arrest her on charges that might include treason.

Narang's voice took her back to that day. How far they'd come from merely confronting a piracy problem that had gotten out of hand, and watching Phil—helping him even—change the course of history.

Kaur watched along with Arya. The exchange hadn't taken long. It was so much bigger in her memory, lasting hours.

Arya's mouth had fallen open. Kaur removed the chip and put it back up on the shelf in the book where it hid. Then she turned to her First Officer.

"Later, I had a secret conversation with Herald Roshni Mishra, on *Aditi*," Kaur continued. "Not on the books anywhere. She offered to keep me in command of *Aranyani* for another year, then move me to a Ship of the Line when Phil's mission was successful. However, this is where a mere Sub-Commander like you has to cross over into the realm of politics."

Arya nodded, as if stricken mute. Kaur understood that feeling. She'd been there many times when everything had first unfolded.

"The Herald is a member of the *Prakaash* Party," Kaur said. "*Beacon*, representing the light of knowledge. Speaker Mhasalkar and Sergeant Chaudhary are from the *Bhavishy* Party. *Future*. Their alliance has always been prickly. Minor parties like *Pahaad aur Baadal* or *Vyaapaar Vaayu* are on the outside, but at any moment, deals might be struck that brought down a fairly fragile coalition and either caused a new government to be formed, or for early elections that might toss out all sorts of folks."

"Who probably should have been tossed out a long time ago," Arya finally spoke.

"Keep those opinions to yourself if you wish to keep your career, Chaudhari," Kaur grinned. "We still remain subservient to the civilian authorities. Even if they are so bent that they have to screw their pants on, as Iveta remarks occasionally."

Arya grinned back and rose from the chair.

"Now what?" she asked.

"It is entirely out of our hands, Arya," Kaur said. "Phil is going to brief the Emperor at his first opportunity. Given *Gloran*, I expect that man to sail to the nearest *Aditi* world, or maybe nearest base considering the fleet he has with him right now, and demand answers."

"Will Phil go with him?" Arya asked.

"Maybe," Kaur shrugged. "If so, we might be allowed as well. And we might not, considering that we represent the perfidiousness of *Aditi* in this matter."

"But we would side with Phil and the *Gloran* Emperor, right?" Arya asked.

"Right up until they pry me out of that command chair and try me for treason," Kaur nodded.

THIRTY-ONE

DATE OF THE REPUBLIC MARCH 24, 412 RAN URUMCHI, CARINAE II ORBIT

Phil would have liked to do this with all the pomp and circumstance it deserved. Grand. Loud. Crowded. Invite everyone, like that first event on *Vilahana*. Without anybody trying to blow up the damned planet.

Get them all in the same room with just enough booze and good food to relax them. Turn Chief Bottenberg loose to cook. The Chief didn't answer to gender. Didn't care. Saw that their highest form of love was in making food for people.

That would be how this should have been done. But beggars can't always be choosers.

So Phil had brought the entire squadron back to Two. He'd found what he needed at Four, for better or worse. He needed to present it to the Emperor of *Gloran* and see if he could keep the man short of the sorts of retaliation that *Aditi* probably deserved for pulling a dumbass, backstabbing stunt like this.

Phil was almost tempted to sail somewhere and demand answers himself. At the point of a gun.

Or just haul everything to *Aditi* proper and have it all out publicly with the leaders of the *Consensus*. On the evening news. Live.

He was not—quite—that pissed.

Today.

The Emperor's shuttle was docking. Rather than send his own GunShip, Phil had let the man bring his chariot over, docking it with good enough seals since *Aquitaine* and *Gloran* didn't use the same standards for airlocks.

Just one more thing that hopefully could change, since the East all used a single design that was ancient. Perhaps going back to something one of Phil's personal heroes, Javier Aritza, might have used.

Beggars and choosers.

He had Heather standing next to him. Xochitl Dar was off to one side, but only because not even Phil could order that woman to not be his bodyguard when meeting outsiders. At least she would remain quiet and invisible. And hadn't argued to bring any of her own troops. Or the *Dalou* samurai she'd been training.

He nodded to her and she winked back, however stone-faced she might be after this.

The hatch opened. Fleet-Captain Povoloi emerged first, with the faintest hint of hesitation in his stride. Phil had requested day uniforms, rather than dress, though he wasn't sure what that meant to Kerenski.

It turned out to be black leather boots with a high polish, just short of the knee. Knickerbockers in a glossy bronze fabric that almost looked like scale mail from the pattern, with a wide, black leather belt. Tucked-in sleeveless shirt with no collar, done in a soft yellow that fluoresced metallically and had horizontal stripes about eight centimeters tall, over a long-sleeved black shirt with a mock turtleneck collar.

The Fleet-Captain, and the Emperor emerging behind him, both wore gold sashes from the left shoulder, with differing chest logos in a manner similar, Phil presumed, to the *Urumchi* patch on his left shoulder.

At least they had both forgone the chainmail-and-plate look that Khan frequently sported in public. Hopefully, that meant that they were not necessarily approaching this meeting with the sorts of bloodthirstiness that he had originally been expecting from *Juvayni*'s commander.

Phil and Heather both bowed to the two men as the four of them came to rest. Dar was off to one side like a caryatid, smaller than everyone else by far. At least physically.

"Thank you," Phil said simply. "I appreciate that this is entirely irregular, but I fear that it is necessary."

Kerenski glanced at Dar. He knew who she was. And what.

"Dar does not gossip, sir," Phil explained.

Kerenski nodded at that. Settled his eyes on Phil. Glanced at Heather mostly just confirm her glower. Povoloi stood not quite facing Heather like bookends. The rest of the chamber was empty.

"So, Kosnett," Kerenski began. "Are we looking at a war with someone?"

Phil normally would have suppressed his grimace behind a bland, neutral façade, but Kerenski was sharp enough to have figured it all out. Not that there were many possibilities that required the four of them to meet thus.

"I'd normally rather not," Phil answered.

"Normally?" Kerenski asked, taken a bit aback. Povoloi actually recoiled in surprise.

"I'll explain in greater detail later, gentlemen," Phil nodded gravely. "For now, I wonder if someone was counting on me standing here trying to talk you out of something. Keeping them from paying the costs of their actions."

Kerenski blinked, but Phil wasn't surprised. The man had come here expecting to meet the diplomatic Explorer Extraordinaire, and instead got the Fleet Centurion who had faced his badly out-classed squadron off with Arlo's invincible Imperial fleet at *Hemet*.

Phil turned to Xochitl now. Nodded to her and watched the tiny warrior pivot and open a nearby hatch. Heather followed her through, then Phil gestured the two visitors after that, himself bringing up the rear.

Dar led them to a small conference room not far from the flag bridge. Phil had gotten it set up ahead of time with both alcohol if necessary and tea and coffee in case this ended up being a meeting that lasted hours.

This time, Dar took up her position in the corridor, exactly in front of the hatch once everyone had gone inside. Iveta had the flag. Anyone causing trouble now would get the sharp end of her tongue.

Or the jagged edge of her sword.

They sat around a square table with just enough elbow room that four people could dine comfortably. Phil was across from Kerenski, with Povoloi on his left. The Emperor's right hand, just as Heather was his.

"To answer your original question, Emperor, we found something at Four that implicates *Aditi*," Phil began, letting some of his anger come to the surface. "I had a meeting with my command centurions because they needed to be prepared for your reaction when it came. Thus, both Cruiser-Captain Khan and Commander Singh of the *Aditi* Cruiser *Aranyani* know."

"*Aditi?*" Kerenski asked. Demanded. Something.

His own anger hadn't been all that deep, but this could be a meeting held in anger. Better to let it all out now, then try to find a good solution, than to try to contain all the ugliness where it would fester.

"Indeed," Phil agreed. "I can show you all the evidence as you desire. Make my people available to answer questions as they come up, with whatever technical aspects you wish to pursue. At the end of the day, the artifact we found in orbit of Four came off an *Aditi* cruiser, recently enough to be a good timing match for the attack on the planet below us."

"No one else intended to frame *Aditi?*" Povoloi asked now, voice hard but willing to explore other options.

Like his Emperor, the man had likely walked in here

expecting Phil to talk them out of reacting, instead of making sure where the reaction was aimed.

"We explored that possibility, Fleet-Captain," Heather spoke up. "The problem is that *Yaumgan* hasn't taken Phil's measure to make sure how he would react. *Dalou* has hopefully turned a cultural corner and has been busy facing their *Ewin* frontier recently. *Ewin* is completely at sea. There are still the former pirates, though our own resident expert has shown us all of her records accounting for anyone who could have done such a thing from *Hamath*. That leaves *Aditi*."

"Why?" Kerenski demanded.

"*Vilahana*," Phil replied. "I have a theory that anything that keeps your attention focused inwards towards *Aditi* keeps the *Gloran* from exploiting what will be massive new trade opportunities in the vicinity of *Vilahana*. Remember, they are neutral and independent because they were always more of a chop shop than anything. Neither *Dalou* nor *Gloran* have any significant colonies in the region, beyond small mining facilities exploiting rare minerals. *Aditi* has relationships with a variety of such systems, because they have tried to trade more than their neighbors, however little it ends up being."

"Trade?" Kerenski asked.

"Another form of military expansion," Phil nodded. "Get worlds hooked on goods from you instead of from their founding system, and they will eventually sever ties, at least culturally."

"Then why would *Aditi* want a war with *Gloran*?" Povoloi demanded.

"Phil's other theory is that someone on *Aditi* is counting on him stopping you from taking the sort of action you would have before us," Heather interjected. "Him stopping you from actually attacking them, while goading you inwards anyway with a sharp stick."

"Counting on you?" Kerenski asked, his voice modulating. "And you suggested earlier that you might not?"

Phil felt his grimace turn utterly feral and savage now.

"If the powers that be at *Aditi* want to poke you, knowing that I won't let you punch them in the mouth in retaliation, what's to stop them from doing it again?" Phil asked. "Or escalating, if diplomats can continue to smooth things over short of shooting at each other? How quickly are we back to that stupid bullshit where an *Aditi* cruiser trades shots with a pirate enforcer until somebody backs off and pays a ransom?"

Both Imperials rocked back in their chairs at that, stunned by Phil's harsh attitude.

He had warned everybody. Most of them had listened. A few had been made examples of, like Russand or Farouk. Or Basant Utkin.

At the same time, Phil had taken this Emperor's measure the other day over juice and small talk. *Gloran* had a reputation for honorable behavior at whatever personal costs one might have to pay.

Kira Zaman, *et al*, for example.

"How would you have handled such a thing a year ago, if you'd discovered that it wasn't really pirates?" Heather asked into the gap. "Or if your spies had uncovered the payments *Aditi* had made to such pirates specifically to do such a thing?"

Oh, that got their attention. Both men leaned forward angrily.

Then Adric Kerenski surprised Phil.

He smiled, leaning back and placing his right palm flat on the table.

"There would have been a war," the man pronounced in that special voice top commanders who are any good cultivate. The one that gets people to do things. "I would have pounced on some *Aditi* colony in a tit-for-tat. Perhaps sent *Arteshbo* and her squadron to maul some *Aditi* cruiser they could sneak up on. Or hauled something bigger, depending."

"The fleet behind you?" Phil asked.

"That is enough firepower to threaten a sector headquarters

fleet, Kosnett," Kerenski said. "Even as you are in the process of upending weapons technology around here. Nobody has built the new ships we are all designing on napkins, so they have to fight me with the forces at hand."

Phil nodded. Kerenski understood that all that tech would mess things up socially for a decade. At least until new fleets came into being.

"And you are supposed to stop us from retaliating?" Fleet-Captain Povoloi asked next, going back and forth between him and Heather.

"That's my current theory," Phil replied. "Sit you down here today. Give you a good talking to overlain with subtle threats to behave or I would sanction you later. Or some stupid bullshit like that."

Again, both men recoiled. They'd been expecting Friendly Phil. That was not the man they were dealing with today.

"What do you intend, then, Kosnett?" Kerenski asked.

"I'm here at your invitation, Emperor of *Gloran*," Phil replied with a harsh smile. "You can order me out of your space. You can order me to attend you at *Derragon*. You can even ask that I wait there for you while you go off and blow somebody up. My patience in that instance is not infinite. At the same time, I feel like somebody owes me answers, so I have considered sailing over to that nearest *Aditi* Sector Headquarters to ask myself. Assuming I don't just haul all my evidence to *Aditi* itself and make people there uncomfortable."

Again, both men flinched. But then, they saw diplomats and explorers as soft people. Occupational hazard, when you were as wound up in your personal, clan, and national honor as *Gloran* could be.

They didn't know the farmers and merchants of *Aquitaine*. The Fifty Families might be important and beautiful, but they weren't the erect spine or broad shoulders upon which the Republic was built. Nor were they the terrible fists wielded on enemies.

That was men and women like Phil and Heather. Like Jessica Keller, the daughter of a starship welder in a civilian dock. Denis Jež, descended from a long-line of pig farmers and sheep thieves, and currently an adopted uncle of the Emperor of *Fribourg*.

"And if *Aditi* responded with force?" Kerenski queried, wonder creeping into his voice.

"*Ewin* tried that," Heather replied before Phil could. "Ask Duke Farouk what happened to his flagship when he pissed my Tactical Officer off."

Dead silence. Silence of the dead. Of the tomb.

Phil was pretty certain that *Hollywood* had hauled Khan's personal reports to *Derragon* after First *Ewinhome*. Phil wouldn't count the sandbox slap fight that had seen the First Minister trapped aboard *Urumchi* and Phil retiring to get help, even if it did get a number. He hadn't fired a shot offensively. Only a few at missiles that might have accidentally locked on *Urumchi*, considering the distance involved.

They would know about Iveta attempting to blow Farouk's boom apart after he had separated from a nearly-destroyed secondary section. In the old days, that was the acknowledged surrender symbol between fools brawling.

Iveta had made the man get on a general comm and publicly beg for mercy. From a woman. *Ewin*'s worst nightmare, as near as Phil had been able to calculate their cultural standards.

"So you would sail to *Aditi* and demand answers?" Kerenski asked carefully. "If that was necessary? And be prepared to offer violence if they met you with scorn or defiance?"

"Hurt dogs howl," Phil said, falling back on an ancient saying that apparently neither man knew, because they looked at him blankly. "If somebody is guilty of a thing, they will be the loudest to cast doubt and make noise to try to distract you. If nobody at *Aditi* did this, they would look at us with confusion and ask what was going on when I show up. If they think they have been caught with a hand in the cookie jar, they might get ugly."

"You said when," Povoloi spoke now.

Phil nodded.

"When," he confirmed. "Personally, I think that we might as well just escalate this right to the top and demand answers. Publicly, so they can't try to sweep it all under the rug and pretend like nothing happened. Let the full *Consensus* know what the folks in charge have been doing in their name, and how they feel about it."

"I thought *Aditi* was your ally, Kosnett," Kerenski spoke.

"So did I," he replied. "I might have been wrong, based on certain behaviors that I find distasteful, bordering on unethical. And gentlemen, I have no higher insult in my vocabulary than to classify someone as unethical, because that means they can never be trusted again in any circumstances. I would have to rethink my entire diplomatic approach to the Balhee Cluster at that point."

He liked the look of fear that came into Kerenski's eyes at his words. Like maybe they'd all been counting on certain outcomes, and not considered that *Aquitaine* might...*change* things along the way.

Aditi was the largest power, however barely, centered inside the hollow sphere and surrounded on all sides by the others. *Yaumgan* might be more powerful, but they remained stubbornly isolated in a back corner, only allowing a little trade, at least until Phil managed to talk them into opening things up.

Everyone had paid pirates to do things to the others. That left them with clean hands. More or less.

"The pirates are done, gentlemen," Phil reminded everyone. "I had expected to have to deal with local bandit problems at this point, just because there are always going to be a few dead-enders unwilling to accept obligations from any society until you hit them on the nose with a rolled-up newspaper or a closed fist. *Aditi* might have been counting on everyone making that mistake in this situation. I think I'd like to go to *Aditi* proper, with your permission Emperor Kerenski, and ask questions."

"My permission?" Kerenski countered.

"I do not wish to give insult by not calling on *Derragon*, having come all this distance," Phil nodded. "At the same time, I believe time is utterly of the essence. The sooner we resolve all this, the sooner we can all get back to negotiating trade agreements that will be better in the long run for the citizens of the Cluster."

"Regardless of the governments?" Kerenski asked.

"People don't make war on their trade partners," Phil said simply. "If nothing else, the merchant and industrialist classes stand to lose too much money, which means people out of work. And angry. My motives are entirely selfish in this matter, because I don't think war is a necessity."

"And if *Aditi* did react with excessive force?" Kerenski pressed.

"I've threatened more than one person with calling home for a Heavy Dreadnought squadron, Emperor Kerenski," Phil said simply. "By now, everybody knows about *Urumchi*. This ship is a Survey Dreadnought, with about one third of the firepower of a Heavy. Eight of those ships, with escorts, so thirty-two corvettes of various configurations. Not even the Grand Fleet Echelon at *Aditi* orbit would be more than a fart in a whirlwind if my boss accepted my recommendation and sent that team here. Might take a bit of time to organize, because *Aquitaine* has never put something that deadly together under a unified command. There is nobody in the Cluster that could stand against it. Nobody."

Eyes blinked. He'd always been vague before, because speaking such a threat came perilously close to making a promise of it. Of crushing someone so badly that he had to stop and rescue all the lifepods himself, because there would be nobody left in local space that could help.

Khandoba was an impressive ship. A fist with three stubby fingers forward, like all *Aditi* warships were designed. Snowballs had a better chance in hell than an *Aditi* Ship of the Line facing *Kongō*.

"So you go to *Aditi*, and demand answers," Kerenski followed up, leaning back again instead of forward and poised for violence. "What then?"

"I don't know what assuages the honor of *Gloran*," Phil countered neatly. "Apologies? Reparations? I would like to think that repatriation might be possible, but I suspect that the women taken might have been disposed of so that their secret could never get out. Had this been a legitimate act of war, they might have been put in a camp somewhere, or scattered to various colonies with gender imbalances. Heather and I have experience with liberating such camps. Here, that would be unethical, but short of murder. I want answers. And I want them public. *Dalou* has had to change. *Ewin* as well. *Gloran* should. If I have to punch somebody in the mouth at *Aditi*, they will change, too."

Blinks. Brain resetting. Recalibrating.

Honor was a predictable pattern to understand. You didn't talk to it from softness or weakness until you had established that the velvet glove still held an iron fist they would respect.

Adric Kerenski had respect in his eyes now. Povoloi looked like someone had sucker-punched him in the kidney. Phil just glowered at them, almost as darkly and heavily as Heather was.

Time passed in silence.

"I will need to see your evidence, Kosnett," Emperor Kerenski finally spoke. "Interviews with the important players, but I don't need to interrogate them myself. Just what you intend to produce when you get to *Aditi* to ask questions."

"So I'm going directly to *Aditi* from here?" Phil asked.

"Yes," the Emperor of *Gloran* smiled harshly. "And I'm going with you."

Phil nodded. He wasn't surprised.

Now, he had to make it work.

THIRTY-TWO

IMPERIAL FLAGSHIP GLANTHUA'S STAND, CARINAE II

Adric had returned to *Glanthua's Stand* in a foul humor. He had toured *Urumchi's* flight bay and seen the box. Read the markings. Understood the implications. Probably better than Kosnett, but Adric had been a grandson of an Emperor, and thus had access to certain things that weren't ever talked about in polite company.

The games that spies and assassins play on one another. Combat diplomacy didn't always involve battle squadrons, after all.

Adric wasn't familiar with that specific ship, but even *Gloran* had such things, often hidden in the penal forces where they could be kept to a lower profile, if a Cruiser-Captain didn't mind being *demoted* to command a spy ship.

Not that Kosnett needed to know how prevalent such things were. Let him maintain ethical standards that would eventually make the Cluster a better place.

A *Gloran* Emperor had other concerns.

He was in his cabin now, having sent A.Q. to round up Khan and Zaman so he could confirm what they knew. There had been time for a quick snack, Kosnett's strange chef having provided a meal truly fit for an emperor earlier.

He was calm. Outwardly. Seething, but that was acceptable. As Kosnett had said, unethical behavior. Was that truly the highest insult?

Dishonorable would be how *Gloran* would describe it, but wasn't that too small? It suggested a personal thing. A cultural belief that might evolve over time.

Kosnett's view on ethics had suggested that some things were always evil, regardless of circumstances or societies.

When he got home, Adric had made himself a note to dig up some dusty professor of philosophy somewhere, dressed in some atrociously-outdated suit, just to ask about such hierarchies. Perhaps *Gloran* needed to expand its thinking to encapsulate the entire Cluster. Or maybe the entire galaxy?

If Kosnett was intent on having a positive effect on the Empire, Adric Kerenski was still likely to be in a position to dictate terms when it got implemented.

What did he want out of the future that everyone was being faced to confront?

Food for thought.

A rap at the hatch interrupted further ruminations.

Adric rose and opened the hatch rather than call or flip a switch.

He towered over Adham Khan, but only in the physical sense. The man had always given off the sense of being an angry badger, willing to go for a wolf's throat if he had to.

Just one of the reasons Adric liked the man so much. Nothing intimidated Khan. His father had been the same way, though perhaps a bit more polished in execution. Might have fit even better into the force that Kosnett had originally assembled, had Artak been still in harness.

Adric stepped to one side, nodding to A.Q. to remain outside for now.

Private conversation, though he had told Tanel everything that had happened on *Urumchi*.

"In and sit," Adric ordered Cruiser-Captain Adham Khan.

There were two chairs, neither with their backs to the door. Khan chose the one that didn't have a mug of tea steaming next to it on a side table. Adric joined him, gesturing to the pot between then.

Khan moved with care, pouring himself a mug and sipping appreciably.

"Kosnett probably showed and told me more than he did you," Adric began abruptly. "What would you counsel in this situation?"

Khan finished sipping, probably to give himself time to frame the words.

"Lau is angry beyond words," he said, speaking of the Command Centurion first. All of his various officers spoke of Lau, usually in hushed and nervous tones, like she might hear them and come hunting for them.

"What are the implications of such anger?" Adric asked.

"At *First Meerut*, she turned Beridze loose with instructions to *dismantle* an orbital battle station with more firepower than one of our battleships, Your Majesty," Khan said.

"In private, now, call me Adric," he replied. "You are here as an advisor, so you need to tell me what I need to hear, not just what you think I want to know."

"Adric," Khan bowed his head nervously, suddenly jumped from a favored Cruiser-Captain to a mover and shaker of the empire in a single word. "*Urumchi* shattered the station and only then did they offer mercy to everyone else, and only if those fools immediately surrendered, because if anybody fired another shot after that, Kosnett would see them all in hell."

Adric had read reports of that battle, though battle was too balanced a word. The station had had no chance at all, once the weak blind side was unveiled.

"Will he show mercy to *Aditi*?" Adric asked.

"Do they deserve it?" Khan fired right back, ever the warrior.

Honor was a thing between equals. *Gloran* pirates had always been few in number, because preying on unarmed shopkeepers and merchants gained one no honor, save only the act of counting coup that youngsters might engage in to prove their tactical acumen and show off.

Most of them grew out of it eventually.

"Kosnett thinks that it is a facet of the *Consensus*," Adric replied. "Political and military leaders in a small, secretive cabal that has not let others know what they did. Or why."

"And I would tend to agree with that assessment, Your —*Adric*," Khan replied. "The *Consensus* is forever going on about their supposed superiority of democratic values, but I will note that any history book you read seems to be filled with the same last names, generation after generation. In that, I would find them even less open to advancement than we are, as you have cousins and brothers of different blood, however much they are family now."

Adric nodded. The smartest Imperial family brought in fresh blood from anybody demonstrating the sorts of excellence to belong. There was nothing worse than growing insular.

Oh, what an interesting term.

Something must have shown in Adric's eyes, because Khan perked up.

"*Insular*," Adric explained. "We work hard not to be, however much *Gloran* itself is on a thin fringe of the Cluster geographically. *Aditi* sits in the center, and looks all ways, but as you note, they do not bring in fresh blood to govern, electing scions of the same houses time and again. What happens if those scions are forever tainted in the eyes of the electorate?"

"The government falls," Khan replied automatically. "New blood comes in, at least for a time while those dishonored work their way back into the public graces. The *Consensus* is all about second chances, after all."

"Much as we are, with the Penal Fleet," Adric pointed out.

Something painful passed through Khan's eyes, and he took an abrupt sip of extremely hot tea to cover it, likely burning his tongue from the way he sucked in air afterwards.

Probably Zaman, being here, though Adric wasn't sure which was taunting the other.

"Second chances," Khan muttered under his breath now, eyes down and unseeing.

"Yes?" Adric asked.

Khan blinked and looked up again, eyes getting a little wide.

"My apologies, Adric," Khan said. "I misspoke."

"Tell me about second chances, Adham," Adric commanded. "What do they mean to you?"

There was something there Adric hadn't expected. Was he to become a confessor tonight, as well as an Emperor? Weirder things had happened.

"We allow mistakes to happen, assuming good intent at the time," Adham replied.

Good intent? Adric focused on the man's breathing and noted a fear that never made it to his voice.

Of?

"Rather than casting a life with permanent disgrace, officers and crew can serve a tour in the penal forces if they wish to remain in the fleet," Adham said. "Assuming success, the taint is wiped from their record and they return to honor and glory."

Yes, that rather did encapsulate it.

"Would *Aditi* offer something similar, if Kosnett is right?" Adric asked, just to see where Adham's mind might wander with such prompts.

The man's father had been excellent at all aspects of command, choosing to retire and maintain a rift with his own son over Kira Zaman's treatment when it all came out in the open.

"Kosnett might see this as an opportunity to crash the *Consensus* government at a time he could control certain outcomes," Adham replied. "*Dalou* is in turmoil, as is *Ewin*. *Gloran* could be, given events. *Zen-Mekyo* is gone, and nothing has yet rushed in to fill that gap, though the trade treaties being discussed might pull merchants across borders."

"Where does that leave *Aditi*?" Adric asked.

"Yesterday, the most powerful, because they marry their central position with stability," Adham nodded. "They could take advantage of everyone else being distracted to expand. Whether that be economically, militarily, or socially, nobody else would be in a position to thwart their aggression."

"Unless Kosnett crashed their entire government and cast down a whole generation of those same people, all in one go," Adric pointed out. "That would force them to turn inward for a decade. Perhaps a generation, depending on who rose to replace them. Is Kosnett that mean?"

"He can be, when provoked," Adham confirmed. "He can also be merciful, as many people can testify, most of whom probably really should be in hell now, but for such withholding of the blade. It would let him control outcomes at *Aditi*. Redirect the entire *Consensus*, who are absolutely the dominant culture right now. Not the most powerful, as they are third behind Kosnett and *Yaumgan*, I suspect, but they would be the kernel around which a new Cluster culture could be accreted, much like a pearl. Even as *Dalou* and *Ewin* do the same."

"I told Kosnett I was going to *Aditi* with him," Adric said with a smile.

Adham blinked rapidly in surprise as he processed that.

"Yes," Adham said quickly. "You should take this entire force with you."

Adric found the emphasis on *entire* interesting. That suggested *Arteshbo* and her squadron, and not just the fleet surrounding *Glanthua's Stand* right now.

"All of it?" he asked.

"Including *Arteshbo*, yes," Adham stated flatly.

"Why?"

There. Bald. Bold. How much intestinal fortitude does my favorite Cruiser-Captain have today?

Adham Khan swallowed. Grimaced.

Something had aged the man five years in the last five

minutes, from the lines that looked to have been etched in Adham's face with an angry hammer and chisel.

Khan put the mug down carefully. Adric wondered if the man's hands might be shaking enough to give something away.

He took a deep breath. Exhaled it just short of a sigh.

"Second chances, Adric," he said simply. "I made a mistake. A profoundly stupid one, at that. Bound up in my own honor and blind to everyone else in the process. I would like a chance to undo it, if I could."

Adric could only think of one event that might really come into play now. He studied this man closely.

"When I spoke with Kosnett, we discussed ethics, Adham," Adric explained. "He seemed to think that there were certain things even more important than honor. That they transcended all cultures, anywhere, and infected them with utterly specific understandings of right and wrong."

He paused there, because Khan had gone white. Stopped breathing. It almost felt as though a ghost had grabbed the man by the nape of the neck and dragged Adham Khan's soul out of his body.

A ghost named Artak Khan, perhaps?

"What have you done that rises to that level, Adham Khan?" Adric demanded in a slow, heavy voice.

"Evil, perhaps," Khan whispered from far away. "Personal greed masquerading as honor. Something. Something I'm certain would cause Lau to strike me down with lightning bolts."

Interesting that he reverted to the Command Centurion. Like so many others. She was the one who frightened hardened warriors. Even more than Beridze.

Having met her in the flesh and taken her measure, the woman wouldn't take one dyne of shit from anyone, anywhere. She was in command of the flagship, and was the right hand Kosnett relied on.

All of Kosnett's senior advisors were women, though Adric

had read the reports that it was the luck of the draw. *Aquitaine* didn't use gender to disqualify people.

Lau would be there regardless. She happened to be female. Nothing more.

Female.

Yes, Adric supposed that Lau might react badly if she heard the truth about Khan and Zaman.

Or had she already?

"What would a second chance look like to Adham Khan?" Adric asked, unable to prevent his voice from sounding like an Emperor now.

"I would undo harsh words spoken in anger and arrogance," Khan replied, finally finding his emotions again. Color began to return to his cheeks. "I would take back the things I said about Kira Zaman that have prevented her from serving you and the Empire as she should."

"As she should?" Adric asked.

"Command Centurion Heather Lau, Your Majesty," Khan said.

As if that said it all. And it might. The woman had infected many people, according to his spies. The daughter of the *Dalou* Hegemon. *Aditi* had placed one of their officers aboard *Urumchi* a year ago and let the woman serve as one of them. That had to be Lau's doing.

"Such things might cost you personally, Adham," Adric reminded the man.

"Ethics demand it," Khan replied firmly. "I have brought dishonor unto myself, my family, and even you by my behavior. Kosnett had it right. I need to own that mistake. To live with it. To undo it, whatever the personal cost."

"Should I remove you from command?" Adric asked, awestruck at actually witnessing the fabled *man falling on his own sword* that usually only existed as a figure of speech.

"If it would serve the Empire," Khan replied. "Perhaps swapping me for Kira right now would be the wisest choice, as all the mistakes are mine, and she should be one of your top commanders and counselors, rather than a fool like me."

Adric found himself struck utterly dumb. And yet, Adham Khan was sizing himself for the blade.

"That is not an action that should be taken in haste," Adric replied.

"It is only hasty when you have not spent as much time as I have recently, contemplating my sins in detail," Khan replied.

"And yet, you are one of my top commanders and counselors, Adham Khan," Adric told the man. "I should not cast that away in haste. Return to *Juvayni*. Prepare yourself and your crew for our mission to confront the lords of the *Consensus* in their front yard."

Khan blinked and seemed to come back to himself from a great distance. Perhaps that angry ghost had been assuaged for now and let the man slip free.

Certainly, Adric had heard of such things, but never once seen such an occurrence in the flesh. Merely the great, oral epics that the bards and scholars kept alive every generation.

Perhaps Adham Khan needed such a thing. The man rose now and didn't look as broken as he had a moment before. He bowed and made his way to the hatch, pausing just outside to bow to someone else just as deeply before the hatch closed.

Adric doubted that A.Q. rated such a thing, so Kira Zaman must be standing there, her jaw probably hanging as far open as it would go.

Adric took a deep breath and considered the other half of this terrible, Gordian knot he needed to solve.

She was standing just outside.

THIRTY-THREE

IMPERIAL FLAGSHIP GLANTHUA'S STAND, CARINAE II

Adric had greeted Khan at the hatch personally, so he rose now, grabbing the man's tea mug and swapping it for a clean one before walking to the hatch to see what other surprises the day held for him.

Kira Zaman, unacknowledged Imperial cousin and Penal Fleet Frigate-Captain, stood there a bit anxiously. But then, Khan's departure had probably ruffled everyone's feathers, as the man had been emotionally on the edge of being unraveled when he left.

Like him, she had gone for the less formal uniform today. Knickerbockers and horizontal stripes, lacking the sash she was entitled to. He wondered if she saw herself being called to account, especially after he had spoken with Khan.

"Come," he said.

She walked past and Adric nodded to A.Q. in the hallway with all the various Security troopers on duty as always.

Adric closed the hatch and turned to watch. Kira had come to rest in the center of the large room, feet apart and hands crossed behind her back.

She wasn't much shorter than Adham Khan, and almost as broad in the shoulders, but lacked that fierceness he brought.

Most captains did. She might have a reason today, being last to tell her story.

"Sit," he gestured. "The tea is still warm, I think."

Adric returned to his chair and settled as she carefully poured herself a mug. He waited. She waited.

The woman could probably out-stubborn him. She had in the past, and he had things that he needed to do.

Kira Zaman really didn't have much left in front of her, save continuing to serve however long he let her. And then retiring at some point.

What would the fleet be like without her in it? Not a thing he had considered before today. Previously Kira Zaman had been a problem to be solved, not a person to be acknowledged.

In those days, he could not acknowledge her. Whoever her father was, he had never spoken up, and her mother was no longer alive to ask. Genetic testing had placed her close to him by blood.

At the time, that had been enough for her to enlist. To serve. To thrive, as much as she could when her choices were so starkly limited.

Like she would let anything stop her.

Adric considered their age gap as he watched her. He was fifty-eight, and on the back side of his prime. She was a generation younger at thirty-four. Thankfully, he had never known her mother, so it was completely impossible that she was his daughter.

At least of the flesh. Of the spirit was a different thing. She had the Kerenski eyes, dark and full of power.

She sipped and outwaited him. Again.

"Adham Khan finds himself in an ethical dilemma," Adric began, picking up this conversation in the middle. Like he had with Kira in the past.

Her eyes flared angrily, but she refrained from spitting on the floor.

Not that he would have begrudged her that today.

"He and I spoke of *Aditi*, and everything that Kosnett and Khan believe," Adric said. "Plus Lau."

Now, Kira's eyes lit up in a different direction. Friendly, hopeful, something.

Command Centurion Lau. Possibly the most dangerous person in the Cluster, because Phil Kosnett wanted everyone to talk and trade and make nice.

Lau wanted people like Adham Khan to understand regret. And people like Kira Zaman to dream.

She refrained from commenting. He nodded anyway, as she was answering his questions in her own way.

"I have told Kosnett that I will be accompanying him when he goes to *Aditi* to confront the *Consensus* publicly," Adric continued, still watching Kerenski eyes dance with inner emotion. "Khan practically demanded that I include your squadron with my fleet when we go."

That got through to her. Even the normally unrufflable Kira Zaman could blink in surprise.

"Why?" she demanded before she could stop herself.

"He acknowledges a mistake he made previously," Adric replied. "Seems to be haunted enough by it that he is willing to accept demotion by his Emperor and the dishonor that accompanies it, that he might make right that which he broke in the first place."

Kerenski eyes got huge. There was really only one thing that touched on all three lives that he could be talking about.

"Artak Khan once told me personally that I should acknowledge you," Adric told her. "That I should promote you out of where you have been trapped by circumstances, the rest of the Empire be damned in the process. Instead, I listened to his son, who made the louder and more compelling case at the time."

"At the time?" Kira asked now, fidgety on the verge of nervous.

All this had been hashed out in public and private alike, several years ago. Settled and done.

Except that Adham Khan had found a template to understand what Kira Zaman could have become, in *any* other culture.

Command Centurion Heather Lau.

"Adham Khan has offered to metaphorically throw himself on his sword, Kira," Adric told her. "He even told me that I should consider swapping the two of you as commanders before sailing off to challenge the *Consensus*, because that would better serve the Empire than a fool like him. His words."

She gasped. Just like Adric would have liked to at the time. He'd had to hold it inside. To present the glorious and terrible Emperor of *Gloran* that Adham Khan seemed to be depending on.

It was not far wrong to say shit had gone entirely weird today.

She was blinking like she had something physically in her eye, instead of a twitch in her soul.

"But I wanted to talk about *Aquitaine*," Adric said, drawing her back from recriminations and might-have-beens. At least for a moment.

"Sir?" she asked.

"In private council like this, call me Adric, cousin," he said.

She gasped again. Like Khan, set down her mug before she spilled it all over herself.

At least Adric finally understood that Lau and Kosnett had already changed the *Gloran Empire*, even if they had hardly dealt with it directly. They had infected Adham and Kira both. The rest would come along eventually.

Change was coming. He could own it, or let it grind him under as he tried to stop it. Because he would fail.

"Khan would undo his denunciations," Adric said. "Meekly accept demotion to the Penal Fleet, or even dismissal entirely, because he thinks you would be better in his place when we go to *Aditi*. Would he be correct?"

Another gasp.

Adric routinely sent the woman to do things, because she got shit done. Not many of his captains could reliably make that claim. She'd gone to *Carinae II* because he needed a force there to frighten off anyone coming back, while sorting out what had happened and how to save the colony. Or rebuild it, as had become necessary.

And he could never admit she had Kerenski eyes.

Until now.

"I don't know," Kira admitted. "He and I have never served in the same system until now. Even when Artak was my Frigate-Captain, Adham kept his distance, probably concerned that dishonor was contagious."

Adric let her have that one. She was not far off the truth he had seen in Adham's unguarded eyes.

"What would you do, if Khan could undo the past?" Adric asked her.

If she became an acknowledged cousin, her wrath on the man could be terrible. And likely correct, considering all the things she might have lost over the last five years.

Kira fell silent. Introspective.

"I had a meeting with Lady Kugosu, daughter of the Shogun," she said, as though shifting entirely around to a different conversation, but Adric assumed it was all connected. That other woman was in the system right now.

"And?" he prompted.

"She and I spoke of trade," Kira said. "That same treaty she had offered to *Ewin*, almost verbatim, with an additional expectation that *Gloran* and *Dalou* both needed to develop worlds near *Vilahana* that we claimed and had largely ignored. She is fourteen years old, and sounds ancient."

Fourteen? Oh, that put an interesting spin on things. Kira

had joined the fleet when she was fourteen. Had set herself on a path on the one thing she wanted that she was allowed.

Had she already served his Empire for twenty years? What would she do next?

"What do you want out of this, Kira?" he asked her delicately.

She could collect a pension and retire. Perhaps had already qualified. It would not be great, but she would not starve. And had an entire life ahead of her, as yet untapped.

"I serve the Empire," Kira told him in a hard, sour voice that had decades of unpleasant memories she had overcome.

"What did Lady Kugosu teach you?" Adric prompted.

Every person Adric Kerenski had ever met had had some lesson to impart, even if nothing more than *but for the Grace of the Creator go I*.

He saw fear in her eyes, but only for the briefest flash before she crushed it.

"That the only limits on us are those we accept, Adric," she replied.

It was his turn to gasp. Audibly. That was acceptable in here. She was family.

She would accept no limits. Not now. Not having met Lau and Kugosu.

Revolution, however tiny now, would only grow.

How long until half of his captains were women? *Gloran* allowed it, then went out of their way to make it harder, stationing women ashore when they became pregnant and not letting them into space again. The few he had were adamantly not going down that path, because they would accept no limits on themselves.

He nodded.

Even emperors could learn.

"You will be accompanying me to *Aditi*," he announced quietly. "I'll detach some of my own frigates to guard this system while we're gone, though I doubt that it would be necessary. It is the survivors who need to be able to look up and see the fleet between them and the darkness."

"How can I serve?" she asked.

"Continue to be excellent, cousin," Adric said eliciting another gasp. "After the *Consensus* is put to rights, we'll take Kosnett to *Derragon* and welcome everyone to our home as we should."

Those Kerenski eyes grew huge as the implications of his words became clear. Our home. Not just his. Cousin of the blood, rather than outcast working her ass off to be better than any other captain under his command.

"And if *Aditi* resents the intrusion?" Kira asked.

"Let them try," Adric assured her.

THIRTY-FOUR

DATE OF THE REPUBLIC MARCH 25, 412 RAN
URUMCHI, CARINAE II ORBIT

Iveta looked up at the message beep from Leyla, seated all of about four meters away. Must be good, if she wasn't talking aloud.

It was the middle of the afternoon shift. Heather had been here for two hours earlier. Iveta had this one, then would turn it over to Pilot Bozhidar Virág in a while. Everyone in the squadron was busy right now, resupplying everything they could beg, borrow, or steal off the Fast Clipper *Mexicali*.

The Pixies struck again, the message read. *Movement orders detaching three frigates from Gloran force. Swapping for* Arteshbo *and her consorts.*

Shit. Harman had cracked another code? This one a military encryption used by the *Gloran* Emperor himself?

Worse, Iveta had been brushing up on *Gloran* military culture, on the off-chance they'd need to fight anybody here. She'd doubted it, but had learned to never take anything for granted because Jessica never would have.

Including Kira Zaman's team on the mission to *Aditi* was tantamount to publicly admitting the truth about the woman's paternity. With *everything* that implied.

She turned to Leyla.

"Wake Phil and Heather if they're asleep," she ordered. "Make sure they see this message immediately, so they're prepared for fallout. Assume *Juvayni* can read it and keep a watch on him."

"We expecting stupidity from that boy?" Leyla asked.

"Expecting?" Iveta countered with a smile. "It's Cruiser-Captain Khan we're talking about."

"Noted," Leyla replied sarcastically.

Khan was an aggressive commander by the standards of an aggressive fleet. An aggressive culture.

He might get feisty right now.

Heather was awake. She replied first, her image appearing on Iveta's screen.

"Turn over to Leyla and meet me in the arboretum," Heather suggested. Sounded like an order anyway.

"Leyla, you have the bridge," Iveta said, rising and moving to the hatch in a single stride.

She got there before Heather, but her cabin was farther aft than the bridge.

They airlocked through into the forest. Like walking on the surface of a planet on a nice day. As long as you paid attention to the rain warnings. Or didn't mind getting wet.

Nobody was around, not counting the Master Gardener who was a ghost in this place, forever just appearing out of the underbrush when he wanted to talk to you.

"What do I need to prepare for?" Iveta asked as they walked down one of the smaller trails. More of a game trail than a path. "What are the implications of *Arteshbo* joining?"

"Two options," Heather replied. "Both her and Khan went to the flagship after he left here, presumably to fill Kerenski in on everything they might have learned."

"Phil or Kohahu," Iveta nodded.

"Right," Heather agreed. "I'm guessing some sort of

breakthrough, at least socially. Otherwise, Kerenski would have left Zaman here to watch the system."

"He discover he has a cousin finally?" Iveta probed.

"Might be willing to admit it, but that means that Khan backed down off his high horse on the topic."

"Our boy Khan?" Iveta was a little shocked.

"I might have been pounding on him to behave," Heather replied. "Maybe something got through."

"I still want him on the farthest wing away from the Imperial force, if we're all going together," Iveta snapped.

"Agreed," Heather nodded. "I expect *Arteshbo* to be held in tight, escorting Kerenski. That was the job of the ships she's replacing, and honestly, I expect she's going to be better at it, if only because she has to stand up in front of the entire Cluster now and prove herself."

"We looking at a future emperor here?" Iveta asked.

Heather stumbled short, like she'd forgotten how to walk.

They were in trees, but comm systems had been hidden everywhere.

"System, this is Heather Lau," she said loudly. "Connect me with Kosnett."

"Phil," he replied a moment later.

"I need you in the arboretum *right now*, Phil," Heather said. "Bring Harinder. We'll meet you at the airlock."

"Coming," he replied.

The line cut and Heather started back the other way. Iveta followed, much more serious than she'd been thirty seconds ago. It had been a throwaway line. Almost a joke.

And yet…

Gloran Emperor wasn't a first son sort of thing. It was an Heir Designate from among a few dozen cousins and relatives, some born that way and some adopted or married into the family to keep the blood hot and smart.

Inbreeding brought down most empires eventually. You

needed to bring in the hungry kids regularly. The feisty ones. Keep the rest on their toes.

That was how the Republic had been able to do all the things they had, compared to the bigger, badder *Fribourg Empire* next door and at war for so long.

They met Phil and Harinder, started down a different trail this time, wide enough to walk two abreast.

"Iveta just had an unsettling question," Heather began.

"Gosh, that's so out of character," Harinder replied sarcastically, grinning from ear to ear as she looked over.

Iveta felt a blush take over and kept her mouth shut. She might have a rep around here. At least it was for more than just being a rabid carnivore.

"Talk to me," Phil said, walking next to Heather a step ahead.

"With Kira Zaman and *Arteshbo* joining this combined forces fleet as we head to *Aditi*, we presume he is acknowledging her birth," Heather said. "She asked if we were looking at a future Emperor here."

Iveta appreciated it when Phil stopped walking as well. Hell of a question. Hell of a weird set of implications.

"They've never had a female Emperor," Phil said unnecessarily.

"And *Dalou* has never had a female Shogun," Iveta said helpfully, causing him to turn around and glare sarcastically at her.

Seemed to be that kind of day, all the way around.

"You will not repeat this," Phil spoke directly at her, ominously. "Heather and Harinder know, but you need to, in light of this."

Shit. Iveta hated it when things got phrased that way.

"Go ahead," she said anyway.

"It is not generally known, but there is a suggestion quietly floating around *Ewin* that Gotzon Solo might be in line to be the next king of *Ewin*," Phil said.

"Solo?" Iveta was gobsmacked. "Isn't he too quiet for those raucous boys?"

"*Gotzon the Quiet*, yes," Phil nodded. "Kalidoona is looking to maneuver things so that his time with us makes him look like the utter badass commander he really is, once you get him out of last century's technology. We're happy to help that way, because he is the quietest prince commanding a ship anywhere. We'd like *Ewin* to maybe learn to move without yelling at the top of their lungs all the time. Or swinging his hands like a cartoon conductor."

"And we're about to maybe go accidentally overthrow the *Consensus* government?" Iveta asked.

"*Yaumgan* might consider revoking our invitation," he grinned. "They might like the world they've built too much to let us mess it up."

"Shit," Iveta said. That seemed to sum it all up.

"Leave no stone unturned," Harinder nodded. "That's the flipside of diplomacy on this scale. Folks were in ruts, and we're going to come along and disrupt everything from under their feet. The pirates had to go down hard. So did *Ewin*. *Dalou* got there on their own. *Gloran* might as well, if we're lucky. That leaves *Aditi* for now."

Iveta wondered if she was supposed to get a new tattoo for being obviously initiated into a much more dangerous inner circle than before. Phil always played things close to the vest, with both Heather and Harinder helping.

Her job used to just be cracking heads together whenever someone looked at her cross-eyed.

Not so much anymore.

Still, Iveta went Tactical. That was her job for Phil.

"So I was telling Heather I wanted Khan on the outer flank farthest away from the *Gloran* fleet when we got there," Iveta said. "Now I want him sideways, them across and back in our rear flank corner."

"If we follow our usual pattern, we would put *Aranyani* on the tip of the spear, in the van," Phil countered.

"No," Iveta said. "That was us sailing somewhere with an invitation and a port call. This won't be. I like Kaur and her crew. And I generally trust them, but this might be that one time where she has to decide whose side she's on. I don't want that conversation happening in the middle of a battle. And I sure as hell don't want her supposedly protecting my bow when I have an *Aditi* fleet squaring up to get ugly."

"Suggestions?" Heather asked.

Iveta considered an idea. Considered how utterly out of character it was.

How nobody would see it coming.

Weren't all the best practical jokes done that way?

"Echelon," Iveta replied. "*Urumchi* and *Viking* as Ships of the Line at the rear. All six cruisers as Strongholds in front of us, with *Hollywood* in the middle next to *Li Jing*. All the corvettes in a staggered jaw formation across the front, with *Forktail* in the center, leading us in."

"*Forktail?*" Harinder asked.

"Anyone starting trouble, and Sugawara is going to be trying to live up to *Morninghawk*'s reputation as a killer," Iveta smiled. "One of *Aranyani*'s class ships might find that they've picked on a rabid chipmunk at that point. Plus I'll be right behind him helping out."

They all turned to Phil now. First Centurion. Ambassador Plenipotentiary.

The Boss.

"You work it out with your people," he told her. "We'll communicate it to *Glanthua's Stand* at the last waypoint and give them time to react. I expect they'll stay in the sort of wolfpack formation they've been using until now, but that just means that I have an entire flank of your echelon secured, so we can put *Shadowbolt* and *Storm Petrel* on that inner wing. I agree about

Juvayni on the edge, but you need to decide if *Li Jing* is next or *Aranyani*."

Iveta nodded. Tactical problems like this were her bread and butter. The entire reason she'd been hired. Been picked over some four hundred qualified others applying.

She'd be keeping Phil safe. And the future Shogun of *Dalou*. And the future Emperor of *Dalou*. And a possible King of *Ewin*.

And maybe a future *Gloran* Emperor as well.

Iveta was looking forward to it.

CONSENSUS

THIRTY-FIVE

IMPERIAL FLAGSHIP GLANTHUA'S STAND, FORWARD LAAGER POINT

Adric had a station on the bridge of *Glanthua's Stand* as they settled in and performed last minute things. He'd visited *Urumchi* and seen the way they separated Kosnett from Lau and Beridze. It felt inefficient. At the same time, Fleet-Captain Povoloi had many things to take care of, all at once, so he was pulled every direction.

Just one more reminder that *Aquitaine* had spent nearly two centuries engaged in a war to the death with a powerful and aggressive neighbor, while nobody in the Cluster had done more than raid each other and chase off pirates on a regular basis.

What would his fleet look like in a decade when he finished rebuilding it?

Nobody built scouts. Not like *Aquitaine* understood the concept. Minesweepers were more common, but even then not vessels entirely dedicated to the concept from the keel up.

He had warships. Certainly, all of the cruisers could extract the pod in back, tucked between the engines like the aft castle of a sailing ship. Combat versions. Carrier. Drone Bombardment. Cargo. Even Diplomatic Couriers designed to haul ambassadors and Emperors in style.

Assuming he wasn't aboard a battleship designed to be his flagship.

Adric didn't think that combat was going to be *Aditi*'s immediate response, but he was also about to arrive with the rough equivalent of three fleets' worth of firepower, considering how he had ordered his own ships to be configured for combat.

"How long are we at this location, Fleet-Captain?" Adric asked.

"Half a day, give or take," the man replied, looking up over the shoulder of a junior officer close at hand with questions on paperwork.

"Long enough to pull captains together for an in-person meeting?" Adric asked. "Kosnett is not on a timer to arrive, is he?"

"He is not, to the best of my knowledge," Povoloi replied. "We can ask. Just our force, or everyone?"

Adric paused, rocked back on his heels mentally by such a simple question. He'd originally intended just his own captains for a last minute pep talk, but perhaps this was a chance to get everyone in a single room. To share his thoughts.

Kosnett was doing this out of pique more than anything, though it was barely slivers shy of an anger worthy of the gods themselves. Adric had chosen to accompany the man, rather than ordering him.

Aquitaine's captains—no, Command Centurions, like Lau— were going to *Aditi* to demand answers for him. But more than that. Because they were following a code of ethics higher than mere government. Mere society.

Right and wrong itself.

"I shall inquire with Kosnett," Adric said, rising now.

He didn't really need to be on the bridge. Might even be distracting folks, though they generally treated him like another superior officer.

Making his way aft with his own Security troopers, Adric nodded to the pair guarding Tanel's office. They opened it and he entered, finding the man's assistant in the outer office. Who then looked up in raw panic.

"Your Majesty!" he cried. "We didn't know you were coming!"

"Let A.Q. know I would like to borrow him and his office to make a call," Adric said, moving to a nearby chair and sitting.

The man vanished through the hatch behind him, emerging almost as fast as it would cycle.

"Please, Your Majesty," he gestured.

Adric left his guards in the outer chamber. They wouldn't relax, but at least they didn't have to intimidate anyone for a bit. That they might choose to was outside his control.

Or was it?

Nobody served on this vessel except a select elite. And yet, he had all the security stations and troops of the lowliest Type Four Patroller in the Penal Fleet. The ships that handled search and rescue and customs duties.

Was it necessary? Even here?

Adric's gait had hitched just the slightest amount as he entered Tanel's office, but he got his face under control again quickly and shut the hatch.

Tanel had risen. He sat as soon as they were isolated.

"Problems?" he asked simply.

Adric took the nearer chair and stretched out his feet.

"I was about to invite all the captains to a final briefing," he said.

A.Q. nodded. It would be in character for him, so the War-Captain wasn't surprised.

"Then Povoloi asked if I meant just our captains, or the entire force," Adric continued, watching the man's face.

It went through a wealth of emotions in under two seconds.

"Would Kosnett allow it?" Adric finally asked.

"I don't see why he wouldn't," A.Q. replied. "Let me talk to his Flag Centurion, so he isn't forced to accept *force majeure* when he's already in a foul humor."

"Exactly," Adric said, rising again almost as fast as he'd sat. "The goal here is to make friends, as Kosnett reminds us frequently. Even if we might be making enemies of *Aditi*."

"They'd have to be allies first, Adric," A.Q. said. "We haven't been shooting at them lately, but that's not the same thing."

"And we might be shortly," Adric said, moving towards the door. "Find out."

He exited, picking up his pet killers and headed aft and up a level to his quarters.

Gloran naval architecture was all about the long, skinny boom where officers and trusted sailors lived and worked, with most of the crew aft in the secondary hull. Battleships had a much thicker neck, in proportion to everyone else. Partly, that was the third engine on a pylon overhead, supplying extra power. But it also let him have quarters out of the way of everyone, so they could get on with their jobs.

His message light was blinking when he got to his salon, leaving the men outside to guard an empty hall that had more guards posted regularly, in case someone thought to assassinate the Emperor.

Adric Kerenski had enemies. He knew that. But he didn't think most of his sailors qualified, as draftees served elsewhere until they decided to remain in uniform.

There were, however, always spies and double agents about.

He kept his door locked once he got inside.

"That was fast," he told A.Q. as the man appeared on the screen.

"I got the impression that they were either expecting it, or immediately welcomed the idea," A.Q. replied. "I'm working with Abbatelli to coordinate, but it looks like we'll have everyone aboard in about four hours. Do we prepare a working dinner on top of it? That's close enough for the wardroom staff."

"Yes," Adric decided. "Arrange officers even/odd so everyone is seated next to two of theirs, if we can stack it that way. Kosnett has just about as many, when you include all the others, so maybe a hollow box with the corners and centers open so stewards can get in and work the inside. We want friendly conversation."

"Understood," A.Q. replied.

"Oh, and one more thing," Adric said.

A.Q. had a look on his face like he'd been waiting for that other shoe to drop.

"Put Kosnett next to me," Adric said. "Kira Zaman next to him, and Lau next to her."

A.Q.'s face went a little white, but he nodded and Adric cut the circuit.

Time to make it public, as it were.

Today, as the old saying went, was always a good day to die.

THIRTY-SIX

DATE OF THE REPUBLIC MARCH 28, 412 RAN URUMCHI, WAYPOINT ADITI TWO

Phil considered the invitation, sitting in his office with Harinder across from him. He could decline it quietly, making this much more of an informal meeting between commanders, though that might prove troublesome later, considering where he was headed. On the other hand, arriving at *Aditi* in tandem with the *Gloran* Emperor would look an awful lot like a treaty relationship, which was something *Aditi* had never managed.

"You are going, right?" Harinder asked sharply as she watched his face.

"Yes," Phil agreed. "But I had to stop and think about it for a long moment. What has Tanel said about the treaty language they've been reading from Lady Kugosu?"

"He sent home for more ambassadors than our own Miliya Gavraba," Harinder laughed. "She's advising them from as much of a neutral position as she can, but obviously he won't trust her that much. Still, it is close to what we'd been offering, because *Dalou* started with our document."

"Which they have since signed," Phil reminded her. "We already have one solid ally here. Two with *Meerut*, though Governor Milose isn't a power to be contended with. Yet."

"Are you planning on mousetrapping Kerenski before *Aditi*?" Harinder asked.

"He might be doing that himself," Phil countered. "What does he say when he has all my command centurions as well as the various local captains together in a single room, just before a major engagement with *Aditi*, military or diplomatic?"

"Do we expect *Aranyani* to break ranks?" Harinder asked.

"No," Phil said flatly. "Kaur is many things, but duplicitous is not one of them. She'll be with us even after some fool of a Senior Director orders her to break from the squadron. They'll cashier her in disgrace later, I expect, but she might have other friends she could call on to see that she's never left out in the cold. That includes us."

Harinder nodded.

"In that case, you need to hit the shower now," she said smartly. "Kerenski specified day uniforms, like they wore here, instead of dress, but you need to look good in front of all of his people. You might also need a haircut tomorrow before you start giving interviews to *Aditi* newspapers."

Phil nodded and shut everything down on his side.

Exiting, he turned to the redneck.

"You shower, too," Phil ordered him. "Day uniform and the smaller travel pack. We'll assume he's not about to poison us over dinner, but I'm avoiding the wine."

"Got it," Markus said, taking off at a jog.

Phil turned to Harinder.

"Why do I feel like this is something of the penultimate crisis of the Balhee Cluster, rushing madly at us?" he asked.

"Because it might be," she replied. "And there is still *Yaumgan* at some point."

"That's why I said penultimate."

THIRTY-SEVEN

DATE OF THE REPUBLIC MARCH 28, 412
GLORAN FLAGSHIP GLANTHUA'S STAND, WAYPOINT ADITI TWO

Heather would have liked to have sent Iveta in her stead, but she knew that was just her general introversion speaking. Bringing Nam and Kohahu would have also been useful, if only to make *Gloran* come face to face with some of Phil's social and cultural changes.

But Kerenski had specified Command Centurions. That included Harinder, because it had included Phil, but it limited Heather's options to maneuver.

As the shuttle docked, she counted noses around her. Two shuttles involved, each taking least-course-paths to gather everyone up. Galia Abbasi off *CC-501* and Erle Kuiper off *CB-502* were on the other one, and had already arrived. Heather was escorting Phil.

The hatch opened and instead of a formal lineup of folks, she found herself facing Fleet-Captain Povoloi alone. Didn't even have his Security Marines with him, though Phil had brought Xochitl. As always.

"Welcome aboard," he said with a nod of his head. "This way, please."

Heather and Dar had been closest to the hatch, so they led a ragtag mob of folks. Dao Zhiou Xue was right behind her from the way that woman's boots clunked on the deck metal. The rest were in softer soles.

Quickly, they ended up in a big chamber, with all the tables taking up one quarter of a larger rectangle, forward, port side. The other half of her team standing around, with the twenty *Gloran* captains somewhat mingling, though still not fully dissolved into a single mass.

That sort of alchemy usually required Phil's touch, but Heather was just wee bit grumpy at last-minute parties, so she ignored everyone and walked right up to Kira Zaman, catching the woman on her back foot, as it were.

"How are you doing?" Heather asked leadingly.

Behind her, all her team began to take her example and dive into the group, looking for friends or making them.

Heather was back in her deportment classes and that first social, when everyone had been so nervous about meeting others and dancing. Good way to break the ice. Still hard on teenage nerves.

She liked to think she was much tougher these days.

"I'm well," Kira said in an uncertain voice.

Possibly a little gunshy, considering that her day uniform had a silver pattern to the shirt instead of the gold that almost everyone else wore, excepting nearby Frigate-Captain Nadim Tikka off *Mardonius* and Frigate-Captain Zeenat Vaishya off *Darius*.

The lesser cousins of the main fleet, just like Kira Zaman was an unacknowledged cousin of the tall man over there talking to Phil, Harinder, and Adham Khan in an animated voice.

"Introduce me to your consorts," Heather softly ordered the woman.

Kira drew them near with a hand, not that they'd gone far off. Tikka was tall and lanky, and had an air of uncertainty about him, like he was still shocked to be in this room. Vaishya reminded Heather of a slightly-taller Khan, more average in height and a little raw and rough, as Khan had been back when he first joined the squadron as the commander of a badass battlecruiser that might have gotten taken down by *CB-502* if he'd gotten unruly.

"Gentlemen," Heather bowed to them as equals, possibly spooking Tikka even more, but a man didn't get to be a Frigate-Captain, even on the penal side, by being shy or cowardly. "I'm just sorry I don't have time to host both of you aboard *Urumchi* for a formal event, our schedule being what it is."

"If I can be so bold, Heather, I would like to hold you to that when we get back to *Derragon*," Kira interjected, catching her two wingmates off guard with a broad gesture. "After all this is settled."

"It would be my pleasure," Heather smiled. That put them a little at ease.

Penal Fleet meant that you had fucked up bad enough to be punished by removal from your command. Possibly demotion from Cruiser-Captain, but usually not. Artak Khan was one of the few who had faced that. One of the fewer who had overcome it to make it back and get promoted as far as Fleet-Captain. But she'd heard some of the legends after pointedly asking a few people who studied that sort of thing.

They spoke of trivialities and inconsequentialities for now, until Kerenski raised his voice and covered the vast hall like a cloak.

"My friends, the stewards inform me that we are ready to dine," the man called loudly. "If you will look at the seats, you will find your name. I have staggered things so that each may meet others, before we ride together in what I hope is friendship, and does not have to turn into battle."

Heather kept her sour grimace inside. She made her way in Phil's direction, figuring that the important people would still be together. It was only a minor surprise that she had Kira on one side and Khan on the other.

Felt like what she'd been up to anyway, keeping the two of them apart and providing den mother and referee.

"I had no idea until now," Khan muttered to her as he pulled out his chair and sat.

Almost sounded like a different man than the Adham Khan she was used to, but Heather supposed that the last year had changed a lot of people. Hopefully for the better.

Maybe an old dog like Khan could learn new tricks as well.

Interesting was Phil on the far side of Kira. And then Kerenski on the far side of that, with the War-Captain beyond. The table was a big, open square shape, so Povoloi ended up beyond Tanel. If she were doing it, Heather would have organized everyone by rank or seniority, and then assigned them one per side going down the list until she ran out of bodies, just to mix things up to the point that someone like Povoloi might end up talking to Isabèl Pan off *CM-507*. Not least senior, but possibly least fascinating normally to a warship hotshot who didn't understand just how engrossing or important mine operations might be when you had the time to mess with someone.

The Balhee Cluster used lots of mines, but in an amateur fashion, as far as Isabèl was concerned. Heather trusted the woman's judgment on the topic.

Phil had turned to Kira to engage the woman in conversation, so Heather decided to bother Khan.

"What are the implications?" Heather murmured quietly, nodding to Kira behind her.

"I offered her my space aboard *Juvayni*, if necessary," the man replied in a tight, almost-inaudible voice.

It was a good thing she was working to be quiet, else Heather might have screamed in frustration or something. Instead, she nodded like it was the most normal thing in the world.

"He chose not to take you up on the matter?" she asked instead.

"So far, Command Centurion," Khan nodded.

Obviously, some serious shit had gone badly sideways.

Heather didn't think she'd pushed things that far off center, but at the same time, everyone was trying to come to grips with everything Phil had done or promised to do to the Cluster by the time he was through.

Gloran might have decided to try to get ahead of Phil's decision curve, as he liked to describe it. Doing things that forced the other guy to react to you, instead of the other way around.

"What would that look like, Khan?" she asked.

"A public apology on my part," he nodded back to her. "Possibly a career-ending one, considering how things went down the first time. I might have been entirely out of line with verbal and personal abuse. I understand that now, but at the time…"

"Gotzon Solo," Heather said simply.

Khan's eyes got big.

"Yes," he said. "Gotzon."

Heather had yelled at the Striker enough about being loud and boisterous in public that he had calmed significantly. This being before she understood that folks back home had considered the old him shy and a little quiet around his peers.

"I'm trying, Command Centurion," Khan said so earnestly she wondered if he'd been replaced by an impostor when nobody had been looking. "Whether I succeed is out of my hands, as it should be. Others will determine my fate."

The way he said it suggested to Heather that he didn't have a high opinion of his chances. At the same time, *Gloran* warriors were defined by their willingness to go down fighting, and win or lose honorably.

Adham Khan was willing.

"Whatever the final outcome, it has been a pleasure having you in my squadron, Cruiser-Captain," Heather told him. "We might have disagreed about things, but I never had to worry about your corner being soft if an enemy pushed. My only concern was keeping hold of the chain to stop you going after their throats when they fled."

Adham Khan, senior Cruiser-Captain badass commander of a flagship, could blush. Heather would have lost that bet, had she made it, but it was the truth.

"Thank you, Command Centurion," he said.

"Call me Heather, Adham," she countered. "We're past the state of formality."

He nodded. Gulped once.

"Heather," he said quietly.

More conversation was cut short by the arrival of stewards before them, with coffee and salad plates, serving the top row first, and then moving outward.

Heather didn't have any clue what was coming next with Kerenski and Zaman, but it promised to be interesting.

THIRTY-EIGHT

DATE OF THE REPUBLIC MARCH 28, 412
GLORAN FLAGSHIP GLANTHUA'S STAND, WAYPOINT ADITI TWO

Phil had a front row seat to the future unfolding, and wouldn't have traded it for anything. On his right, Adric Kerenski leaned forward to make small talk with Kira Zaman, seated on his left. On the surface of things, just another politician, albeit one with a significant naval background, talking to one of his subordinate captains.

"Kira, how would you rate the formation of the two squadrons, as we settle into this laager prior to arriving for our mission?" Kerenski asked.

Kira glanced up at Phil—all of her height seemed to be in her legs—and then turned her attention to the Emperor when Phil nodded.

"It is my understanding that *Aquitaine* ships by themselves can travel through Jump significantly faster than anyone else," she began, again glancing at him for a quick nod. "The other ships slow them some, but they have had a year of sailing together to tune things and organize themselves so that everyone arrives together. Additionally, they always tend to maneuver in a flat diamond, rather than the Echelon of *Aditi* or the Wolfpack of *Gloran*. Our present force was organized from various elements that happened to be present at *Derragon* and *Carinae II*, so they have not worked together as much."

"Should we consider organizing squadrons such as yours to better train?" Kerenski asked.

Again, perfectly normal. Unless you were asking an unacknowledged bastard daughter of the Imperial House. Commanding a Penal squadron attached to the main fleet for a mission.

Then it was less normal.

"*Arteshbo*, *Mardonius*, and *Darius* have trained together significantly," she replied carefully. "Even as command staffs have rotated through. The crews are sharp and know what to do in an emergency."

Phil kept his commentary inside. She'd risen probably as far as she could, unless something drastic changed. Which seemed not only possible now but likely from the way Kerenski was approaching her.

The other two Frigate-Captains had been in place for about a year or so each, so had another year before they could be paroled back to their old jobs. Other senior officers came and went as well, with only Kira Zaman being the fixture.

If she was that good with what one presumed were second-string officers and crew, Phil could only imagine what she'd have been like in the main fleet. Or aboard this vessel.

He'd have hired her, because she might have given Heather a run for it.

"I agree, Kira," Kerenski replied, surprising both of them. "I wonder if we have gotten a little stodgy, too set in our thinking. Kosnett here has already delivered a new outlook to many of our neighbors. Perhaps we should take advantage of the opportunity to make some changes in how things are done in the Empire. I look to *Dalou* as an example of what can be possible, when one looks forward, rather than wallowing in the past."

Phil wondered where he would have gone after that, but food and drink arrived just then, interrupting things. As a way to get your audience on the edge of their seats, Phil was hard pressed to think of a better example, as he and Zaman were both dangling painfully, but unable to comment.

He shared a glance of commiseration with the woman and settled himself for some coffee.

THIRTY-NINE

IMPERIAL FLAGSHIP GLANTHUA'S STAND, FORWARD LAAGER POINT

Kira wondered if burning slivers of bamboo, inserted under her fingernails and left there, would have been less painful.

Was her cousin toying with her now? Dragging her into the limelight just so he could torture her? He had promised change, but not until they returned to *Derragon*. Implicitly promised to admit that she was a relative.

Not just an embarrassment to one of his kinsmen.

She ate mechanically, because food had been put in front of her and there had been times when she was a child where there hadn't been enough food. Nobody starved in *Gloran*. A few came close.

Dishonor didn't help. Hadn't helped her mother's cousin who had been willing to take an orphaned waif in and protect her as much possible.

Kira had left at fourteen to let the woman return to something of her own life, remaining in touch as a niece who called whenever she was home long enough.

At one point as they ate dinner, Heather leaned gently into her shoulder, as though holding her upright. Nothing more. Human touch.

Gloran was not a touching culture. They did not hug. They were not tactile.

Kira drew strength from that simple act though, and made it through the main course. Managed to keep her head up when the two beings battling for her soul wanted her to either retreat entirely and flee, hiding in retirement where no one could find her, or challenge Adham Khan to personal combat, just so she had the memory of him either fleeing from her, or getting his ass kicked.

Either would keep her warm when she was an old woman.

She could not square that her cousin was going to acknowledge her. Not after everything. Perhaps accept her as an excellent commander. Cruiser-Captain of a penal force.

But truly accept her? Embrace her as the cousin everyone already whispered about?

Enough years of hope spurned had turned something sour in her soul and she could not envision it, even now.

Instead, she found herself wondering about the woman Nagarkar, who had transferred to the *Aquitaine* fleet and served in green and black. Or Lady Kugosu, poised at that same point where a young bastard cousin had put on the silver, black, and bronze of the penal forces to serve as much as they would allow her.

Maybe she would return to *Derragon* and remove the uniform for good. *Gloran* was no longer enough. Not the place she had grown up.

There were other lands she could visit. Other dreams she could chase.

Other navies where perhaps she could serve.

And Heather had leaned into her shoulder, as if she understood. Perhaps she had. Perhaps Kosnett had seen in the woman what others saw in Kira Zaman, and realized how powerful it could be.

Command Centurion Lau commanded his flagship. His

entire battlefleet. Even a notorious prick like Adham Khan had been brought to heel by the woman.

That also warmed Kira's soul.

Dessert had been cleared. Simple sweet pastries with dried fruit, but a treat nonetheless to a poor child on the wrong side of the palace wall.

Her cousin rose now, drawing all eyes and stilling tongues. He gestured everyone to remain seated, even as several were in motion to join him standing.

"This is not intended as a council of war, my friends," Adric called to the room. "All of you are already committed and need no goading on my part to do your duty. If anything, you teach me what duty means, considering everything each and every one of you has overcome to be here tonight."

Kira kept her face stern as various others glanced at her. *Gloran* captains tended to be hostile. *Aquitaine* friendly. Everyone here knew her story. Only a few would she count as allies, and almost every one of them in black and green.

"A crime has been committed," Adric continued harshly, letting his tones turn darker and drawing all the captains here closer.

Gloran had been insulted. *Aquitaine* knew outrage. *Aditi* would have hard answers to give before this was settled finally.

Adric paused there, looking one by one at every man and woman in here, going around the square until he finally landed on her and Kosnett.

"*Aditi* has the truth, one way or the other," Adric continued finally. "We are not sailing there for a war, but for answers. At the same time, they may object to the truth coming out. May deny and obfuscate. May even attack us for the audacity of asking. That, my friends, is the mark of desperation, not of honor. We could have sailed into one of their own lesser worlds and unleashed utter devastation, but we are going to their government for answers. For truth."

Kira wondered if everyone had stopped breathing, or just

her. Adric Kerenski was magnetic when he chose to use it. That was one of the reasons he had been chosen as Emperor.

He could make you *believe*.

"At the same time, there is always risk in war," Adric continued. "Accidents and casualties happen in war, even at the best of times. We are going to confront someone who may object violently to our mere presence, let alone our questions. With that in mind, it behooves your emperor to make some changes before we get there, lest it be too late later."

Oh. Fuck.

Kira listened as Adric pushed his chair out of the way and came to rest exactly standing behind Heather.

Between Kira Zaman and Adham Khan.

Heather was looking over her left shoulder, no doubt keeping Khan in her sights for a punch to the mouth from the way she was poised.

"At one time, it was whispered that Kira Zaman was a bastard of the Imperial House," Adric raised his voice to the rafters. Not just overriding the murmurs but crushing them. Conquering them. "Medical sciences have assured me that she is in fact a Kerenski, though no man has been willing to acknowledge that before today. We all know that one of us was responsible, but somebody was a coward."

He hung them there, waiting for silence to return. Kira noted the stewards hovering around the outer edge of the scene like raccoons at the edge of the firelight. Or mice.

All the wolves were warm by the fire itself.

"A case was made against Kira Zaman, when one of my commanders sought to have her brought in from the cold she had known all of her life," Adric called now in dark, heavy voice. "Adham Khan, you will rise."

Forty mouths gasping simultaneously made an ugly sound, like a ripe melon dropped from a third-story window onto a stone floor below to rupture hollowly.

Kira leaned and turned to watch her greatest nemesis stand.

No, second greatest. Somewhere, a kinsman of Adric Kerenski knew the truth and refused to admit it. Had refused for thirty-five years. Might have taken his lies to his grave, as many of her suspects were dead now.

Khan stood at parade rest before his Emperor, feet apart, hands clenched behind his back, head up as though expecting the man to rip the sash from his chest. To strike him down with fists or blades.

Like Khan deserved.

"Artak Khan counseled me to accept Kira Zaman, when he himself was rehabilitated into the fleet and promoted again," Adric called to the room. "At the time, he asked the favor of me, but his own son was still head of clan, and objected. Artak Khan bowed and withdrew the request. Have you spoken to your father since, Adham?"

"I have not, Your Majesty," Khan bowed. "Command Centurion Lau commanded me to send him a letter of apology, which I have done, but we have moved too quickly for a reply to come."

Kira looked around and realized that she wasn't the only one with their jaw hanging open. Even *Aquitaine* officers who knew Khan were stunned.

"The Command Centurion?" Adric asked, turning in surprise to Heather after looming over her. "Thank you."

Heather nodded but didn't speak. Kira wasn't sure she herself had words.

"What would you say about Frigate-Captain Zaman today, Cruiser-Captain Khan?" Adric turned his implacability back to the man.

"That I was wrong, Your Majesty," Khan admitted. Publicly. In front of his own peers. In front of the Empire and the galaxy. "That I was blinded by hubris and arrogance. That the old ways had served us well for centuries and should be hewed to in such a setting. That was a mistake then. It is a mistake now. My mistake. None other."

Kira wondered if her heart was about to explode, as it started racing madly, faster and faster.

"Cousin, Adham Khan admits to a failure of his judgment," Adric declared *putting a hand on her shoulder and publicly calling her **cousin***. "What do you say?"

Kira had to grab a glass and take a drink, because her mouth had gone entire dry. Others felt the same, from the number of hands suddenly reaching.

Kira put the glass down and pushed her chair back, rising to stand next to the taller man. She was eyeball level with Khan. Heather had turned her way now. She felt Kosnett's eyes on her back.

Five years ago, she'd have gladly seen Khan's blood on this deck. That was exactly what both men were offering her today. Khan's public dishonor. Payment for hers. Possibly his death.

Today?

Heather sat there between them like calmness itself. Kira drew strength from that. From the touch earlier that had been no more than a shoulder bump between friends.

Friends? Could she get away with that term? Except that Heather had gone out of her way, time and again, to accept Kira. To make sure men like Khan accepted her. To order a hotheaded, hardheaded fool like Adham Khan to apologize to his wronged father. And then get the man to actually do it.

"Something Lady Kugosu told me, when I met with her back at *Carinae IV*, comes to mind now," Kira found herself saying, almost automatically. "*Aquitaine* brings with it change. The old ways, as Khan noted, are just that. Old. Yesterday's solutions to yesterday's problems. If we are to be part of tomorrow with our various allies, things must change. Attitudes must change. Society itself must change. Adham Khan admits that his judgment was flawed, but only when seen through new eyes in this new future. He was right then. He is not right now, and acknowledges that."

She looked up at Adric and waited for some hint. Some clue

as what he wanted, before pronouncing doom on Khan. Whichever doom would be the most painful.

Kira wasn't sure which answer would hurt more at this point. She had already won.

They both turned to Khan instead.

"I did what I thought was right," Khan reminded everyone in a steady, if emotional voice. As if anybody didn't know that whole story. "It was not. The dishonor is mine entirely. What punishment would serve your will, your need, your Empire?"

Until this moment, Kira hadn't believed. Had not processed that Adric had been right. That Adham Khan was willing to fall on his own sword in public.

She could break the man. With just a word. Adric was literally offering her Khan's head on a platter if she wanted it.

Would it change anything about her past? Would it make her not an orphan at eight? Not a sailor at fourteen? Not a penal commander at thirty-four?

Nothing about her past could be changed. Nothing about Khan's, either. He had been driven by a chauvinistic vision of his honor. All of *Gloran* seemed to suffer from that, to the point that allowing any man to touch her physically had threatened to end Kira's career. Even a hint of pregnancy would have been sufficient grounds for those grouchy fools.

Lady Kugosu had been right. There was only the future. Only what she would make of herself, if she wasn't limited to what scraps her cousin's system would allow.

"You acknowledge my paternity, Adham Khan?" she asked in a voice loud enough that even the cooks probably heard her.

"I do, Kira Zaman, of the House of Kerenski," Khan bowed deeply to her.

Kira turned to Adric, her cousin. *Her cousin.*

"I am satisfied," she said simply.

Adric put a hand on her shoulder again and squeezed. She covered it with hers for a moment, then turned enough to lean some of her weight on Heather.

None of this would have been possible without the Command Centurion. Simple as that.

Kira turned again and took her seat, feeling the warmth of Kosnett's smile as she did. And the other command centurions. Even a few captains, however surprised and hesitant.

Khan sat at Adric's gesture, leaving only an Emperor standing.

"My friends, this is what honor means," he called in a voice heavy with emotion. "We have known it our entire lives, but rarely does it teach us new things. *Aditi* has forgotten. We go not to punish them, but to remind them, because we are in the right."

FORTY

DATE OF THE REPUBLIC MARCH 31, 412 RAN
URUMCHI, APPROACHING ADITI

Heather had Nam and Kohahu on the bridge with her today. Nam had earned a spot under the gunner, Hào Boyadjiev, supervising the Pulse-Two Gun Captains in what might be a battle against her own kith and kin. Kohahu was still learning, but had earned her spot for what she'd done to help Kira reach a mental and emotional breakthrough.

Fifteen soon, and teaching her elders how it was done. She'd be scary if she stuck with naval studies and commanded a warship in the Shogun's service before taking his place in another twenty years.

About the same age as Kira was now.

"Pilot, call the count," Heather said automatically as she watched the countdown timer that everybody had on their screens.

"Thirty seconds to Emergence, Command Centurion," Bozhidar replied in a formal voice.

"Iveta, you have Tactical, but we are in lockdown until provoked," Heather reminded the woman, and everyone else on the internal comm. "Phil's dropping us closer than *Gloran*, so that the locals are more inclined to talk than shoot. They may still shoot after talking."

Heads nodding. Everywhere they'd been until now, it had been iffy if anyone would escalate. *Ellariel-jo* had brought in three battleships, but they'd later admitted to nervousness on their part. Still, enough, considering that Phil hadn't brought all of his corvettes.

Unlike today.

The only ship missing right now was *Morninghawk* itself. *Forktail* had a chip on their shoulders about that. As they should. It was one of the highest bars to clear that Heather could think of.

Right up there with *Auberon*, *Vanguard*, and the Expeditionary forces Keller had taken to *Buran*.

Hell of a comparison. Accurate though.

"Emergence," Bozhidar called.

Some people claimed to feel like falling into or out of a warm bath at that instant. Heather felt it in her bones these days, a sharp spike of pain gone before it even registered, but enough to bring her out of a solid sleep, were she trying.

Icons started appearing on the screen as everyone emerged and checked in.

"*Aquitaine* squadron, this is Kosnett, aboard *Urumchi*," Phil's voice filled the airwaves. "I have the flag. All vessels stand by and maintain alert status until notified otherwise. Same as if we were back at *Ewin* that first time."

Heather counted the chuckles around her. Both times, they'd landed long and waited for trouble. Both times, trouble had found them, though only once had mattered.

About half a light-second behind her, more icons filled the screen as *Arteshbo* and her consorts appeared closest, with *Glanthua's Stand* behind them.

"Phil, we're being hailed by an extremely nervous Port Authority on channel seventeen," Leyla spoke up, face down on her screen and tracking anything and everything moving.

Heather flipped her screen to that channel and noted that Phil had left it open, but muted everyone but himself.

"Leyla, is *Gloran* able to follow things?" Heather asked.

"*Pixies* might have gotten involved," Leyla glanced up and grinned. "I can neither confirm nor deny such accusations."

As with weapons and JumpSails, the locals had a few things to learn about cryptography, though she was utterly loathe to let Harman explain himself to anybody outside this vessel. They might catch on at how easy he found it when he got bored.

Which was much of the time.

"*Aditi* Port Control, this is First Centurion Philip S. Kosnett of the *Republic of Aquitaine* Navy," he said in that special tone you only got when the man was angry. "I have come to consult with the *Consensus* Caucus. My forces will remain at anchor here until such time as they are available to chat."

"Leyla, what's the delay?" Heather asked.

"About two and a half light-seconds," she replied. "Just shy of three to the ground."

"You have brought a warfleet into *Aditi* orbit without notification, First Centurion," the woman on the line replied. Nervous. Maybe angry.

Darker skin than Kaur, but not much. Shorter hair. Rounder face. Big eyes.

"I brought two fleets, Port Control," Phil answered sharply. "These are extremely important questions."

And he left off the part where one of them was obviously a major *Gloran* sector fleet, with a vessel identifying itself as bearing the Imperial Flag itself.

Most serious questions.

"Current moorage coordinates noted, *Urumchi*," the woman at the other end said, when it finally dawned on her that things had gone well above her pay grade. Above almost everybody's pay grade. "Please maintain current heading and orbit until notified. I am contacting my superiors."

Phil muted the line from his end when the color band around the outside changed to dotted lines.

There weren't many folks above the Port Commissioner on

the other end of that line, if Heather was remembering uniforms correctly. Most of those were elected officials with pretty titles.

And dirty hands.

"Leyla," Iveta spoke up. "Tag every vessel in orbit and redband them as soon as anybody so much as moves. Any direction. Any reason. Not many high enough in the gravity well to Jump. I want to know anybody trying. I also want to know any military force moving."

"Understood," the Science Officer replied crisply.

Unnecessary order, in Heather's mind, but she supposed that Iveta was having class for Nam and Kohahu on how to handle Tactical on an *Aquitaine* warship.

Just in case either woman needed such personal knowledge later.

"Boss, I just got a heads up from my *Pixies*," Leyla called. "Ground just sent orders to *Aranyani* to break formation and head inward to rendezvous with *Khandoba* in low orbit."

"I'll handle it, Leyla," Phil said over the general line.

Heather nodded and started plotting locations of enemy cruisers and Ships of the Line.

Aditi might have just shown their hand.

FORTY-ONE
ADITI CRUISER ARANYANI

Kaur turned to Arya.
"Repeat that?" she said.
"Fleet Command just sent us an order to break formation, Kaur," Arya said. "Ordered us to move into a spot right in front of *Khandoba*'s squadron."
"Anything else with the message?" Kaur asked.
"An unspoken *or else* seemed prevalent," Arya looked up and scowled.
"Who signed it?" Kaur asked.
"Senior Director Parvez," Arya replied. "Oh, I have Phil calling. Stand by. Oh. Shit. You need to take this, maybe in your office."
"Negative," Kaur said. "If we're at that point in the game, all of you need to be aware of what is happening. Put him on my personal screen. Everyone listen."
"Hello, Kaur," Phil was there a moment later. "I'll explain later, but I've already read the orders Senior Director Parvez just transmitted. What are your plans?"
Phil had read them as fast as Arya had decrypted them? Had they broken the main *Consensus* codes? Oh, my.
"I had considered challenging his authority to issue such

orders, Phil," she replied instead, understanding what that would mean. "I'm currently attached to your command until removed. They can't have any reason to suddenly order me out except guilt. An acknowledgment on their part that they already know why I'm here."

"It's not worth your career to buck them right now, Kaur," Phil told her carefully.

"No, that's where you're wrong, Phil," she countered sharply. "It is exactly the oath we all took as officers, regardless of the uniform. As Emperor Kerenski notes. That's why I was at *Vilahana* that day when you arrived. Trying to do the right thing. Same goes here. Doubly so when the *Gloran* Emperor himself is willing to ask questions instead of just blowing things up. I want answers. They will supply them. If my career is worth anything, I'd like them to tell me exactly what that oath is supposed to be about."

"Understood," he said. "Given the circumstances, would you like to take the flag and handle these negotiations?"

Kaur wasn't the only one that gasped on her bridge. Phil was offering her the chance to go out in a blaze of glory if she wanted. But what was the alternative? With a quiet whimper?

She considered it for a long moment. Looked at the surprise on Arya's face. The shock on Indra Korrapati's, who had taken Nam's spot as Kaur's Weapons Officer. The determination on Jagadish Mishra's.

"Yes, Phil, I think it would be appropriate," Kaur replied.

Phil nodded and Kaur clicked the line that connected her with both the squadron as well as the entire *Gloran* fleet currently settled behind them.

"*Aquitaine* forces, this is Kaur Singh aboard *Aranyani*. I have the flag," she said simply. Sternly. Calmly, even, though her heart was racing. "Arya, open a line to Senior Director Parvez aboard the station. Stand by to retransmit the entire conversation unencrypted on Channel One."

Arya's jaw dropped open, but she could at least say later that she'd been following orders. Might get both of them arrested at the same time, but then again, it might not.

What was their oaths worth, after all?

Senior Director Parvez appeared. Kaur knew the face, but couldn't say she'd spoken more than a handful of words with the man in her life. Political commander, at the top of the scale where he met with the government rather than commanding ships or even fleets.

The image on her screen gave the impression of being tall and corpulent, as so many of them were when they got to that level. No longer working hard to stay in shape. Enjoying the fruits of their career.

In her head, Kaur only whispered quietly about the amount of corruption she'd mostly turned a blind eye to in her time. Five and ten percent deals under the table for such petty things as contracts to service warships in somebody's particular port station rather than another one. No-bid contracts.

Back scratching that didn't look all that impressive with the sorts of eyes Kaur brought to the field of battle today.

"You were given specific orders, Commander," he said bluntly. "Is there going to be a problem?"

On her various screens, no squadrons were currently maneuvering to become hostile. But then, nobody had been expecting this, and they'd outrun any messages if there had been a spy who could spill.

Still, blaze of glory.

"First Centurion Kosnett is currently seeking the whereabouts of the *Aditi* Light Strike Cruiser *Kartikeya*, Senior Director Parvez," Kaur replied in a flat, bureaucratic voice. "He has placed me in temporary command of this combined force. The First Centurion would like to ask the captain of that vessel some pointed questions. Perhaps read their flight logs. The *Gloran* Emperor has accompanied us today. He also has questions, which is an improvement over his original intentions.

Who would be the correct person to come aboard *RAN Urumchi* for such a conversation?"

She muted the line and just sat there, scowling. The lag was long enough that she could see the impact of her words in the way his nostrils flared angrily. Followed by a hint of concern in his eyes.

He stared at her for a few more seconds, possibly remembering that she was in the process of disobeying a direct order.

Or worse, ignoring it entirely. She had the flag today. That was for the entire, combined force. *Aditi* might have more warships in system and local orbit, but they were not currently organized in any manner to be a threat to Phil. Or the Emperor.

Trying to become such a threat was an admission, too.

This was as high as the stakes got, but she could just continue to broadcast everything in the clear. As she was doing. Phil was poised to unleash havoc. Angrily.

And Parvez knew the name *Kartikeya*. That much was obvious. His eyes didn't have the blankness of ignorance when he considered that name, like an innocent man would.

"You are disobeying an order, Singh," he tried instead, perhaps remembering how the conversation had started, all of twenty seconds ago.

"Yes," she admitted. "I'm willing to be Court Martialed over this, Senior Director. I will ask my associates to testify in open court. Demand it, as a matter of fact. Or we can just broadcast everything to the entire system, right now on every channel a ship like *Urumchi* is capable of overloading. You haven't answered my question."

She hit mute on her end so he didn't hear her growl. Not yet, anyway.

All of the *Gloran* captains and a great many of her friends had looked askance at her after the truth had come out. *Kartikeya* was an *Aditi* vessel, after all. Supposedly a friend.

Parvez glowered at her.

"You can come aboard the station and we'll talk," he snapped.

"No," Kaur snapped back. "You and whoever else can come aboard *Urumchi*. Or *Glanthua's Stand*. I haven't asked Adric Kerenski which he ship would prefer. It was his world that was attacked. He may demand that you attend him on his flagship. Phil Kosnett offers neutral ground. At least for now."

As in, Phil might decide that he has to take sides in this matter. You probably wouldn't like that outcome, either. You might come to regret a great many things, if you decide to make Phil Kosnett your enemy, because he's made friends with the entire rest of the Cluster.

Somebody off-screen at that end had obviously waved a hand to get his attention, because Parvez's face turned that way. Sound stopped as they muted so he could be told something.

His scowl turned a little white. Then a lot white. Like maybe somebody important had called on another line. Or been listening and wanted to know more about why *Kartikeya* was an important enough name that the *Gloran* Emperor was personally involved.

"Stand by, *Aranyani*," he said abruptly. "We will get back to you shortly."

And he cut the line from his end.

Phil was back a moment later in the internal line.

"Nicely done, Commander," he said. "Subtle. Threatening without being threatening. Penetrating in the right quarters, and problem-causing in others because folks will want to know more."

"Do we expect a reply quickly?" she asked.

"No," he shook his head. "I think we've opened the perfect can of worms for them to have to deal with for now. I expect that folks will need to talk for a bit. I would recommend that ships stand down one alert level and start rotating crew members on watch shifts."

"You would recommend?" Kaur asked, confused.

"You have the flag, *Aranyani*," he smiled. "What are your orders?"

Oh. That's right. She had the flag.

"I think you should take over at this point," Kaur replied.

"Gladly," Phil said, cutting over to another line.

"This is Kosnett, I have the flag," Phil said. "All vessels move to your orders for holding pattern for now, while we await developments."

Kaur breathed out heavily. She'd just committed the most polite mutiny she could think of. And even threatened her superiors over an open line. But it had been worth it.

She had upheld her oath.

Let the rest of them say that.

FORTY-TWO
CONSENSUS CAUCUS CHAMBER

Roshni Mishra had managed to retain her rank and position in the government as Herald, perhaps third in overall rank to Speaker Jasvinder Mhasalkar, through all the complicated maneuvering that had arrived with the *Aquitaine* fleet and beyond. Jasvinder's *Bhavishy* Party had the most seats in the Assembly, with her *Prakaash* small enough to only be a distant second place. Too small if she decided to see which of the small parties would support her in a small palace revolution.

For what it was worth.

The Caucus itself was in session now, sixteen faces around a table with nobody but a few personal aides allowed in the room.

Jasvinder had his beloved gavel in hand. All eyes were currently turned to Administrator for War, Avinash Bachchan of the *Vyaapaar Vaayu* Party. He was almost a legacy hire at this point, having held the job through three and a half administrations because nobody could ever agree on a replacement for the man.

That might have been a mistake. If the words coming out of his mouth right now were even half-true, he'd screwed up badly. Bachchan finished explaining what he'd done and rattled down to empty.

"So," Jasvinder snarled angrily as Bachchan wound down. "In your infinite wisdom, you annihilated a *Gloran* colony, just as Kosnett's forces were preparing to visit *Derragon?*"

It even sounded like Jasvinder hadn't given such an order, but Roshni couldn't imagine that dinosaur going that rogue.

"It's not the first time we've done so," Bachchan snarled back just as viciously. "Don't get sanctimonious with me, Mhasalkar. You've been involved in the other such raids we've sanctioned. Or hired pirates to commit. All of you, as a matter of fact. There are no clean hands in this room."

Roshni felt the rage that those two men broadcast and considered how it would look when somebody leaked the details of this meeting.

Someone always leaked. It was almost a competitive sport, to see if you could get the best press for your side or to cast some enemy in the worst light possible.

She wasn't sure how much uglier this one could get.

Roshni let the silence hang as people muttered at each other, and flashed back to a meeting she'd had with Jasvinder and the Assembly's Sergeant at Arms, Nilima Chaudhary, back when Kosnett had first come to speak to the Assembly and the *Consensus*.

She had warned both of them then that the time had come to clean up their acts. To divest entirely from their various under-the-table shenanigans and prepare to face a situation where criminal corruption wasn't going to be acceptable.

Apparently, they hadn't listened.

She leaned forward as the two men continued their staring contest, her motion breaking the stalemate and drawing eyes to her instead. As intended.

Jasvinder had held the Speakership for almost a decade, making deals and swapping governing alliances as votes moved things around. It helped that his *Bhavishy* Party tended to lean towards the same cultural conservatism that propelled the *Consensus* most days.

Most days.

This felt different. And ugly.

"Why?" Roshni asked simply, eyes moving back and forth between the two men.

"What do you mean?" Bachchan demanded angrily.

"You obviously had a reason to do this," she said patiently. "To order this attack. What was your logic? Or is it that you simply didn't expect anyone to put the pieces together?"

"We've already reinforced the sector capital at Voida," Bachchan snapped. "They'd have hit someplace like Niani or Ikrilph, according to our calculations. Nowhere important."

"Why?" she pressed. "You've just explained how prepared you were, not why you provoked *Gloran*."

"To distract them," Jasvinder interjected with exasperation. "To make *Gloran* angry. Not thinking straight. The pirates make an excellent foil for such a thing."

"There are no more pirates, Jasvinder," Roshni replied tartly. "Kosnett broke them."

"There are still some running around," he said.

"No," she shook her head. "If you'd actually read any of the intelligence papers, or paid attention in the weekly briefings, you'd know better. *Kosnett broke them*. All of them. Maybe you have bandits, but even then, could you have picked a dumber patsy than *Hamath Syndicate*?"

"What?" the Speaker roared at her. "They must be made to take the blame."

"Why?" she returned to the question that seemed to do the best job of getting under people's skin today.

"Do you know what that woman is doing?" he demanded.

"Which woman are we talking about this time?" Roshni asked. "There are a lot of women involved in this situation."

"She's in orbit right now!" he snarled. "With Kosnett!"

"That barely narrows the field."

"*Hollywood* Ward," he finally said. "The woman is building a new communication network with Kosnett's blessing!"

"Why is that a problem?" Roshni asked. "Did she turn down a demand for a bribe or something for an operating license? Or do you see her as competition for something you wanted to do instead?"

Oh, that was an interesting reaction.

Roshni had known Jasvinder for more than two decades at this point. Knew how to get to him. When she wanted to, which wasn't often.

If he ever realized where his weak spots were, Jasvinder might do something about them, after all.

"She can't be allowed!" Bachchan interjected into the row, like maybe those two were up to something and had perhaps forgotten to tell everyone else about it?

Not the first time.

"It's Kosnett's operation," Roshni replied with a purring smile that she extended to the rest of the Caucus, just to see which way those folks were leaning right now.

Egomaniacs, the lot of them. Herself included, as she wasn't that rude to suggest otherwise. Most of them, however had their petty grifts and official hands in cookie jars that kept them fat, happy, and rich.

Jasvinder Mhasalkar had too solid a grip on power to be unseated.

Or did he? She started counting noses and noticed that a tide had shifted at some point in the last few minutes.

Wavering.

Dangerous waters.

"Kosnett will be gone soon," Jasvinder snapped. "Whatever promises he made to a bunch of pirates can go right out the airlock with him."

Roshni considered the monumental stupidity contained in that sentence. Grand even by Jasvinder's normal standards.

"So you poked *Gloran* to keep his attention occupied?" she asked him, walking some of the others slowly through logic that might be too complicated for them. Depending on how drunk they might be at this moment.

"That's right," Bachchan replied. "Like usual. The only difference was that there were no pirates immediately available for hire, so we did it ourselves."

"And you don't see where that might be a problem?"

"What's he going to do?" Jasvinder demanded. "Attack us? Start a general war with *Aditi*? Of course not. Kosnett would never allow it!"

"Really?" she asked, ladling on the sarcasm so thick she might end up with it all over her hands. "Then why are they both overhead right now with full battle fleets?"

About half the room gasped. Not always the brightest. Here to protect their holdings and their various party's interests, rather than really govern. Jasvinder kept most of them bought off with Administrator positions or slush funds.

"Attack us?" Bachchan roared. "We'll destroy them!"

"Like King Doysan did at *Ewinhome?*" she countered. "That was only part of Kosnett's fleet, along with a much smaller squadron of Kalidoona's ships. This is everyone. And Kerenski brought more than twenty ships. Granted, some of them small, but still…"

She leaned back just so she could watch the two men squirm a little. Mutterings around the table turned into yammering and accusations as she listened.

Jasvinder finally had to slam his precious gavel down to get people to shut up.

"Why is Kosnett here?" Roshni asked as Jasvinder drew a breath to start lying again. "Why is Kerenski?"

And the noise started up again. Noses scenting the wind shifting and maybe starting to tack against it.

If they could.

"We can bring more force than they can possibly withstand!" Bachchan roared over all of it.

"So?" Roshni sneered at the man. "Isn't that as good as

admitting that you ordered an active duty fleet cruiser to annihilate a *Gloran* colony while planting evidence that the *Hamath Syndicate* did it? What's everybody else going to say?"

"Who cares what they think?" Jasvinder roared just as loudly as Bachchan now. "They'll ignore us and maybe pile on if we decide to start attacking *Gloran* worlds. *Dalou* is always looking for loot."

"Are you even listening to yourself, Mr. Speaker?" Roshni roared back at him. "Do you hear what you just said? *Dalou*, expansive? Since when?"

"*Urwel*, for example!"

"*Urwel*?" Roshni leaned into the verbal blow with a harsh laugh. "Their own world where they've finally decided to build a trade station? That *Urwel*?"

Jasvinder blinked. Maybe something in his brain short-circuited. It was hard to tell.

"Or did you think that maybe *Yaumgan* would see an opportunity to slice worlds off a frontier that they have held tenaciously for more than a century?" She pursued him like a wounded buck. That was what he was. Roshni could almost smell blood in the air. "Or *Ewin*, where Kosnett just crushed part of their fleet and signed treaties of trade and friendship? All of them have, by the way. If you started a war right now, I'd be more willing to believe that everyone else would be on Kosnett's side. Didn't Kaur Singh tell Parvez to get stuffed when he ordered her to break ranks? What do you think Kosnett has up there? All of the nations of the Cluster, including the pirates, former pirates, whatever. Hell, the Crown Prince of *Dalou* is aboard *Storm Petrel* with Kosnett's force. The apparent heir to the Shogunate is aboard *Urumchi*. Are you people all morons? You're going to start a war with *Gloran*, at the precise moment when Kosnett has everyone on his side!"

Jasvinder had to hammer the table hard enough that his precious gavel might have broken. Certainly, at some point the pitch of the banging changed.

Roshni looked at the others around the table and felt the wind shift again. Jasvinder was breathing so hard you might think he'd just run a marathon, though as fat as the man was, just walking to one of his mistresses' bedroom might be too much effort some days.

Just another reason Roshni kept her body in shape. It helped with the mind as well. Saved her from doing stupid things like not realizing the galaxy had changed.

"Did you decide to start a war with *Gloran* and possibly *Aquitaine* and the rest of the Cluster for any reason besides greed and personal stupidity, Jasvinder?" she asked in the deadly calm that had finally fallen.

Up until now, he might have thought he could get away with it. Or blame someone else.

Gasps. All the way around. Government-breaking gasps.

"And what are you going to do about it?" he demanded.

Roshni considered. Counted noses around her. Wondered about leaks to the news reporters no doubt already baying for a story.

The ancient term was *Le Beau Geste*. The Grand Gesture. Usually stupid. Frequently suicidal.

Always glorious. Especially counting those noses. And feeling the wind in her hair, at least metaphorically.

"Mister Speaker, the *Prakaash* Party can no longer support the government," she said formally. "Shortly, I will be tabling a motion of No Confidence and demanding an open, public discussion and vote on the matter."

She leaned back, smiling as everything erupted in noise yet again. Jasvinder's gavel broke off in his hand this time. She liked that symbolism. Maybe she would campaign on it, as this was likely to lead to early elections, one way or the other.

Broken gavels, broken promises. Yes, that would do nicely on a campaign poster.

She'd warned them to clean up their act. *Prakaash* had. Apparently *Bhavishy* and *Vyaapaar Vaayu* hadn't.

Looking around, both representatives of *Pahaad Aur Baadal*, the Mountains and Clouds Party, were nodding. Her own people were solidly behind her. A few party rebels in *Bhavishy* might see this as their chance to evict Jasvinder from his role as Party leader that he had held so long. Maybe she could quietly encourage a few Turks to go after Bachchan as well.

Kosnett had laid it out clearly. *Aditi* could be on the right side of history tomorrow.

Or the wrong one.

FORTY-THREE

DATE OF THE REPUBLIC MARCH 31, 412 RAN URUMCHI, ORBITING ADITI

Phil had retired to his office to get some work done, with Markus outside, probably reading. Unlike vid shows, things never happened quickly when politics occurred. Even major fleet engagements that only took up a few pages on paper usually ran hours of realtime when you looked closely at the event log, with long stretches of maneuvering and such between actual action.

So he looked up sharply when the hatch opened unannounced. Markus stood there with a tablet in one hand, immediately stepping to the other side of the desk and handing the device to Phil.

"You need to see this live," he said as the hatch closed.

Then the big lug sat down in the chair and leaned back. Must be good. Markus was usually a little more spit and polish than that. Most of the time.

Okay, sometimes.

Phil looked down at the machine. Video poised for play. Looked like something broadcast from *Aditi* on public airwaves. Trust Markus to have picked up a gadget like that when he was here last. Probably had several, so he could take them apart and study the innards.

Markus was like that, too.

Phil hit play and watched the woman newsreader stare into the camera with haunted eyes.

"Breaking news from the Capital, in case you are just joining us," she said in that breathless way that they all had mastered by the time they got promoted to the cushy job. "The *Prakaash* Party has broken with the government and announced a vote of No Confidence, to be held tomorrow. Spokespeople from *Pahaad Aur Baada* and *Van* Parties have also put out statements in the last hour that they will support *Prakaash*. Furthermore—wait, I have an update. We're about to go live to our reporter in the field for a special scoop."

The screen cut and Phil recognized Roshni Mishra now. He even recognized her office, deep in the bowels of the capital building itself.

"This is Ashwin Kulkarni," a young man appeared in the screen. "I'm currently talking with Herald of the Assembly Roshni Mishra in her office, regarding her statements about no longer supporting the government of Jasvinder Mhasalkar. Madam Herald?"

The camera shifted around to Roshni again, looking almost triumphant in the way she seemed to glow.

Phil assumed that somebody had turned their back on the woman at the wrong moment and gotten a knife in the kidneys. She had never come off as a bad person, but a smooth operator and a deadly foe.

"Thank you, Ashwin," she said, turning those dark, charismatic eyes to the camera like she was already in a campaign commercial.

Maybe she was. If she was voting against her own government, there would likely be snap elections pretty quickly. Phil wondered if Mhasalkar would stay on as a custodian, like usually happened in *Aquitaine* elections.

Then his mind flashed back to the Horvat Affair that had brought down the government back home. And gotten a number of people thrown in prison for a long time for what was adjudicated as treason at the time.

Phil had had more than a little involvement in such a thing. He supposed that he might bear some responsibility here.

Of course, if politicians stopped doing bad things under the table, they wouldn't have to worry about police coming to arrest them when it all came out.

Roshni had paused just long enough to spike the camera. Looking like a Speaker should? Maybe.

"I have just come from an Emergency Meeting of the Assembly Caucus," she said, like it was an announcement rather than an interview, but Phil wasn't sure it wasn't. "Certain details that heretofore had been unknown to me were brought to the attention of the Caucus. Tomorrow, I will be introducing them without security clearance to the Assembly itself, as part of the explanation for why *Prakaash* is no longer supporting the government and will be moving into the opposition immediately. There will be a vote of no confidence at that time under extraordinary circumstances."

"Will the government fall?" the reporter asked, breathless with anticipation that he had the inside scoop.

Phil wondered if the *Aditi Consensus* was about to come apart on him. Or just finally grow up and stop acting like bullies to all their neighbors.

Nice enough folks, but he wouldn't trust any of them with his last beer, as the ancient saying went.

"That is up to Jasvinder at this point," Roshni said with the kind of smile that a shark would have been jealous of. "Based on the outcome of the meeting, I and my people will have nothing to do with it. I believe that many other parties will feel the same way. When the news comes out, I wonder if his own party will continue to support him. Or Administrator for War, Avinash Bachchan of the *Vyaapaar Vaayu* Party."

Phil heard the gasp from the reporter and nodded to himself.

Roshni was about to play hardball. She'd impressed the shit out of him on that topic when he'd first met her.

"Madam Herald, can you give my viewers some clue as to what information you will be introducing into the public record tomorrow?" Ashwin Kulkarni asked now.

"Certainly," she said now, somehow finding yet another level to dial up her smile and intensity. "Put simply, the government of Jasvinder Mhasalkar, in the person of Administrator for War Bachchan, ordered the attack on the Gloran *Carinae II*, one that destroyed the colony. We have the evidence, and will make it public tomorrow. That's all I really have for now. Thank you."

Boom.

He looked up at Markus, noted the wide eyes on the man.

"Get Harinder in here," he said.

Markus moved instantly, standing and opening the hatch. Harinder happened to be almost there from the other side.

"He already knows," Markus said, sliding out and to one side as Harinder entered.

"Shit," Harinder said from the doorway.

Phil handed her the tablet.

"Get that video transmitted to everyone in both squadrons immediately," he ordered. "Just in case somebody wasn't monitoring the right channel. Then contact *Glanthua's Stand* and ask the Emperor to stand by for a day so we can see how it all shakes out."

"Government falling?" she asked.

"Horvat Affair, all over again, maybe," he nodded. "You remember how that went down, so prep everyone here. Iveta can be extra paranoid for a day or two, but I don't think we're at risk. Still, maybe we should back off some, like it was *Ewinhome* below us, just so we don't get caught up in the collateral damage. Careers just ended over that admission on Mishra's part."

"Phil, people are likely to go to prison for that," Harinder countered.

"All the more reason to let them sort it out themselves," he said. "Getting that out in the open and making them deal with it means that they might take the opportunities to clean up some other things. Possibly even sweep out a lot of those old farts and bring in some new blood. Creator knows the *Consensus* needed something like that, even before this. I just need for Kerenski to not decide that he needs an extra kilo of flesh over this as well."

"I'll talk to the War-Captain and see what they think," Harinder nodded. "And brief folks. You want to make a statement in an hour or so, once we all start listening to the planetary news along with everybody else?"

"Yes," Phil agreed. "And let Kerenski know that he might want to address the joint force at that time as well. I doubt he'll have anything to say to the ground or the Assembly at this point, but I'll keep our options open."

"The Emperor address the Assembly in open session?" Harinder asked sharply.

"Not until I know what he'll say," Phil smiled. "At the same time, it might ratchet things down a few levels. There have to be a lot of folks a little twitchy right now, with this much potentially hostile firepower in orbit."

"Understood."

She stepped back and closed the hatch. He located Heather and opened a line to her quarters once he knew she was awake and relaxing.

"What's up?" she asked as she came on the line.

"Mishra just admitted on the local news that *Aditi* did it," he said. "Harinder has the video going out to everyone. You and Iveta stay on rotating shifts for now, in case I need one of you with Tactical on no warning, but that's paranoia, not concern."

"We here for a few days and then withdraw to *Carinae*?" she said.

"Or *Derragon*," Phil nodded. "Kerenski has to decide if bringing down the *Consensus* government will be enough, or if he wants to go after the *Consensus* itself."

"We likely to help, if he does?" Heather asked.

"Not if he shoots first," Phil clarified. "If *Aditi* does, they probably have it coming."

"Good enough," she said.

Phil cut the line and leaned back to think.

He'd come in expecting to have to have nasty, public arguments with folks. Folks who might have forgotten that *Aditi* was only a nice place on the surface of things. And like the others, the presence of *Aquitaine* seemed to be a catalyst to break loose a lot of old friction.

First Lord Naoumov had given him those secret orders to make sure that the entire cluster was brought forward, technologically as well as socially and politically, because at the end of the day she couldn't definitively say that Denis Jež was wrong. That the Republic would never fall and transform into *Imperial Aquitaine*.

Phil wasn't so sure. No, that was a lie. He was almost positive, but that it wouldn't really happen in his lifetime.

Unless there was a way to watch frogs being boiled so slowly that nobody noticed. Was that what Denis had seen?

Phil remembered things back when he'd joined the fleet out of Academy, about the time that Jessica Keller had started making a name for herself as the greatest commander of her generation. Back when overall fleet command had been split between the Noble Lords and the Fighting Lords, a split partly reflecting the origins of the officers of said fleet, when about half had come from the so-called Fifty Families that really made up the social and cultural elite of the Republic.

The other half had been folks like him, Jež, and Keller. Middle- and lower-class kids with aptitude and dreams.

Kasum had broken the power of the Noble Lords. Removed a great many of them from power. Horvat had accidentally helped that, because so many of the folks that had gone down with him at the time had also been those sorts of folks.

That left a lot of aggressive ones behind. In command, with

CONSENSUS

Keller and her squadron all retired for good now, getting on with their lives.

That also left people like Phil to try to read the tea leaves of history and make smart choices now, because they might not play out in his lifetime.

If he was lucky.

The future of the galaxy might come down to Adric Kerenski at this point.

FORTY-FOUR

IMPERIAL FLAGSHIP GLANTHUA'S STAND, ADITI PLANETARY ORBIT

Adric was back in his cabin, ruminating. The hatch chimed and he rose to answer it, finding both A.Q. Tanel and Kira Zaman standing there. The former was to be generally expected. The latter was a surprise he found welcome, which startled him even more.

Adric gestured them in and walked back to his chair. The others followed and closed the hatch. He pointed at the chair. Kira took it. A.Q. dragged another one close. They sat, though it took her a moment of hesitation.

"There is news, Adric," A.Q. said without preface.

Kira looked a little shocked, but Adric supposed that she was used to the pomp and ceremony of the Empire, having never before been admitted into the sorts of rooms where actual policy was made.

That needed to change, since she was his cousin. Officially.

She had the Kerenski eyes, after all.

"Talk to me," Adric replied.

"*Urumchi* sent us a package not too long ago," A.Q. said. "Video feed captured from a local news channel. Interview with Roshni Mishra."

"The Herald?" Adric asked.

"The same," A.Q. nodded. "She basically admitted that the *Consensus* ordered the attack on *Carinae II*. Said that tomorrow, local time, she would be voting no confidence in the government and making everything public."

"What's the reaction on the ground been since?" Adric asked.

"Bedlam on all channels," A.Q. grinned now. "I wouldn't have believed it, but Kosnett knows these people in a year better than we did in a lifetime. I've had all my captains on maximum alert with orders to able to unleash every weapon possible on five seconds' notice since we dropped out. Kosnett just waltzed in and everything fell apart without a shot fired."

"Without a shot fired by us," Adric corrected him. "I've met Mishra diplomatically a few times. Hard woman. Mean, when she has to be."

He turned to Kira and his brain registered that she was still wearing the silver uniform shirt of the Penal Fleet rather than the gold he and A.Q. had on. He'd need to change that, along with a lot of other things, when he got home.

Hell, did he need to even maintain that whole second navy? And who was this weirdo even contemplating such radical suggestions?

"Kira, I'm sorry I haven't fixed your uniform yet," Adric said simply. "This might be a perfect time for you to become a personal representative of the crown, talking with the fools on the planet below us."

"Send me in silver anyway," she replied calmly. "You can put me in gold later, with an official announcement. We don't necessarily have time for that now, if all this is true."

Adric nodded. She was not wrong.

"We'll know tomorrow?" He turned his attention back to A.Q.'s face.

"Maybe before then," the man replied. "I suspect that Mhasalkar is busy polling all his friends overnight down there. If Mishra went public like that, she just became the government's enemy, and the Speaker might be bleeding more votes than he can afford right now. They might boot him in the morning, then ask someone like Mishra to call elections while she's caretaker instead of him."

"It's not enough," Adric said.

"Didn't figure it would be, Adric," A.Q. replied. "At the same time, Kosnett was the one who came here to demand answers, and we came along to help, rather than the other way around. What's he going to do? Remember, he was the one pissed off enough to arrive uninvited and maybe expecting a hostile reception. We're just a lot of extra guns if they choose to get rude about it."

"This was a crime, A.Q.," Adric decided. "Kosnett's word, but it fits. This was not an act of warfare. This was cold-blooded murder. I want scalps. At the same time, maybe they can be individuals, if *Aditi* is willing to throw the masterminds to the wolves like us."

"It still doesn't rebuild *Carinae*," Kira spoke up sharply. "We all assume that the people who disappeared were all murdered afterwards, rather than sold into some sort of slavery, but there have to be answers there as well. Maybe a few did survive. And the *Consensus* need to make *Carinae* right. Either they rebuild it, or they pay for the reconstruction."

"You think they would?" A.Q. asked sharply.

"I think Kosnett might make them, if they wanted to stay on his good side," she replied. "As you said, we're observers to his mission. He wants justice. What does that look like? What does it taste like?"

Adric leaned back. He didn't know.

At the same time, he really didn't know Kosnett all that well. Still, he had a connection there, considering Kira and Heather Lau.

"Kira, you take charge of this," he said. "All of it. Become my personal representative, right here, right now. Contact *Urumchi* and go aboard as soon as you can. Talk to the

Command Centurion and Kosnett and get their assessment. We need more than a simple apology here, but less than a war with the *Consensus*. I wasn't expecting anything like this, so I'm not really prepared to immediately move to the next stage of whatever is going on. Plus, the *Consensus* will need a day or three to sort themselves out. We might even need to withdraw most of our squadron while that happens."

She'd gone a little white around the edges, but Adric supposed that wasn't unexpected. A month ago, she'd been his chief troubleshooter, even in silver, because that was the best he could do for her at the time. At least without starting a revolution at home that he hadn't been prepared to wage.

Good thing it had gone ahead and shown up on his doorstep in the form of *RAN Urumchi*, then, wasn't it?

"Most?" Kira asked carefully.

"I feel comfortable leaving *Arteshbo*, *Mardonius*, and *Darius* here," he smiled now. "Don't I always send you to get things done, cousin?"

She blushed at his words, but that was fine. He and most of the rest of her cousins owed her for a lifetime of unnecessary pain and suffering as an outcast.

Unnecessary. Adric might even go back to the scientists and see if there was a way to narrow down her parentage. They'd never bothered before, when her mother had refused to say anything about a child with Kerenski eyes.

Maybe there was another crime Adric needed to have a long discussion with someone about. Her father, if he was still alive.

"In silver?" she confirmed.

"Only because I don't have time to make it gold with the sorts of pageantry you deserve, Kira," Adric nodded. "Take Tikka and Vaishya in silver as well, just to make an extra statement. I suspect that I need to fix that when I get home as well, but it won't be done with the snap of my fingers. Too much that needs to be prepared before silver uniforms disappear for good."

"For good?" she gasped.

A.Q., too.

"For good," he nodded. "Command Centurion Lau got Adham Khan to publicly admit he was wrong about something. Adric Kerenski can do no less. If *Aquitaine* promises a new future to those who are willing to grasp it, then *Gloran* needs to be there with *Dalou* and *Ewin* when it happens. *Aditi* can rot for all I care, as long as they do apologize and make things right. You and Kosnett need to tell me what right is."

She blinked rapidly. Possibly a bit overwhelmed, but that would be a temporary thing. She would probably have processed and be ready before she left his cabin. Kira Zaman was like that. That was why he sent her to do things.

The woman got shit done.

"Now," he rose, gesturing. "You two plot things out and make them happen, understanding that I'll support you. Get Kosnett and Lau to sign off on it. Maybe even demand a new peace treaty between *Gloran* and *Aditi* like *Dalou* signed with *Ewin*. I've read it and it doesn't really commit everyone to anything but behaving and working towards a future of trade and friendship. If you can arrange meetings with the Kugosu daughter, we can sign that same sort of treaty with *Dalou* as well. Hell, even the threat of that boxes the *Consensus* in pretty hard, because that's three of their frontiers now aligned against them. Or trading without them."

A.Q. had risen slower than Kira, but his mouth fell open faster. They both stood there slack-jawed for a long moment.

"Go," Adric ordered, shooing them to the hatch and out.

Alone, he returned to his tea. It was still warm, even.

He sat and ruminated. Kosnett was a blunt instrument. A ten-kilo maul swung overhead. Lau was a shiv, getting in where you didn't even know you had gaps in your armor.

Deadly combination. He could see how they'd drawn the rest of the Cluster into their wake. *Dalou* had even sent both a

Crown Prince and a potential Shogun to keep watch on Kosnett. And learn from him.

Hell, even the pirates were here in an official capacity. *Hamath Syndicate* and everything.

Adric considered his current situation. Yes, it was good.

He rose and keyed the comm.

"Bridge, Povoloi," the Fleet-Captain replied instantly.

"I want to talk to the woman called *Hollywood*," Adric said.

FORTY-FIVE

ABOARD FLAGSHIP URUMCHI, ADITI ORBIT

She was always going to be *Hollywood* Ward, but the piracy side of things was fading even more rapidly than Kim had ever imagined it might. She was in a conference room with Lau, Lady Kugosu in her official capacity, and Frigate-Captain Zaman of *Gloran*.

Nobody else. Not even Phil or Harinder, bizarre as that seemed.

But Lau was in charge. Nobody had any doubts about that.

"Should Kaur Singh be here?" Kugosu asked as they settled.

"Not until we know what *Aditi* intends to do about the news yesterday and the politics today," Lau replied. "That bombshell has only begun to cause collateral damage, and Kaur isn't deputized to make deals. Not like the three of you."

Hollywood nodded. She wasn't Dexter's official heir. At least not yet. Maybe his right hand. Minister of Trade and Communications, once his government actually got their shit together well enough to have such formality. Maybe even diplomats, though not today.

Today, she had her network of ships racing madly around carrying news from capitals to *Meerut*. They hadn't even had time to start establishing lateral spokes. Just hubs back and forth.

Kosnett had suggested anchoring all lines with a hub out of *Aditi*, but she was more inclined to move her base of operations no farther than *Urwel* at this point. That let her hit three sides quickly, once she got three old Pickets trained up and operating.

Aditi was going to be a mess.

"So why are we here?" *Hollywood* found herself asking. "I mean, I understand that Kerenski specifically asked me to attend. And to come to *Derragon* with everyone, but he didn't give me a lot more details than that."

"Kira has most of it," Lau replied, nodding to the Frigate-Captain in the silver stripes of the Penal Fleet. An acknowledged cousin, at that.

"*Aditi* has screwed up on a grand scale," Zaman spoke slowly. "The First Centurion came here to demand answers of the *Consensus*. None of us were expecting a palace coup, which is really what Mishra's work amounts to. My cousin demands more than an apology, but less than a war with *Aditi*. He has tasked me with talking to Heather and the First Centurion for answers. He wants you here, *Hollywood*, because you will bring trade."

"Me?" *Hollywood* recoiled. "I'm in the communication business."

"And that means that news will travel," Zaman nodded. "People will travel, seeking their fortunes, if the pirates are gone and the Five Nations are starting to open their economies up to others. *Dalou* broke that dam open by signing a deal with *Ewin*. The Emperor has tasked me with negotiating something similar binding *Dalou* and *Gloran*. That secures borders and facilitates trade."

"I have one ship running to *Derragon* right now," *Hollywood* replied. "That's a long flight to *Meerut* and back."

"Indeed," Zaman replied. "I wish to see if we can work a deal for one of your ships to run directly to *Aditi*, and a second one to either *Ellariel* or the nearest sector capital."

"*Urwel* too far?" *Hollywood* asked.

"*Urwel*?" Zaman was lost.

"Lord Morninghawk has established a formal *Dalou* colony not far from *Toulouse* and *Belamel*," Lau spoke up now. "Phil is working with Kim to create a triangular communications run between those worlds, connecting *Ewin*, *Aditi*, and *Dalou*."

"Kim?" Zaman asked, more lost.

"*Hollywood*," Lau said. "Her real name is Kimberly Ward. *Hollywood* is a much longer and more interesting story, but you probably need to get her a little drunk first to hear the good parts."

Kim blushed. She'd only been a little tipsy. And comfortable talking to Lau about certain things.

"Oh," Zaman said. "In that case, I am Kira. It is a pleasure to make your formal acquaintance, Kim."

Kim nodded and smiled.

"*Urwel*, huh?" Kira asked.

"Faster, if you wanted to get information to *Ewin* and *Dalou*, I think," Kugosu spoke up. "Possibly *Aditi* as well, considering that anything fed in at the top has a tendency to take a while to get to the frontiers, whereas things can be absorbed upwards quickly. Plus, that helps anchor things, at least until we have a better treaty understanding of how everyone will deal with *Vilahana* and whatever *Dalou* does."

Kim turned to the youngest woman in the room. At least by age. Still one of the sharpest wheelers and dealers Kim had dealt with. But if you grew up in that sort of world, it was probably required.

"So, I need two contracts then," Kira said. "One for a new run to *Urwel*. The other a treaty like you have with *Ewin*. Maybe a third that lets us collaborate on founding or building out colonies around *Vilahana* where they take a narrower view of law and order."

All four of them laughed at that. *Vilahana* had a reputation Cluster-wide as a chop shop where anything was possible if money was on the barrel top first.

"Joint colonies?" Kugosu asked. "And before I forget, I am Kohahu."

Kim and Kira both nodded and smiled. Felt more and more like a social thing. One that just happened to be altering the center of gravity in the Cluster. Like Kosnett had threatened to do.

"Joint colonies, yes," Kira said. "Neither of us have much experience with that sort of thing, being more centrally run and administered than *Aditi*. And I'd rather not ask *Aditi* to get involved as yet. They have to earn my trust at this point, and Adric Kerenski has put me charge, rather like you, Kohahu."

Kim had a momentary spike where she wondered if Kira Zaman might be the next Emperor after Kerenski. Hadn't ever happened, but there was nothing in their laws against it. Just their culture. Same as *Dalou*.

Kohahu would be an interesting role model then, flipping things on their heads.

No, Heather was the role model that all of them were striving to emulate. Even Kim.

"I'm happy to talk about a deal," Kim told them both. "Kosnett has been funding me to this point, along with a few folks back at *Meerut*. *Ewin* isn't ready to do anything worthwhile, but perhaps we should talk about a funding scale for governments wishing to extend my network? Based on a daily rate for ships and maintenance?"

"When will you start carrying commercial cargo or paying customers?" Heather asked abruptly.

"After everything else is settled," Kim replied. "Maybe I'll charge a freightage rate for hauling diplomatic couriers around first, but Phil wants folks used to me being a neutral party. Nothing in his treaty language, however, stops former pirates currently rusting in dock at *Meerut* from making commercial runs, if the two of you are open to such a thing."

"Is it wise?" Kira asked, concerned a shade.

Gloran was heavily armed and took a dim view of piracy.

Smuggling had been an entirely different conversation, back in the day.

"It gives them something to do," Heather interjected. "There are good sailors there. Without a better hobby, some will fall back into banditry, as Phil has warned. But if they can run cargo between *Dalou* and *Gloran*, at least at the beginning, then add *Ewin* and *Aditi* later, it puts them to work building up everything they've spent the last century tearing down. Personally, I think it is an idea with a lot of legs that you three should explore."

Kim studied the Command Centurion. She didn't note any falseness to the words or tone, so presumably Phil Kosnett was speaking here.

Kim smiled at Heather.

"I need a contract with you, too, Command Centurion," Kim said merrily.

"Me?"

"You've been running your Fast Clippers home for supplies for the last year," Kim said. "They come back with news and orders, but at some point, you'll be going home. I need to have a ship running to whatever the closest border capital is. Maybe *Ladaux* as well."

"In which case, you'll need to talk to Phil and get his official assistance setting up a long run back to *St. Legier*," Heather said. "Casey will support you, but nobody is going to take your captain seriously when they drop out of Jump. Even with an *RAN* transponder code."

"Casey?" Kim asked. The other two leaned in, just as lost.

"Centurion Kasimira *zu* Weigand," Heather grinned. "*RAN, Retired*. You know her better as Emperor Karl VIII of *Fribourg*. She's a penpal of Phil's, so he can get you that introduction."

Kim felt her stomach drop a little at those implications. She'd heard him talk about the woman in a personal sense, but hadn't really grasped that he might actually be friends with her.

Then she looked at the other three women and saw the shape of the thing Phil Kosnett had wanted her to create.

Seeing the smiles on Kira's and Kohahu's faces, she was pretty sure she could make it work.

EPILOGUES

EPILOGUE: MISHRA

RAN URUMCHI

Roshni noted the formal honor guard as she exited the shuttle and stepped onto Kosnett's flagship. What a visiting head of state got back home, from the level of formality and pomp. Not at all what Kosnett normally preferred, so Roshni wasn't sure whether he was treating her as the new Speaker, even in a temporary role until elections sorted things out, or subtly mocking her by having a small band playing military tunes quietly in one corner, as over one hundred sailors stood in formal lines and dress uniforms on both sides.

Kosnett's tiny bodyguard, Xochitl Dar, was there to greet her as Roshni looked around. The Centurion bowed, then stepped close, pivoted, and grasped her forearm to lead her to a stage risen out of the flight deck.

As she got close, Roshni noted that all of the other captains from his squadron were present. The ones from the Cluster, rather than the command centurions. *Ewin*. Two from *Dalou*. *Yaumgan*. The former pirate Ward. Three captains from *Gloran*, plus a fourth up on the riser.

Most of the *Gloran* fleet had returned home, leaving only three penal frigates to deal. Normally, *Aditi* would have been deeply insulted. Even when they deserved it. But the squadron commander was an acknowledged cousin of Kerenski. There were stories and implications there that Roshni needed to understand, but that was a thing for later as well.

Command Centurion Lau and Commander Singh stood on either side of Kosnett as she got close, with Frigate-Captain Zaman beyond Lau. Again, possibly honor. Possibly the most perfectly subtle mockery. Roshni wasn't sure. And today was not the day to push.

Kosnett was letting them off easy, as far as Roshni was concerned. He hadn't even asked for a kilo of flesh. Just money and assurances of criminal prosecution of the fools who had ordered the attack on *Carinae II*. And the captain of *Kartikeya*, who should have mutinied when given such illegal orders.

Rather like Kaur Singh had.

Roshni came to rest and bowed. Kosnett and his two aides returned it just as deeply.

"Welcome, Speaker Mishra," Kosnett boomed his voice over the chamber. "Thank you for coming."

"Thank you for the invitation, Ambassador," she countered, addressing him politically rather than militarily.

His military force was impressive enough. What he'd done at the negotiating table, time and again, was something to behold.

She turned to Singh.

"Commander, thank you for everything you have done, as well," Roshni continued. "Yours is the example that I hope all officers everywhere look up to."

Kaur blushed. That was good. She had done better than anyone had expected. And kept *Aditi* out of a war with both *Gloran* and Kosnett. One that might have gone general with everyone else remembering old scores they needed to settle with the *Consensus*.

As it was, *Aditi* was behind on deals that *Gloran*, *Dalou*, and *Meerut* had already begun signing.

Aditi needed to move if it didn't want to be left out.

EPILOGUES

She'd warned Jasvinder and all the other old fools. Most of them hadn't listened.

Their loss.

"If you would be pleased to accompany me, Speaker Mishra, we will move to sign the new peace treaty between the *Aditi Consensus* and the *Gloran Empire*," Kosnett said. "After that, a small reception, to be followed by a formal dinner being cooked by Chief Bottenberg."

Roshni found herself looking forward to that meal. Kosnett's chef was simply amazing.

Cooking, as the highest possible form of love.

Roshni bowed again and allowed Dar to lead her over to a long table that had been set up with printed copies of the official apology, reparation payments agreement, and trade and friendship treaty that had already become the law between *Dalou, Gloran, Meerut,* and *Ewin*.

Aditi needed to not be left behind.

Frigate-Captain Zaman moved to the far chair and sat. Dar led Roshni to the nearer one. There was a pen. Three documents. And the entire future of the Balhee Cluster. All laid out and waiting for Roshni Mishra, Caretaker Speaker of the *Aditi* Assembly.

She was reasonably certain that her party would have the most seats after the election. She'd already spent the last year pushing for law and order in a variety of topics, as well as trade. That had resonated when Kosnett had caused people to dream.

Hopefully, she could keep the gavel when it was done. If not, at least she'd gotten the *Consensus* out of the stupid, fucking mess that Jasvinder and Bachchan had blundered into, may both of their sorry asses rot in prison for a generation.

The regular formation of sailors dissolved and Roshni found herself with an audience, including all the local captains witnessing for their respective governments. She picked up the pen and made a careful production out of signing things as Dar kept them organized.

Then the small Centurion carried each document the two meters to where Zaman was seated, handing her each one to sign and then collecting them back up.

The small woman turned to face the crowd finally.

"First Centurion, it is done," she called in a formal voice.

"Thank you," Kosnett replied. "Ladies and gentlemen, this calls for a celebration."

The crowd cheered and Roshni felt the weight of history slide off her shoulders like a greased monkey.

This could have gone so much worse, but for Kosnett.

EPILOGUE: ZAMAN

TYPE FIVE HEAVY ARTESHBO, DERRAGON

Kira had met him at the airlock personally, just so she could watch the eyes of her Security Troopers goggle as the Emperor himself came aboard with only two bodyguards and no aides. They'd managed to escort her and her guest back to her office without tripping over themselves, but an unnatural number of crew members had found an excuse to be in the main corridor, mostly as witnesses.

She wouldn't remain in command of *Arteshbo* much longer. Probably. Perhaps she would, and the whole crew would trade the silver for the gold.

A new empire had dawned over the last month.

They were alone in her office now. Kira had gestured Adric sit behind the desk, but he refused so they ended up in the two chairs on this side of the room, knees almost touching.

"I have read all your reports," Adric began. "You have justified my faith in you a thousand times over."

"However?" she asked, catching the hint in his voice.

"I'm going into business with *Dalou*?" he asked with a twinge of concern.

"No," Kira smiled. "The Empire and the Hegemony have

both chartered a joint development company operating out of *Ladaux* under *Aquitaine* law."

"The difference?" he pressed.

"You, as head of the Imperial Household, control enough shares to appoint one director to the board," Kira replied. "The Hegemon has the same number of shares. The *Republic of Aquitaine* has the third minority stake."

"I'm reasonably confident I don't understand," Adric said with a prompting smile.

"Heather Lau has an amazingly well-developed business sense that she doesn't talk about," Kira smiled. "Or the right advisors. Kohahu Kugosu, Kim Ward, and myself represent a majority of shares in a separate, private partnership that owns the rest of the development company."

He studied her now.

"Minority stakes," he said.

"Many of the worlds around the mouth of the Cluster, close to *Vilahana*, are technically unclaimed," Kira said. "Or the claims are dubious and generally unrecognized. Thus, piracy has been rampant through there. *Gloran* and *Dalou* have the best claims. This corporate agreement allows both nations, with the assistance of *Aquitaine*, to sort out such things, and start developing those worlds, with an eye towards trade that will be coming."

"And the three crowns are minority owners," he continued dubiously.

"It keeps each of you engaged for a profit motive," Kira smiled. "Kim is a most sneaky woman when there is money to be made. Her crew has also invested as an entity."

"Why?" he finally asked.

"We're backwards barbarians, Adric," Kira turned serious. "That's what *Aditi* and *Yaumgan* considered us before *Aquitaine* arrived and showed everybody what the future could be like if we'd gotten our heads out of our collective asses. *Dalou* is moving that way. *Ewin* might. Pigs might fly, but they might.

EPILOGUES

That leaves us to either step up or be left behind. *Dalou* or *Ewin*. Simple as that. Phil Kosnett made sure that Harinder assigned legal affairs staff to help negotiate things, even when Kohahu and I were representing private individuals, because he believes very strongly that money will be what drags everyone else around. If they can get rich, they won't want to go back to the old ways."

"So you're going to be rich, young lady?" he asked her with a smile. "As a member of the Household, you will never want."

"Adric, nobody ever starves in *Gloran*," Kira fired back now, maybe a little angry. "The Standard Income guarantees that and allows warriors to train. But that doesn't mean I don't remember my childhood deprivations. Bad meat and pasta intended to keep us alive. When this gets going, I might be in control of more money than you have right now. I will never want. But I will never have to rely on someone else, either."

He shut his mouth, presumably chagrined. The Imperial House was more of a concept than a place. Scions lived in luxury so they could learn and train. Become leaders. Captains. Governors. Emperors.

"So what does Kira Zaman want?" he asked after a few moments. "At one time, I would have expected Adham Khan's head on a stake in the corridor outside, but you walked right past that and never looked back."

"I don't need it, Adric," she replied. "I've spent too much time around Heather, Kohahu, and Kim. We're going to make the Balhee Cluster a better place. The rest of you can keep up. If you can."

"And I'm on your board of directors for now, so I'll stay involved," he nodded.

"According to Harinder, it will work, because at some point we will have to have a biannual board meeting somewhere, which means you and Jirou Kugosu will be there as private citizens," Kira said. "No politics. No diplomacy. Tea and finger foods. Worse, if Kohahu is serious, she intends to marry Crown

Prince Shingo at some point, meaning the future Emperor of *Dalou* will be there as a mere spouse attending."

She watched that implication course through his eyes. *Gloran* and *Dalou* had always largely ignored one another. *Aditi* in the center and *Ewin* on *Dalou*'s other flank, plus the mouth of the Cluster leading into nothingness.

At least until a shark appeared out of those dark depths with a message.

"What about *Aditi*?" he asked her. "We're cutting them specifically out. Won't that make enemies?"

"According to Heather, *Aquitaine* intends to approach *Aditi* in another decade or two about selling their minority stake to the *Consensus*, putting them on the same footing as you and *Dalou*," Kira grinned. "I told you Harinder had some sharp people on her staff. They have this gamed out a generation or more."

"In that case, extremely well done, Kira," he smiled at her happily. "What happens if I decide I want you as an heir at some point?"

Kira blinked. Almost felt her brain reboot.

"What?" she managed weakly.

"Heather is right, you know," he grinned. "You might have been in command of *Glanthua's Stand*, had your father been willing to acknowledge you at the start. Your talent and hard work is why I kept sending you places when I needed things done. I sent you to *Aditi* for results and you got me a treaty, an apology, and enough funds to rebuild the colony. And that was before you went off and decided to take over the Cluster with your new friends. It would be criminally negligent of me not to put all that on the scale at some point. I won't say it is a done deal, because you haven't met some of the others in the running, but I'd have no regrets adding you to that short list. None whatsoever. Which brings me back to the first question. What does Kira Zaman want?"

"She wants to belong," Kira said, falling into a weird third person. "All of her life, she'd been an outsider, looking in the window while standing out in the snow, watching while others feast."

"I'm sorry," he said. And seemed to mean it. "No more."

"There are others," Kira felt a hint of anger inside now. "It is not enough to save one little girl. I'm sure I have other cousins whose mothers were paid off and sent packing, never to be seen again. And it isn't just the Imperial House. It is an entire way of life, Adric Kerenski. An empire that produces results like that. The Penal Fleet is just an expression of something fundamentally broken. It all needs to change."

"Then it's a damned good thing that I know just the person to tap, isn't it?" he smiled. "Exactly the right advisor, with all the relevant experience, to lead all of us out of that darkness and let us explore what *Gloran* could have been. Should be. Will you, cousin?"

She stopped to consider it. The implications. The hard work, but when had something like that ever stopped her?

"I will," she answered. "Do your damnedest."

"I don't have to, Kira," Adric said, holding out a hand that she took. "You will."

Kira Zaman nodded.

She would.

EPILOGUE: KOSNETT

DATE OF THE REPUBLIC MAY 3, 412 RAN
URUMCHI, ORBITING DERRAGON

Phil was in his office. Harinder and Iveta were in charge outside. He and Heather were having some warm, spiced port to celebrate. Just the two of them. It had been one hell of a month.

"So what are you and your disciples doing as an encore?" he asked, mostly just to watch her hackles rise for a moment before she caught the grin on his face.

"Very funny," she grumbled.

"Truth, though," Phil countered. "I'm sorry that you couldn't pull Nam in there, but that wouldn't have worked out for all the reasons Harinder and I have gamed out. *Aditi* needs to arrive late, behave themselves first, then ask nicely to be included."

"I think it will work," Heather replied.

"Oh, I'm sure it will," he nodded, taking a drink of the excellent bottle Adric Kerenski had delivered as a *thank you* for so many things. "Harinder put her heart and soul into it, once you explained the shape of the thing you wanted to build. You've nailed down more than two hundred degrees of arc across the mouth of the Cluster into a free trade zone. Throw in *Ewin* in a few years and we're closer to three hundred and twenty. And that's before *Aditi* fills in the core section."

"That leaves *Yaumgan*," Heather nodded, also taking a drink.

"When we started, I expected *Aditi* and *Yaumgan* to be the ones best suited towards building what I needed out here for the First Lord," Phil said. "I am a little tickled that *Dalou* and *Gloran* might drag both of them along instead. That will make the entire Cluster stronger, because the formerly weak cousins will be doing the hard work for me."

"You think *Yaumgan* will emerge from their shell?" she asked.

"That, I cannot answer," Phil shrugged. "They are philosopher-kings charting a radically different cultural path from everyone else in the Cluster."

"Because they aren't native," Heather noted.

"Indeed," Phil agreed. "I presume armed refugees from farther west who managed to escape whatever calamity befell them then, like the ancient Jews fleeing into the desert from that one holy book. Hopefully, Pet will let you go and investigate all that, one of these days. Or Whughy, when he takes over as First Lord."

"That a done deal?" Heather asked. "Would you want it instead? Or after Whughy?"

"I've thought about it," he nodded to her. "Wondered what I might do if I was responsible for the entire navy. Not sure I'm suited to it, temperamentally. I'd rather teach."

"Or advise, like Jež?" she teased.

"There's that," Phil grinned. "Pretty sure Casey would offer me a job there if nobody wanted to hire me around *Ladaux*."

"Pretty sure I can name a few capitals around here that would happily take you," she grinned back.

"No, most of them would rather have you, Heather," Phil said. "I'm the terrible warlord come to disrupt all their lives. The smart ones looked at their previously-bereft daughters and saw

EPILOGUES

those young women dream for the first time in their lives. You are the role model to a big chunk of this space."

She grimaced, but didn't argue. He didn't figure she would. Heather just wanted to do her job and have quiet time to escape people. He got that. At the same time, her standards of professionalism had already inspired a generation of officers back home.

The Balhee Cluster might deify her eventually. As they should.

A lull occurred. Port was sipped. It was good.

"So *Kyulle* and home?" she asked.

"Those are my current mission parameters from the First Lord," Phil nodded. "Granted, every run home for socks and fresh cream gives her the chance to change that, but nothing in recent dispatches has suggested any drastic change. At the same time, we are far out on the end of the logistics train, so who knows what ship might drop out of Jump tomorrow with an emergency somewhere. Wouldn't even have to be Pet Naoumov, either. *Hollywood* has people. As do several others. But yes, another week or so here finalizing things with Kerenski and Zaman, then I intend to haul everyone to *Kyulle*. Probably return once more to *Aditi* itself, just because it really all started there."

"No," Heather spoke sharply. "If you intend to finally break up the squadron, we need to be at *Vilahana* when you do that. Invite *Morninghawk* and a few others. That was where this adventure really started. You just sent the invites to people from *Aditi*. You need to impress *Vilahana* into their minds when they think of us, so that nobody ever decides to make those sorts of choices again."

"That reminds me," Phil perked up. "I have a note from Nam that her team might have invented a thing so radical that even *Aquitaine* might be interested. Harinder put me down for three hours tomorrow morning for a briefing and demo. Wanna come?"

"Probably shouldn't miss it," Heather said. "I've been so busy at the negotiating table that I've lost track of those projects. What are they up to?"

"Markus gave me a thumbnail view," Phil said. "They managed to *locate* a tractor beam emitter like Wulfa had."

"*Locate*," Heather grinned.

"They call him a dog robber for a reason," Phil nodded. "I don't ask. Better all the way around. Anyway. Something that combines elements of a Shield Projector, a tractor beam emitter, and Iveta's Ghost Mode. Ought to be able to force most seeking weapons to change target and hare off after a false image. He thinks that only specially-programmed missiles would be able to avoid being blinded and fooled, and that you'd have to sacrifice at least half your warhead to do that."

"Are we back to Lady Moirrey's *Mischief*?" Heather asked. "That kicked off a huge arms race everywhere, right up until Bedrov upended the whole war all by himself."

"I think that Pulse technology effectively kills firebirds and missiles as offensive weapons," Phil said. "That means people have to build things more like Expeditionary classes anyway, so maybe the titan bolt and power tap become predominant, at least until they figure out how to shrink their equivalent of a Type-4 down or buy them from us. Even the days of *Ewin* and *Gloran* dabbling with snubfighters is probably over, and they stay with things like GunShips or Type Four Patrollers. Either way, everyone spends a decade designing and testing new ships, then a generation building them. I'm hoping that they forget about war in that time and spend all their efforts getting rich. Thanks to you."

"I'm just the messenger, Phil," she reminded him tartly.

"You are," he agreed. "But the message has been heard. Listened to. Understood, even. I've cracked skulls together and blown more shit up than I care to, because sometimes it was the only way to control the situation. And the ones I expected to be my problem children, *Dalou* and *Gloran*, ended up being the ones that didn't require guns. You got them to trade, Heather Lau. Brought key players into a single room and gave them the protection to dream about something even more revolutionary than peace. Remember that, when you're sitting on my side of the desk and I'm on a beach somewhere with Xue Yi sipping rum drinks and enjoying the sunset."

"You'd be bored out of your mind in week," she teased.

"Summer break from teaching," he laughed. "Or summer vacation away from the office. Sure. The point stands."

"You think I'll be there, one of these days?" Heather asked.

"I'm counting on it," Phil replied. "I think the entire Cluster needs it. Maybe the rest of the galaxy."

READ MORE

Be sure to read the next books in the First Centurion Phil Kosnett series!

Encounter at Vilahana
Consensus at Aditi
Hegemony at Dalou
Princes at Ewin
Empire at Gloran
Domain at Yaumgan

Available at your favorite retailers!

ABOUT THE AUTHOR

Blaze Ward writes science fiction in the Alexandria Station universe (Jessica Keller, The Science Officer, The Story Road, etc.) as well as several other science fiction universes, such as Star Dragon, the Dominion, and more. He also writes odd bits of high fantasy with swords and orcs. In addition, he is the Editor and Publisher of *Boundary Shock Quarterly Magazine*. You can find out more at his website www.blazeward.com, as well as Facebook, Goodreads, and other places.

Blaze's works are available as ebooks, paper, and audio, and can be found at a variety of online vendors. His newsletter comes out regularly, and you can also follow his blog on his website. He really enjoys interacting with fans, and looks forward to any and all questions—even ones about his books!

Never miss a release!
If you'd like to be notified of new releases, sign up for my newsletter.

http://www.blazeward.com/newsletter/

Buy More!
Did you know that you can buy directly from my website?

https://www.blazeward.com/shop/

Connect with Blaze!

Web: www.blazeward.com
Boundary Shock Quarterly (BSQ):
https://www.boundaryshockquarterly.com/

ABOUT KNOTTED ROAD PRESS

Knotted Road Press fiction specializes in dynamic writing set in mysterious, exotic locations.

Knotted Road Press non–fiction publishes autobiographies, business books, cookbooks, and how–to books with unique voices.

Knotted Road Press creates DRM–free ebooks as well as high–quality print books for readers around the world.

With authors in a variety of genres including literary, poetry, mystery, fantasy, and science fiction, Knotted Road Press has something for everyone.

Knotted Road Press
www.KnottedRoadPress.com

Made in the USA
Columbia, SC
23 November 2022